Love Me, Kiss Me, Kill Me

For Linda —
A good book &
always a great
friend —
Lynda Alexander

Love Me, Kiss Me, Kill Me

Lyndi Alexander

Hydra Publications

ISBN: 978-0615684222

Hydra Publications
337 Clifty Dr
Madison, IN 47250

www.hydrapublications.com

For all those who persist in the face of danger, who open themselves to the possible, and who carry through their commitments till the end.

CHAPTER ONE

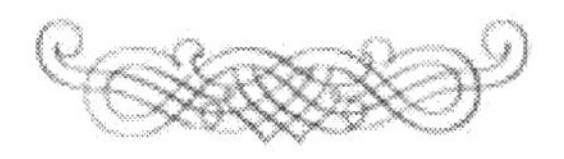

Of all the corpses I'd seen in six years as a news reporter, Lily Kimball's hit me the hardest. Found in a drainage ditch along Route 24, two inches deep in snow, she wore only a shabby pair of Banana Republic jeans and a red jersey shirt, a dried clot of blood on her forehead where she'd taken a header into a discarded bottle.

In the half-light before dawn, two CSI-types crouched in front of the body taking pictures and samples, thick parka vests protecting them against the thirty degree early March chill. Each breath left their cold lips as a mist of water vapor.

"Damnedest thing I ever saw," the lead investigator said to the waiting medic from the volunteer ambulance service, "Why the hell would some girl be out here in the middle of a snowstorm without shoes, without a coat?"

Good question as far as I was concerned. I was freezing my butt off, despite a hoodie under my jacket, black sweat pants and fur-lined boots. I couldn't return to the office until I had some answers. So far, all I had was her name, thanks to the CSI techs .

No evidence of blunt trauma, no gunshots, no bruising—it didn't even look like the girl had been tossed out of a car. I angled my pad to catch the headlights of the cop car and scribbled some notes, numb fingers slipping on the pen. "Your tech pulled a bank debit card from her pocket. Maybe she needed cigarettes or something." I gestured toward the lights of the 7-Eleven a mile or so further along where the road intersected with Declan Highway.

The officer's glare roasted his techs for sharing information, then he eyed me. "Who're you again?"

"Sara Woods, for the *Ralston Courier.*" I tilted my laminated badge so he could read it.

He squinted at the black and white picture of a pixie-like brunette with a slightly crooked smile, then compared it to my pixie-like face, much more florid in the wintry wind. I tried for the smile, too, in case it helped. "New blood, huh?"

"Just started. I'm covering for O'Neal this weekend."

The officer chuckled. "He'll be pissed. He loves dead bodies." The medic snickered along with him and they walked away, back to the running patrol car. The *heated,* running patrol car.

With a disappointed shiver, I observed the techs. They hadn't disturbed the body much, other than to rule out major trauma. Lily's skin was icy white, her black hair patchy, so thin it lay atop the snow. Bony stick fingers and toes were dark red, almost violet, from frostbite at the bare tips. It seemed like she'd just fallen over into the ditch. Just let go, dead.

Satisfied with their photos, the techs turned over the stiff body. The girl's pale, sightless eyes stared into the gray miasma of the late winter sky. Nausea crept from my stomach toward my throat. She had to be about my age, twenty-something; about my size too, although those fingers were wickedly thin. What would have compelled me to leave home in a blizzard, half-dressed, ending in a frozen ditch with my life sucked out?

I didn't know what could cause such desperation.

But the goosebumps that rippled across my skin told me it was still out there, lurking.

CHAPTER TWO

I hate being marginalized. Studying the scene, I found my opening : the junior officer, relegated to walking the perimeter to chase off the random gawker. The guy huddled, arms crossed, in a heavy navy blue parka at the far edge of the area lit by the headlights. Tall, his smooth baby face tipping me he was not long out of the academy, he had close-cut dark blond hair and narrow-set eyes the color of tin. He looked cold, and walking up to him, I said so.

"No kidding. Is that why you're a reporter?" he asked, "Those great powers of observation?"

A smile was in his eyes, so I grinned back. "Sometimes I amaze even myself. My name's Sara Woods." I held out my hand.

He glanced over to the patrol car, but his superior was still gabbing. "Brendon Zale," he said, and he shook my hand. "Heard Tom say you were a rookie."

"New at the *Courier*. I reported for the *Pittsburgh Post-Gazette* before I came here." I hoped the lack of specificity would make me seem experienced and wise, even though I was only twenty-seven . I also hoped he wouldn't realize what a jump it had been from a 186,000 circulation paper down to the *Courier*, a local paper of about 20,000. That would raise questions. "Anything interesting about this dead girl I should know, Brendon?"

"Her? I have no idea. But that makes four." Brendon kept one eye on the patrol car. "O'Neal covered the others. One on this road, two out on State Road 18. One just outside her house in October last year."

"Serial killer?" I wrote as fast as my chilled fingers would allow.

"Nope. All died of natural causes. This one looks pretty much the same."

"Natural causes? All of them?" That lurking feeling seeped in under my jacket with the cold and I actually looked over my shoulder to make sure no one was watching.

"That's what the coroner said." The door of the patrol car opened, and Brendon stiffened. "Better move on, now." He scooted away from me like I had the plague.

Catching the other cop's heated glower, I stepped back and raised my voice. "Yeah, thanks for nothing!" Muttering, I walked away toward my car. Hopefully that got Brendon off the hook.

The one he'd referred to as Tom came striding toward me. "We'll have a press release later, when we've got something to tell you. Step back and let us do our jobs now, all right?" He didn't even bother to use his 'polite' smile.

"Keeping the city safe, right? Good work." I glanced pointedly at the dead girl and got in my small silver Chevy Aveo, the one Jesse had dubbed "the Hamster." Tom eyed me as I pulled away, and I chastised myself for not sucking up enough. Not only was I the new kid, I was a girl. Unless you were Edna Buchanan, cops hated to see females working on scene. Especially in small towns.

Murder was apparently men's work.

The LED display in the car showed it was nearly seven a.m. in beautiful northwestern Ohio. The body hadn't been discovered until an hour past today's deadline, so that meant the television stations from Lima and Toledo would have been all over it for their morning broadcasts. That gave me all of today to deepen the story, to prove that people could still gain something from reading the morning paper that the Internet wouldn't serve up in a neat package with a click.

Jim O'Neal, the paper's long-time crime reporter, was away in Columbus researching legislative history of police department funding, or something equally dry and boring. Tom was right; the rotund, bearded writer would be kicking himself. But at least I had access to his other stories for background, and this girl's name, Lily Kimball.

It wasn't but three miles from the scene to the *Courier* offices on Larchmont Street; it wasn't far from anywhere to anywhere here. Ralston was a quiet town, a 'nice' place to live and work. The outlying people farmed for the most part, while generations of family members worked side by side at the mobile home factory. The whole city of 14,500 could likely have fit in my beloved Pittsburgh Strip District. Memories of breakfast at DeLuca's, tapas and dry red wine at Ibiza on East Carson Street, my bright little apartment in yellows just inside the North Hills, the reminders dribbled in until I found my throat choking up as I pulled into the paper's lot. I didn't dare glance at the rear view mirror for fear Jesse's ghost would be there, accusing me.

Stop.

Stop remembering. Close it off. Survive.

I took deep breaths, forcing calm through my nerves, gradually relaxing. Ralston was only a waypoint, I kept reassuring myself; an emergency landing, a place to find my feet again after the divorce I'd never wanted.

When I had myself in hand, I left the car and hurried inside.

The *Courier* had seen its heyday long before, maybe in the 1960s or 1970s, when people still read. The lobby's carpet, once brown or tan, had worn to a threadbare beige. Circulation sat off to the left, a mish-mosh of heavy old desks stacked with computers and phones that rang in the same whiny, complaining tones as their callers. Oft-painted stairs with a black rubber mat stapled to them went up from the center of the lobby to the second floor, which housed the news and editorial departments. To the right were the classified and advertising sections, the real heart of the paper.

I remember my first journalistic years, working for the high school paper in a small Cleveland suburb, when I was still naïve enough to believe that publication of a newspaper was about news. J-school at Kent State had quickly disabused me of that notion; papers were about income from ad sales. If there was space afterward, then the publisher let some news fill the remaining column inches. Most journalists, however, ignored this, letting self-interest and their egos make them the stars.

I certainly wasn't immune.

Hurrying upstairs to my little gray upholstered cubicle, I found myself the first reporter in. I turned on the computer to let it warm up and went for some coffee so I could do the same.

"Sara? My office!"

My eyes rolled almost without volition. Of course Gloria was there. The paper's editor, working on her twenty-fifth year of tenure, would probably be buried in the damn building someday. "Coming!" I replied. I filled a ceramic cup with scalding black coffee and wrapped my fingers around it, letting the blissful heat thaw them. With any luck it would happen before Gloria Wilson stopped talking.

Not likely, though.

I trudged along the short hall to Gloria's office, the glassed-in front revealing a row of overstuffed file cabinets and piles and piles of sturdy boxes stacked from ceiling to floor along the far wall, barely avoiding the window to the outside. That remained unblocked, to support Gloria's tobacco habit. Whenever Gloria craved a cigarette, she'd defy company policy and crank open the window enough to blow smoke outside, to the amusement of the half dozen writers. No one called her on it to her face. No one would dare.

"It's another of those girls, isn't it? Natural causes, right? Natural causes, my ass!" Gloria stood behind her desk, which was also piled high with to-do baskets. A woman who'd passed over to the dark side of fifty some time before, Gloria still dressed for success, her smartly cut brown hair fading to gray, tortoise-shell glasses precariously perched on top of her head as she paced in agitation. "Tell me about her!"

I shared what limited information I had. "The cops weren't very helpful."

"Then you damn well make them helpful!" Her brow furrowed with displeasure. "Our readers have a right to know!"

I had to smile. At least every other day of the two weeks I'd worked here, Gloria lectured us with fervent opinions of eras past, tales of the times when she started out, the Woodward and Bernstein era, her namesake Ms. Steinem and Betty Friedan, who'd opened the way for women, as liberation moved forward in the form of civil rights for all and the country crawled out from under the oppressive Nixon years.

I mean, no doubt it had been a great time for journalists; so all the professors had assured us. But since then freedom of speech and the press had been kicked to death by the Bush administration and The Patriot Act. And small town cops still thought women belonged off the streets. Jerks.

"I know," I finally replied. "Actually one of the guys referred me to O'Neal's other stories. That was my first order of business when I got back, besides ditching the ice cube imitation." I raised my cup. "So if I could get on it…?"

Gloria snapped her glasses back into place, dismissed me with a curt nod and picked up her Blackberry, her thumbs tapping away. I returned to my assigned desk. Its flat gray surface held no personal mementos, no photos, nothing to personalize it like those in cubicles around it. No sense in making it 'home' when it wasn't.

I dug through the newspaper's online morgue until I found the stories about the other women. At first glance, they had nothing in common. One was a teacher, one a housewife, the other a fast food service worker. All were under forty. One was married. Two were mothers. They lived in different areas of town. Nothing to tie them together.

So what about the new one? I opened a web browser and ran the name Lily Kimball through a people search on the Internet. Apparently there was a blues singer of the same name in the country, but that clearly wasn't the person found frozen on Highway 24. No local address or occupation that I could find.

The debit card had been from Huntington Bank. I glanced at the clock; not even seven-thirty. No one would be there for another hour and a half. I sipped the coffee, found it cooled to an appropriate temperature, then gulped down about half of it. I'd been up since four a.m. and I'd need more to stay coherent until I could pull this story together. I finally shucked my coat and shuffled down the hall to put on a fresh pot.

~*~

By the time anyone arrived, I'd rifled through O'Neal's Rolodex, trying to track down likely sources of information and had made a few calls in to some of his sources. Dedra Rhodes, the summer intern from Bowling Green, came in armed with a dozen donuts from the mom and pop place on the square downtown. "You're early!" she said, her voice shrill with perky joy. The blonde reminded me of a St. Bernard puppy—awkward, bouncy, all legs, and about to burst with boisterous excitement.

"Dead body," I said with some pride.

"No way!" Her bright blue eyes widened with what I hoped was hero worship.

"Way." My smile faded as I considered Lily's fate and the odd feeling I'd gotten standing there in the cold by her lifeless corpse.

"Dish it, girlfriend!" She cozied onto the corner of my desk, pulling an oversized purple sweater close around her. She opened the pristine box of donuts in my direction. "Don't take the chocolate one. It's for Mitch."

I considered Mitch Calvacca, a New York Italian and the paper's sports editor, whose first reaction to meeting me had been a hungry glance at the ring finger of my left hand. When I caught him looking, he just gave me a 'bad boy' smile and a cocked eyebrow. It wasn't likely that he'd get any of my time. I hadn't bothered to let him know.

"Why are you sucking up to Mitch? You don't even cover sports." I selected a maple frosted round, licking a bit of frosting from my fingers.

"He's an editor," Dedra confessed, biting her lip. "I just…you know. I need all the friends I can get." She took a cream filled monstrosity and closed the box. "Besides, I'll do anything to avoid another assignment tramping through cow barns. I totally ruined a pair of Michael Antonio boots." Her lip slid outward in a soft pout.

"Cow barns." I chuckled at her misfortune, inwardly praying I'd be spared any such assignments.

"Seriously." The girl sighed and poked at her pastry. "So what about the body?"

I told her what I had. "Everyone seems to think this death is linked to those others, but no one can say why. Nothing on the surface matches up."

"Ooo, maybe they're all getting poisoned at some restaurant, but no one knows they're going there. As long as it's not that vegan place out by the college. I love that place!" she gushed, crossing her legs.

"What place?" An amused contralto came from behind us. I turned to discover the lifestyle section editor, Melissa Jones, a woman over sixty, certainly, if her pure white hair was any evidence. Soft but not fat, she favored long flowery skirts and gave off vibes of some mysterious vitality. If she were in a European village, I would have pegged her as the town Sybil. She just had that way. She walked up behind me, leaning close as she inspected the donut box. "*Fresh Horizons*. The vegan place. We're just debating who's killing all these women!" Dedra said, a vibrato of excitement tingling her voice.

"More likely these donuts are killing people than healthy food!" Melissa said, closing the box lid. "All sugar and oil. Nothing redeeming in a one of them!"

"Exactly," I smirked. "That's why we eat them." I leaned back and felt a pinch in my spine. Immediately a set of muscles in my back tightened in practiced response. I groaned. "Not again!" I stood up and twisted slightly, trying to get the old physical therapy moves to release the spasms.

"What's the matter?" Dedra's expression bunched into a frown.

Melissa was close, very close, and she reached out to lay a hand on the offending area. "Let me see," she said.

I gasped as I felt heat where Melissa's hand passed. "What are you doing?"

"Just checking things out." She poked her thumb into my mid-back vertebrae and twisted gently, then moved down each one and did the same, until she reached the waistband of my slacks.

"But you didn't even hardly move!" Dedra cried, clearly confused.

"Sometimes I don't have to," I said, grunting as Melissa pushed a little harder. Thing was, as her hand moved along, the spasm was relaxing; I voted to hang in until she was done. "I had a car accident three years ago in the winter, someone T-boned me. I had surgery and physical therapy and all, but it's just never been the same. If I move just right, I pull something out of whack and then it's usually two or three days with heat packs and muscle relaxers to get it back in gear." I paused, pleasantly surprised, stretching just a little as the pain faded away. "That really feels better. Wow. Thanks, Melissa."

"I'm happy to help." The old woman beamed. "You know, I learned that technique at the Goldstone Clinic here in town. They teach other practices for self-healing. You should really check them out." She ran her hand down my back again, and I felt the heat pass again. "Do you want me to make an appointment for you?"

I turned, something in that sudden offer seeming very forward. Dedra, too, had a bemused look as she studied the old woman. "No, thanks. I can handle my own doctoring."

Melissa broke into a sunny smile. "Sorry, of course you can. Don't mind me! I just get a special treatment, like a bonus, if I refer someone, you know? When you get to be nearly seventy, every little bit of health counts, you know?"

Her skin was almost free of wrinkles, her fingers, knuckles not twisted or thickened with arthritis, her dark eyes sparkling with vigor. "It must work for you."

"It's a lifesaver," she said.

"Do they treat migraines?" Dedra interrupted. "Because, you know, I've got migraines that are killer."

"I believe they do. I've got some of their flyers on my desk. Just a minute." She disappeared around the corner of the cubicle. I set the donut aside, a little guilty about eating it after all this healthy talk. Dedra winked at me and took the box out to the common area next to the coffeepot.

Melissa reappeared with several glossy, full color flyers for the Goldstone Clinic. The cover had a photograph of three beautiful women in lab coats, and the motto, "Devoted to serving our community by bringing you good health."

The caption introduced the tall chignoned brunette as Dr. Francesca Ruprei, a medical specialist from Europe, with a host of letters after her name. She was flanked on the right by a petite elfin brunette with huge dark eyes, Sheila Morgan, identified as a nurse practitioner, and a muscular Amazon, dark blonde hair pixie cut, who looked like she took no nonsense, on her left. The Amazon's name was Ulrike von Dorn. The brochure didn't say what she did. Anything she wanted, I thought, in the parody of a bad joke.

Ralston wasn't exactly mainstream medical America, so I was intrigued that a European doctor would tend to the citizens of this small town. It sounded more like the kind of practice one would find in South Side Pittsburgh, or Beverly Hills—something fluffy and indulgent for those with the money to spend.

I flipped to the inside, finding a list of maladies treated by the clinic's professionals, office hours and location on Declan Highway, out west of town, according to the tiny map. Not too far from that 7-Eleven I'd spotted earlier.

There was also a list of techniques available, from petrissage to shiatsu to Reiki energy treatments, and art depicting spheres of energy extending several feet around a dark silhouette of a human body. Inside the silhouette were seven colored circles that ran the gamut from red at the hips up through white at the top of the head. The copy suggested it was possible to adjust one's energy fields as easily as a chiropractor adjusted the spine.

Now this was ooga-booga stuff for sure. What? No magic mushrooms? No animal sacrifices? I smothered a nervous laugh that insinuated itself in my midsection as I promised Melissa I'd check it out. Gloria's bellow for Dedra shattered the tense moment. Melissa vanished back to her desk.

Dedra giggled. "Government by decibel. Yikes." She hurried off to see what Gloria wanted. I stretched a little, back and forth, still amazed at the relief Melissa had given me. That had been the fastest an episode had ever resolved itself. I glanced at the flyer again. Maybe I would check it out. It couldn't hurt.

CHAPTER THREE

It was nearly two p.m. before the police issued a press release. Annoyed as I was, I set my feelings aside. The way to get the story was to act on the information as soon as possible.

Unfortunately, the only real lead was the dead woman's neighbor. I went out to her apartment, one of eight in a small brick building on a two-block alley downtown. The older Mexican woman, who wouldn't give her name, reluctantly shared the fact that Lily had been to the emergency room two days earlier while feeling under the weather.

I tapped my pencil on my pad at my desk, frustrated. The only thing harder than getting information from the police would be getting information from a medical facility, under all the new regulations. "Now what?"

Gloria passed my desk and paused a moment.

"I have some connections at the hospital. Why don't I put in a call for you?"

I bristled first, not wanting to be indebted to anyone. In Pittsburgh, I'd had some clout. My name opened doors. But I had to acknowledge that here I hadn't yet made enough contacts to do that. "Sure, thanks, Gloria."

A few minutes later she came back with a note. "Here. See Dr. Rick Paulsen. I've arranged for him to be available for an interview for the lifestyle section this afternoon. When you're there, I'm sure you can bring all your wiles to bear on him." Her tongue flicked over her lips, then she smiled. "He's very good-looking."

"As long as he has the information I need, how he looks doesn't matter to me," I told her.

But I was wrong.

When I walked into the hospital—pitifully backwoods after some of the steel and chrome medical facilities I'd visited in Pittsburgh—I was the focus of a number of eyes. "Can I help you?" chirped the candy-striper at the front desk.

"I'm looking for Dr. Paulsen."

"Isn't everyone?" The girl's eyes gleamed with interest. "Are you a patient of his?"

"If I were, I wouldn't tell you," I said, adding a frigid note to my voice. It worked. She sat up straight. The warm light vacated her eyes and she looked down at the schedule in front of her.

"Sorry, miss. He's on duty now. The emergency room is down the hall to the left. See the nurse at the triage desk."

"Thank you." I smiled in an effort to remove the sting of my earlier rebuff. She was just a kid. A kid with a big crush, apparently. First Gloria, now the volunteer? How gorgeous could the guy be?

I checked in at the desk in the ER, and waited, foot tapping, pondering some clever way to pry loose information about Lily. After several seconds, I noticed a blond, broad shouldered man in a white coat, sapphire gaze appraising me. He couldn't have been much older than forty. His tan spoke of southern beaches, not wintry landscapes. Step aside, Dr. McDreamy, I thought, trying not to stare. This one was the real thing.

As he caught me noticing him, his lips broke into an impish grin, his amusement shining through his eyes. "You're looking for me, I take it?"

If I could have snapped my tongue back into place like they did in cartoons, I would have. Absent that technique, I just squirmed a little.

"I-If you're Dr. Paulsen. I'm Sara Woods from the *Courier*." I walked over to shake his hand, but he pulled his hand back.

"We don't shake here any more. Nothing personal, just precaution. Germs, you know. Who would have thought we had those?"

His straightforward manner put me at ease, though I didn't dare relax. I'd always been a huge sucker for blue eyes, damn it. Maybe because everyone in my family had brown, or because of Brad Pitt, my high school crush, or just because I needed to be contrary. But blue eyes always twisted my heart into knots; blue like Jesse's.

"Come to my office. We'll have some privacy there." As we walked down the corridor, the tall doctor was a magnet for the attention of nearly everyone we passed, most of the women and even several of the men. His gaze frequently flicked to my face, and I almost felt he could detect my frenzied internal battle.

He held the door to his office open to let me go in first, then closed it behind us. The office was standard hospital doctor issue, at least according to Hollywood style. The windowless room held the uncluttered wooden desk, walls covered with expensively framed certificates proclaiming Richard Allen Paulsen's credentials and a cum laude designation from Case Western Reserve University. But the room's crowning touch was a withered schefflera on the credenza, its pot wrapped in contrived gaiety of red foil, rather like lipstick too bright on an aging prostitute.

He caught my eye on the plant, and opted for a rueful smile. "My mother sent me that over the holidays last year. I do much better with my human patients."

"I'm sure that's comforting."

He stepped smoothly behind the large mahogany desk with an economy of motion, a seeming well-oiled machine. I guessed he was or had been an athlete, just by the way his body moved. He had a real presence, too, almost charismatic. No wonder he inspired the devotion I'd seen already. even without his blue eyes.

"It makes me feel better, anyway. Have a seat." He gestured to the two sage green upholstered chairs across the desk.

"Thanks, Doctor."

"I'd rather you call me Rick. Unless you're expecting a diagnosis."

"Oh, well, Rick, then," I said, fumbling for my notebook. I was glad he invited the informality, since I was ostensibly here for a personal interview to fill Melissa's pages. Something light, fluffy, vaguely naughty, I guessed, nothing too hard to pull together. I sat where he'd indicated, first perching on the edge of the seat, then sliding back to a firm landing. I should look comfortable, but lean forward slightly, so as to inspire confidences. If I could just get past those eyes, I'd be fine.

Rick sat in the heavy tall-backed brown leather chair behind the desk. He studied me, and I studied him. Finally I asked, "How long have you worked here in the emergency room?"

"Nearly five years," he answered, an underlying amusement making me wonder how deeply he was reading my attraction to him, "Yes, I find emergency medicine extremely satisfying. Yes, I enjoy the adrenaline rush of trauma cases, but it's hard not to take patient deaths personally. No, I wouldn't prefer another specialty. Yes, there's an increase in strange things during full moons."

I stopped writing about halfway through his speech, realizing he had anticipated my next questions. "You must have done one of these interviews before."

"Three, maybe. Or five. Since TV has inspired people to find out all about emergency room hotties and our raunchy sex lives in the drug and linen closets? Yes, definitely the flavor of the week."

In spite of my determination to be professionally distant, I laughed at his self-deprecating humor. Good for him. "I hadn't even gotten to that yet!"

"I can wait if you like." He picked up a pen and fidgeted with it. "I'm sure your angle is different than the last fellow who was here. He was more interested in blood and guts."

There it was. My opening handed to me on a plate. "Actually, I have a blood and guts kind of question for you." I leaned forward even more and looked him in the eye, calling it brown, green, hazel or any color but blue. "About Lily Kimball."

He pulled back, his smile fading. "What about her?"

I could see questions in his eyes. Was I here to accuse him? To crucify him in some way? I spoke up quickly to get past his fears. "I was at the scene this morning. I've been trying all day to find out something about her, anything, any reason why she would have been out there in the cold."

His fingers tightened on the pen he was holding until they were red. "Tell me what you saw."

"She was so thin," I said. "Pale, except for damage from the frostbite. She wasn't wearing any winter clothing, just a jersey and jeans. She didn't look like she'd been hurt, stabbed, bruised in any way. Just…limp."

Rick hadn't moved while I spoke. His gaze had become more intent, like a microscope focusing in on a specimen for examination. "Which way was she walking?"

I closed my eyes a moment, orienting myself to the road. "She was on the west side of Route 24. If I had to guess I'd say she was heading for the Declan Highway."

He paused, silent, contemplating.

"Was she your patient?"

My pen hovered over the pad as his stricken silence continued. I wished I could read him as easily as he seemed to read me. I'd shared more, perhaps, than I should, but all that information would be public record on file at the police department. Whether they chose to do more with it than shelve it away depended on outside information. Like whether Rick Paulsen had contributed in any way to Lily's solitary winter death march.

The doctor straightened slowly. "Give me your hand."

"Excuse me?" I looked down at my pen in confusion. Hadn't he just said there was no hand-shaking?

"Please. Give me your hand." He held out his right hand impatiently.

My head cocked in curiosity, but I transferred the pen and pad to my left hand and reached my right out to him. "I thought—"

"Shh!" he ordered as his hand closed around mine. His skin was so warm. His palm and fingers gently manipulated, squeezed, sensed. Yes, somehow I felt he sensed me through his touch. As I watched, we both came slowly to our feet, tied together by those hands. He laid my palm, open, against his, and it almost felt like electricity running between them. When the tingle became obvious enough to be disturbing, I jerked back, dropping my reporter's tools.

"What was that?!" I demanded.

"Lily was my patient," he said. The non sequitur threw me a second, but I couldn't take my eyes off him. He walked out from behind the desk, walked around the chair where I'd been sitting, studying me. "She came here Tuesday night, weak and dehydrated. We kept her here as long as she'd stay. I wanted to admit her, but she insisted on going home."

Stunned he was telling me confidential patient information, I concentrated on memorizing it, as I didn't want to break his narration by reaching for my pad on the floor. "What had debilitated her so much? Did she have some illness?"

He stopped, lost in thought, hands on the back of my chair. "No. Four months ago, the first time I met her, she'd just arrived from Cleveland for a visit with her aunt. She was a bright and vibrant girl getting ready to audition for a ballet company in Chicago. It was a dream she'd had all her life."

"Bulimia?" It seemed a logical choice. I'd read about girls who starved themselves to become the ballerina's ideal of ethereal waif.

"Tendonitis. That's all. Just…tendonitis." As he spoke, his face flushed, and his hands clenched into fists. "Just damned tendonitis!" Lightning fast he reached for a stack of files atop a metal cabinet behind him and sent them flying. "Bastards! They killed her!"

Mesmerized, I watched the papers float down and settle on the gray carpet. He froze, staring at the floor. The door flew open, no doubt in response to the shouting. A middle-aged nurse in multi-colored scrubs inspected me as if I were a terrorist.

"Dr. Paulsen? Is everything all right?" She mother-henned her way into the room, bending down to collect the scattered contents of his files, glaring at me while she gathered them into piles.

He seemed to slowly pull himself together, almost as if he were recovering from a shock. He stared at me a minute, then shook his head. "You need to go."

"But—"

"You heard the doctor," the nurse said, immediately applying herself to the task of removing me from the office. "Out."

"Just a minute!" I protested, lunging around her stiff arm to grab my purse and the pen and pad off the floor. I turned to Rick in supplication. "I didn't do anything!"

"Out!" she insisted, shoving me toward the door.

The doctor finally looked at me. "There's something about you," he said. He half-reached for me, then turned away. "We'll talk again."

The nurse succeeded in getting me past the door frame, and she promptly slammed the door closed, nearly hitting me in the face. The loud bang drew the attention of everyone within twenty feet and they all stared, curious expressions of all kinds wondering what this woman in her leather jacket could have done to offend the doctor.

"No," I muttered, thoroughly mystified, "there's something about you! You're a crazy lunatic." I walked away toward the parking lot, proudly waving the tattered shreds of my dignity. I might not have gotten the story I'd expected, but I had something. I had something.

Now all I had to do was find out what that 'something' was.

CHAPTER FOUR

God bless small towns.Rick Paulsen hadn't told me much, but he'd told me enough. An aunt. Ballet. Chicago. I started with my landlady, Thelma McCracken. She was a correspondent for the *Courier* back in the Ford and Carter years, updating the county on 4-H and women's club achievements. She'd been thrilled I rented the little second-story apartment in the upstairs of her home. She also knew just about everyone.

"A ballerina?!" she gushed. "I love Swan Lake. Just love it. Harvey took me to see it at the University back in 1965. Now who do I know who loves ballet? Let me see…"

I waited, nerves on edge, as she reminisced, her hands moving slowly through the mechanics of making a pot of Earl Grey. She'd insisted on brewing it, and my experience over the past few weeks was that once she started, nothing dissuaded her from the painstaking, step-by-step process. I just prayed that she could multi-task long enough to make the tea and think about ballet at the same time.

But the tea was delicious.

Thelma directed me to a cashier at the IGA, an elderly woman who fancied heavy black oxfords. She didn't know Lily, but she knew the second victim, a woman named Gina Levin.

"She bought cheap diapers," the cashier complained. "It wasn't but fifty cents more for the good kind. No wonder that baby always had diaper rash."

"Diaper rash. Right."

"They found her just after Christmas. Frozen stiff, just off Declan. She was a student at the tech school, learning cosmetology." The town crier in her came out, and she waxed rich in detail. "She was half eaten, if I remember, dogs or wolves or something. They had to ID her by dental records between the decomposition and the missing skin—"

"Ugh!" My own skin crawled just listening. "Okay, thanks. Geez!"

She gave me the address where I could find Gina's estranged husband. I made a note, but right now I was set on Lily's trail.

The county library had a branch in Ralston, and the librarian was a voluptuous redhead with the ridiculous name of FiFi LeMew. I'd been in to check out a couple of medical thrillers by my new favorite author, CJ Lyons. Every time

I'd been at the counter, FiFi had been in hip-deep gossip with whatever locals had been there. Sure enough, she remembered Lily.

"That girl, she was so sweet. She was always checking out first readers for her niece. She's dead, you say? What a shame. Did you know she was going to be a ballet dancer? She was bound for Chicago, I heard. Came running here with a broken heart, but she was going to change the world!"

FiFi picked at her bouffant hairdo with a couple of perfectly-manicured fuchsia nails, and looked at me slyly. "Broken hearts. A lot of those going around, isn't that right?"

I gave her a quelling look. "Her aunt's name?"

"Marnie Tattersall." FiFi smirked. "But you won't find her."

I raised an eyebrow. "Why's that?"

FiFi leaned close, and whispered with great drama and excitement, "She ran off with the washer repairman!"

Trying not to groan, I took the book I'd checked out as a cover and started for the door. It was nearly five p.m. and I had two hours left before Gloria expected a story.

Bastards! They killed her!

Rick Paulsen's words kept replaying in my head. Who did he mean? More important, why hadn't he come forward to share his theory with law enforcement? Was he complicit in the act? And what was all that touchy-feely stuff about?

I sipped coffee and started typing. The press release covered the basics, and I'd learned enough about Lily to flesh out some semblance of a story. I cribbed details about the other victims from O'Neal's previous stories, which were well-researched, their tales of being found dead, without reason or a common thread among them shedding a little light on each of the women. Ten inches. I needed more.

I picked up the phone and called the police station, hoping to get someone on the line authorized to tell me something I didn't know.

"Ralston Police, Zale speaking. Is this an emergency?"

I couldn't help smiling at the great seriousness with which the young man filled his "official" voice. "Not an emergency," I answered.

"Please hold." The line went silent for a minute or more, then he came back. "Please go ahead."

"Brendon, this is Sara Woods at the *Courier*. I needed a little more information for my story. Who's providing updates?"

"Updates?" His voice tightened with confusion.

"Updates. You know, new information after the first release." In Pittsburgh the Bureau had a designated officer who posted regular briefings so the media could stay on top of significant events. In a town this size, a dead woman on the side of the road would certainly qualify.

"Hang on." The sound from the receiver was muffled, like he'd covered it with his hand. "Tom? You have any updates for the paper?"

I heard the beginning of a heated response, then the line went silent. I waited for a few minutes, my fingers idly editing the piece on the screen. Brendon came back on the line, his tone chastised.

"No updates. The coroner will issue a report when he gets around to it."

"When will that be?" I craned my neck to get a look at the clock on the wall. "By eight?"

He snorted. "What planet are you from? We'll be lucky if it comes in by next Thursday." There was a staccato burst of yelling behind him and he hung up.

Before I could do more than hang up, there was a burst of yelling behind me as well. Gloria.

"Let's go, Sara! I need what you've got now or you lose the space above the fold."

"All right, all right!" I gave the story a final paragraph saying that more information would be available once the medical reports were in, and filed it. When the words cleared my screen, I growled and rubbed my forehead. It wasn't my best work. I didn't like turning in work that I felt wasn't ready, but what was I going to do when the system didn't suit me? Saturday, O'Neal would be back and I would revert to covering schools and community news. He could worry about his crappy information flow.

Dedra looked over from her desk with a smile. "You survived," she said.

"Almost." I stretched, the tension from the long day settling into the muscles of my back as it always did. My daily routine included a set of flexibility and strengthening exercises to help relieve the situation, but most days I ended up in pain by the time the sun went down. I winced as a stab of agony ran along a nerve toward my hip, and I desperately tried to break the connection by standing and twisting around.

"Oh, my," Melissa Jones said as she passed by on the way back to her desk, her pages signed off. "You're practically radiating. I swear, you'd benefit from some time at Goldstone."

"Maybe so. Maybe so." It had been a hell of a day. Maybe something new would just do the trick, as I'd found with my super-anti-inflammatories. I didn't take them often, which seemed to exaggerate their effect when I did. "Maybe just a massage. That'll help."

"Tell them I sent you, would you please?" Melissa smiled, her face losing about fifteen years in the process. "I need that bonus!"

"Sure I will."

Gloria came back in, gave me a thumbs-up and continued through to her office. She reached for the window crank and opened the window. A few seconds later, I saw the faint trace of smoke outside the glass. It gave me a chuckle.

"Are you really going?" Dedra asked. "If you really are, I'll make an appointment too. I need to kick these damn migraines."

"All right. I'll call." I dialed the number off the brochure and easily made two appointments for the next day. As I hung up, I caught Melissa's approving eye.

"You'll be glad you did that," Melissa said, smiling so widely her canine teeth showed. It disturbed me a little, that Cheshire Cat grin. But she went back to her office, and that was the end of it. I let the picture fade from my mind.

The noise level in the newsroom doubled as the post-deadline show began, the time when reporters kicked back after the rush to get the paper out, a release of tension that often got out of hand. Chris Brown and Mitch Calvacca came back where my desk was, most interested in talking about Lily's gruesome death, and as their conversation got raunchier, I got irritated, the stress twisting my muscles tighter.

Finally I announced to Gloria that I was leaving for the night, since I'd been out streetwalking at four a.m. The phrase, of course, caught the attention of the overgrown juveniles and I departed to wild laughter. Men. Jerks. The two words just seemed to go together.

CHAPTER FIVE

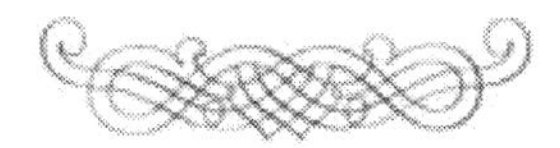

"I'm glad we decided to come today," Dedra confided as we pulled into the parking lot, slowing to avoid afternoon traffic zipping by on the busy highway. "I worked late last night. I had to interview the city manager about the employees' new managed care health plan. Made my head hurt."

I smiled in empathy. I'd had a hard night, too, one that had ended in several muscle relaxers and a glass of wine to kill the worst of the ache. As I climbed out of the car, taut muscles shot through with fresh pain. I parked my silver sedan in front of one of several large evergreens outside the fairly-large one-story brick building. The clinic was pleasantly landscaped, tulip greens poking up through the ground, though they weren't yet in bloom.

Inside, the reception area was decidedly upscale, the sophistication again surprising me. The advertising budget must have been huge, including all the advertising and billboards I'd seen, which seemed incongruous in this small town. But here, the office had real plants, maintained by a service from the look of them, as well as tall silk flower arrangements in red and black, and deep pile salt-and-pepper carpet, none of which were inexpensive. The waiting chairs were covered in what looked and felt like black leather, separated by glass and chrome tables. It was much more Manhattan than mid-America. Weird.

The glassed in panel at the desk slid back and a pleasant dark skinned woman greeted us. I noticed her perfect complexion, face radiating a healthy glow. She handed out two clipboards, with a form that appeared standard on each, requesting name, address and insurance information, and medical history.

Now this routine I knew. Paperwork never quits.

As I wrote down answers as simple as I could formulate them, my gut reluctant to tell too much, I noticed several female staff members behind the glass, all very attractive. They seemed fascinated by the two of us.

Several other women waited in the reception area in various states of agitation; it wasn't like these nurses had nothing to do. They just stared. Odd. Very odd. Avoiding the women's gaze, I hurried to complete the forms, copying insurance information from a brand-new card in my wallet.

Dedra, not so distracted by the weird vibes, finished first and took her clipboard to the window. She was immediately escorted inside by a white coated woman who didn't say a word. Several of those waiting muttered and fidgeted at Dedra's seeming preferred status, then returned to what they'd been doing: picking at a fingernail, humming to themselves, one girl chewing on a long piece of her shoulder-length hair.

I had a strange feeling that perhaps a psychological clinic might suit some of these patients better than a good massage. But then I was no physician. I had a hard enough time dealing with my own job, thanks.

I jotted down the final responses and took the clipboard to the window. A tall brunette in a white nurse's uniform trimmed in red ushered me inside. She introduced herself as Rona and reached for my hand, holding it while she showed me to the exam room. *What was it about people and hands in this town? Medical people of all of them should know how dirty hands were!* Maybe it was part of the treatment. Some kind of touchy-feely thing. They could paint me blue and call me Macaroni, as long as it worked.

The carpet cushed under my feet with each step. As we went farther along the hall, I noticed a faint scent of a spicy incense in the air, but the exact flavor was hard to pin down. Abstract oil paintings lined the walls, bearing angry, thick strokes of paint, jagged thrusts in vertical lines of red, gray and black. I did not like them in the least, but they were strangely compelling. I had to tear my eyes away.

"Dr. Ruprei is the artist," Rona said, noting my interest.

"They're very expressive."

"Doctor has many interests. I don't know where she finds the energy—or the time," Rona added quickly.

As we moved further into the rabbit warren behind the scenes of the fancy waiting area, I caught glimpses of rooms filled with gleaming steel equipment and well-padded exam tables.

At what appeared to be a small nurse's station, two nurses were in conference with a man, his black suit coat a contrast to all the white around him. As we passed, he turned to look at me. Whatever he'd been saying stopped in mid-word, and his gaze, the rich color of dark chocolate, became more intent. His hot stare was almost physical against my skin, and I stopped a moment, riveted in place.

Rona realized a beat later I was not following her and physically took my arm. "This one is for Dr. Ruprei," she said, reproach thick in her voice.

"Ah, of course." His potent look flicked away, and I felt like I could move again. "I'm sorry." Thin lips divided over perfect teeth, a smile without much warmth.

Rona guided me away from the man, who watched us all the way, and placed me in an examining room, taking a computer pad out from under her arm. Perching on an examining table always made me uncomfortable and conspicuous, so I took the chair to the left. The doctor could deal with me on equal ground.

In an impersonal voice that didn't match her cultivated expression of friendliness, Rona took the usual medical history, pulse and blood pressure, tapping information into her laptop. She seemed especially interested in any hereditary illnesses, which was a new one for me. None of the orthopedists had asked about that. When I questioned her, she simply replied it was part of the form.

She also wanted to know where my immediate family was located. I told her, somewhat reluctantly, that my parents had died from natural causes, and Rona quickly added that information to the chart.

Maybe they did things differently where this foreign doctor came from. Where was that again? Eastern Europe? I asked Rona for clarification.

"Yes, she studied outside Belgrade, in the former Yugoslavia," Rona said, preoccupied with her notes. "She took additional training in New England when she came to America, to better serve her American patients."

My thoughts drifted back to the man in black. "Did she come to this country with her… husband?"

Rona eyed me a moment, then shook her head. "Doctor has never been married. She has devoted her life to her work."

"Is that guy out there one of your doctors, too? He's hot!" I smiled, trying to encourage a little sociability.

Rona tucked her stylus in her front pocket, and her smile faded. "Doctor would be the one to best explain her credentials. She'll be with you soon." She dug in a free-standing white metal cupboard for a hospital gown. "Please put this on. You can put your clothing there." She pointed to a chair nearby, then left, sharply closing the door behind her.

Well, excuse me! I thought. Alone in the room, I studied the standard charts and diagrams of backs and spines, a beautifully colored print describing reflexology, and another of Dr. Ruprei's disturbing abstracts. This one nauseated me slightly with textured swirls of black and crimson, swirls that drew my eye and wouldn't let go until I'd followed them down, down, down…

I was startled back to reality some time later, I didn't even know how long, when the doctor entered abruptly, laptop in hand. She was even more stunning in person. Her fully auburn hair shone, wrapped tight in a chignon, and gold flecks splashed her brown eyes. She seemed perfectly proportioned, in good physical condition, as far as I could tell, and there was stiff starch in the folds of her white lab coat.

"So, little Sara. I see you took Melissa's advice and came to visit us. You'll be glad you did." She set down the laptop and read over the history. "You have pain in your back from a car accident?" The doctor's English bore a faint piquant accent that added to her air of distant mystery. I gave her the rundown of my previous treatment once again. She shook her head, sounding disappointed.

"The standard course, nothing innovative. It is no wonder pain remains with you. Sit up on the table," the doctor ordered, patting the shiny leather. I'd noticed the table wasn't exactly a medical model, and not chiropractic, either. It was flatter than the former and higher than the latter. Though I'd been on my share of both, I'd never seen one like this. I climbed awkwardly onto the end.

The doctor reached in a drawer next to the table for a small instrument that looked like something from a science fiction show, a double-pronged handheld device with a meter on top. After she untied the gown, she slowly moved it up and down my backbone, close to the skin, then made some notes on the computer.

"What's that?"

"It is called a Nervoscope. It measures heat given off by imperfections in the balance of your spine," Dr. Ruprei said in a slightly chiding tone. "Now, lie on your stomach." The doctor helped me switch around on the table, making sure my modesty was protected at all times, then examined my spine, her fingers warm on my back, making a couple of minor chiropractic adjustments. She hummed to herself as she worked, then stepped back and paused in thought. I thought she was finished and began to get up, but the doctor laid her hand firmly on my shoulder.

"Not yet! You young people are so impatient!"

"Sorry," I said. Some of the territory was new here, but I hadn't been dazzled yet. Other doctors had done this much – *well, not the whack-o-meter thing.* And "young people"? How much older than me was this woman? She didn't look a day over thirty-five.

"All right. Take off your shoes and lie on your back," the doctor commanded.

How is she going to treat my back while I'm lying on it? I wondered, giving it a shot. That's why I'd come, after all, to see what I could see.

"I'd like you to close your eyes and breathe deeply. Try to relax," Dr. Ruprei said in her clipped accent. She turned on a CD player, from whence issued ocean sounds and soft new age music. Then she rubbed her hands together briskly, eyes closed, hard enough that they must have been warm from the friction.

Even though my eyes were closed, I could sense the doctor standing at the end of the table where my head lay, her hand just above my forehead, continuing her odd humming. I'd learned to breathe in yoga class, and fell into the gentle cycle that never failed to make me relax. I lost track of time, awareness of the doctor's presence fading into the music.

The doctor moved along the side of the table to my midsection, and a tingly buzz filled that area under her hand, like the feeling when your foot's asleep and blood is restored to it. She continued to move very slowly down the side of the table past my legs, until her warm hands reached my feet, where she pulled and stretched my toes, massaging the skin between the joints. *Weren't there a lot of reflexology points in the feet*? My mind wandered, lost somewhere among the incense, the music, the sound of the waves, and those wonderful warm fingers.

"Sara? Sara! It's time to go."

"Hmm?" I blinked awake, a little dazed, feeling almost drunk, but without the usual euphoria associated with alcohol.

"Your treatment, it is finished. You did very well," the doctor said, smile lighting her face."Oh, I—" Embarrassed, I sat up slowly and nearly fell off the table, waves of dizziness passing over me. Dr. Ruprei put an arm around me and held me up till my head stopped spinning. It felt like the one time in my life I'd given blood.

Weak, yes, but my back didn't hurt. *So the operation was a success...but would they lose the patient*? I felt an odd giggle rattle around in my head before my mind started to wander again.

A rank ammonia smell under my nose burned my focus back into existence immediately. "Hell, no!" I said and I shoved the offending object away. I blinked and felt more like myself.

"There, that's better," Dr. Ruprei said, tossing the ammonia ampoule in the shiny black wastebasket. "Let me check your blood pressure." The doctor fastened the cuff and began to puff up the black cloth, holding her finger up for silence as she listened. "It's a little low," she said, after she loosened it, "but it will be fine. Your color is back to normal. How do you feel now?"

"Is something wrong?" I bristled, not liking to feel out of control, particularly in a medical office.

"Not at all. I have adjusted your energy field to realign the unbalanced parts." Dr. Ruprei pulled down a retractable chart on the back of the door. I recognized the picture from the clinic's brochure, the colored circles that accompanied the spine in a straight line from the top of the head to the groin.

"These are the chakras," the doctor explained, pointing down the line of circles. "'Chakra' is an ancient word which means 'wheel.' The chakras are centers of energy. When all is in balance, the energy flow from one to another is effortless. But when the system is out of balance, the energy needs are erratic and cause physical pain. Your back hurts more when you're under stress, doesn't it?"

"Of course." I studied the picture, trying to decipher the print at each junction.

"When injured parts are out of synch, whether physically or energetically, it takes more energy to maintain them," the doctor explained, perfectly manicured nails tapping out a rhythm on the poster as she spoke. "I was able to realign the energy down the lengthwise meridians, to share the burden more evenly."

It wasn't the hokiest explanation I'd ever received, and several steps up from one chiropractor I'd had, who attached me to electrodes to stimulate painful muscles.

"Do you feel ready to leave?" the doctor asked, not impatiently. "I don't want you to pass out as soon as you step outside."

"I'll be fine." And so saying, I was determined to be. Even though I still felt disoriented, I covered it and let her walk me to the lobby. Dedra awaited me, slumped into a chair, eyes half-closed, looking drained. The others in the waiting room were gone.

"Here's a CD for each of you," the doctor added with a smile. The art inside the case had another of the stark colored paintings as its cover. "These will help you relieve stress. Play it just before you go to bed at night, let it help you get to sleep."

"Thanks," we both murmured obediently.

Once she'd left us, I leaned closer to Dedra. "Are you all right?"

"My headache is gone," Dedra said shakily.

"You look like hell."

"So do you."

"Let's get out of here." A glance behind showed me that several staff women, and the man in black watched us through the glass window. I opened the door for Dedra, wanting nothing as much as to clutch her arm for support, knowing we’d look like two old women walking together down an icy sidewalk.

But my back hadn't felt better since the accident.

CHAPTER SIX

I drove Dedra home, and she invited me in for tea. I was exhausted after our session at the Goldstone Clinic, but Dedra looked even worse. I hated to leave her that way.

We both moved somewhat arthritically from the curb toward the slate-gray house where Dedra rented a small first-floor apartment. The steps leading to the white-painted door that was Dedra's separate entrance were freshly swept of the coating of snow that covered everything else. She unlocked the door and tried to open it, but even a heavy shove failed to move it more than a foot.

"Damn it," she said, peering around the door. "My boxes must have…Hang on." She slipped in through the narrow space. I heard heavy cardboard scraping, then the door gradually opened, Dedra leaning heavily on the frame. "Welcome to my humble abode," she said dramatically, with a small bow.

I stepped in, amazed. Open boxes perched on the few pieces of well-used furniture in the small front room, and piled on top of each other in the middle of the floor. A trail of clothing snaked through from the couch into a back room. The only clear space was a small kitchen table that held a laptop and several used mugs. Something smelled like it had been left out of the refrigerator much too long. "Has your house been ransacked, or is it supposed to look like this?"

Dedra smiled an apology, ducking to gather up the clothing, which she tossed into another open box. "Haven't finished unpacking yet."

I wouldn't have been surprised to see rodents darting among the debris, but I didn't. Yet. I stepped gingerly over to the table and took a stack of books off one of the chairs so I could sit. My head still felt a little light, my muscles not quite under my control. As I stopped a moment to check in with my body, though, I felt fluid and warm, with a sense of well-being. "I thought you said you'd been here three months."

"I have. I just can't decide what I need." Dedra crossed to the area which passed for a kitchen, two short counters lined with a dorm-sized refrigerator, a microwave and a hotplate. "Herbal or regular?" she asked, digging into the cupboard above the makeshift stove.

"High-test for me, thanks. Something with spice, if you've got it."

"Definitely caffeine," she said. "I'm just wiped out." She took two flowered cups from a shelf over the sink and looked in them, then rinsed them out quickly. "Damn spiders," she muttered.

I watched a parade of ants come in under the wooden window frame, where they gathered for a convention on a withered peach on the counter. "You need to find a man with a fanatic OCD complex."

"I know, seriously." Dedra filled the cups with water and put them in the microwave, then set out a box of flavored teabags. "I wouldn't dare bring my mother here. She'd give the big lecture about how I wasn't in college any more, and I needed to grow up and…" She rolled her eyes as she trailed off. "Parents." She twisted her features into an expression of disgust.

"You don't miss them till you don't have them." I watched her flit from surface to surface, unable to quit moving. "You must feel better."

"I do, actually. That headache was coming, I'd felt it all night. When the pain sets into the muscles that deep, you know, it's usually a done deal. I just have to sit and wait it through. But Chal managed to fade it out just by placing his fingers on my forehead."

"Chal?"

The microwave pinged and Dedra set the steaming cups on the table. She dug in another box on the counter and came out with a handful of sugar packets from McDonald's and some white plastic spoons. I grinned, remembering my post-college days, when money was tight enough that ketchup as a vegetable actually sounded possible. She blushed and sat down. "Chal Talman. Oh my God, what a hunk."

"The guy? You had the guy?" I described the man in black, and she nodded.

"I'm jealous. He's hot. What did he do?"

Dedra stirred three packs of sugar into her cup. "I don't remember exactly. He put on some elevator music CD, and then he had me sit in a chair, and he just set his hands on my shoulders, moved them around a couple of times. Sort of like a massage, but not really. The pain in my neck subsided, though." She shrugged, tucking her legs under her. "How about you? You're moving a little stiffly."

"Better now, I think." I stretched out my arms, twisted a little. Definitely better. Stronger, actually. Unreal how I'd reconciled myself to expect the constant pain. The absence of it was a bit shocking. "I had the head doctor. Dr. Ruprei. You know, she used that CD too. I wonder if that's the same one she gave us to take home."

"Maybe." Dedra pulled hers from her tattered backpack. "I hate New Age crap."

"I agree it's not my favorite. But I do like to meditate, and that music tends to relax me."

"So they didn't creep you out there? All that touchy-feely stuff?" Dedra shifted in her chair and hugged her knees close to her chest.

"What do you mean? It's a medical clinic. There's going to be examinations and manipulation of bones and things." I knew what she meant. The nurse, the doctor, both had touched me much more often than I'd expected.

Europeans as a whole had a reputation for more body contact between friends and associates than Americans; maybe it was just their way.

"This was different. First the nurse, who kept smoothing down my arms and back after she asked me all her usual questions. You know, patting me, like I was a dog." She demonstrated by running her hand down her arm, shoulder to wrist. "It felt cold the first couple of times she did it, then by the end, it was warm, almost hot."

"Hmm. That's an odd technique. Not what happened to me, but we had different complaints, you know?"

"I guess."

"Maybe it's just part of their treatment, a therapeutic touch. Like all those studies that show old people living alone need hugs frequently, to help stimulate their immune system? Every time they are touched, it gives their own healing powers a kick in the pants."

"Oh, I remember reading that," Dedra said.

"If everyone in the clinic is vested in helping your treatment, if they're working together, then that makes sense."

Dedra swirled the tea in her cup. "Did you ever give blood?" she asked.

My breath caught in my throat, and I nodded slowly.

"When he was done, it felt just like I felt after that." Dedra looked at me in earnest across the table.

So we'd both felt depleted of life fluids? I sat back, feeling the solid chair behind me, my feet on the floor, again solid, something I was sure of. That reaction — an odd one. Surely more than a coincidence. But the clinic practitioners hadn't done anything that could be envisioned as removing blood, or plasma or anything. No needles, no medications, no….

A cold rock about the size of my fist formed in my stomach. Something wasn't right. Something frightening. No. My journalist's ear for accurate wording nagged at me. Not "frightening." More—disquieting. The feeling the moment just before opening the dark and scary door. Waiting to see what was going to grab you.

What was making me so uncomfortable? I felt so much better, so in tune with how my body was supposed to be. No pain! But at the same time, there was something. Maybe just the novelty of the new age healing—chakras and reflexology and acupressure. Previously, I'd gone the strict medical route. This was different. I had the opportunity now to get some information on it, particularly if it was going to be practiced on me.

I realized with a start that Dedra had babbled on, and I made a conscious effort to catch up with the random thread.

"I'll have to thank Melissa for recommending the place," Dedra was saying. "If I can get rid of a migraine that quickly, I'll do it in a minute. Besides, if I can see Chal more often, my life is destined to improve dramatically." She giggled.

"I wouldn't mind seeing him myself." I thought about that brief burst of heat when our eyes met. More than a spark there, I was sure of it.

"Oh, no you don't. He's mine." Triumph spread her grin wide.

That made me laugh. "You did get first shot." A quick memory of the nurse's admonition to the man, *This one is for Dr. Ruprei*, passed through my mind, and I wondered if that was strange or if I was just paranoid by now, thinking about the oddities. "And those paintings," I said.

Dedra blinked. "No kidding. They were—I mean, you couldn't stop looking at them."

"Or the staff. They were all…really beautiful." As I said it, I realized it was true. All the women, even the man in black—Chal Talman, I reminded myself—had thick, shiny hair, smooth, perfect skin. They were fit and proportioned perfectly.

"I noticed that, too. Huh." Dedra finished her tea. "You want another?"

I shook my head and stood up. Dedra had reclaimed some of her usual perk, and I had things to do. "No, I'd better go home. I plan to take it easy tonight, though. You should, too."

Dedra groaned. "I can't. I've got a city council meeting to cover tonight. You're so lucky! You get homicides, and I get old fogey guys with bad breath!"

"They're not all so bad. What about Mark Stewart?" I thought about the young city councilman who'd declared himself a candidate for state senate a couple weeks before. He was an attractive and intelligent man, as far as I could tell.

"Oh, him. Yes. With the trophy wife and the 2.3 perfect children."

I laughed. "That might put a crimp in those plans. You should ask Gloria to consider you for some more edgy assignments." One thing I'd learned in my years in the business: sometimes you had to create your own opportunities.

"Maybe. Gloria likes my work, I can tell. But she's been more like my mom than an editor. She doesn't have a family of her own, you know, so she kind of adopted me, I think." As I moved to go, Dedra grabbed her wrist. "Why don't you come back later? We'll have a sleepover."

The thought of rodents occurred to me again and I pulled away with a polite smile. "Maybe when you decide what you're unpacking, or even packing, I will. Thanks for the tea. And for going with me."

Her face registered her disappointment, but she stepped back. "See you tomorrow then."

"You bet." I pushed the door open, avoiding the cardboard obstacles, and walked out to my car, feeling stronger with each step. Before I climbed in the car, I took a risk and thoroughly stretched, arms horizontal, then diagonal and to the sky. No trace of a pinch. Whatever the doctor had done, it worked.

~*~

The next day, I hardly got into the *Courier* Building before Melissa Jones scurried into my cubicle. "Well?" she asked. She came to me and laid a sympathetic hand on my shoulder.

"Well?" I replied. "Dedra and I went. I feel fine. Thanks for recommending them." I pulled away from her grasp. "I told them you referred me, like you asked me to."

"I'm glad you went. I'm sure Francesca was pleased. I told her she needed to meet you." She studied me with sparrow-like dark eyes, bright and covetous.

"Fran—Dr. Ruprei, you mean?" That was a little familiar. "You know her socially then?"

"Socially?" Melissa recoiled as if I'd pushed her. "No. Why would I know her socially?"

My brow furrowed. "Well, you did call her by her first name. That would indicate some knowledge deeper than just as a practitioner."

"Oh. Well." She seemed to scramble for an explanation to hide behind. "I've just been going there, to the clinic, since they opened. Three years it's been there, and when it first opened, just Fr—Dr. Ruprei, fresh from Boston, and a secretary. Now she has a whole lovely staff. Aren't they lovely girls?" Melissa's over-conciliatory tone dripped like honey, smothering me.

"Perfect specimens," I said. I set my case on my desk and turned away from her.

After a moment of silence, she made some fluffy comment about being glad I felt better, and she hurried away. I turned and looked at the empty space she'd left, curious about her conversation and her motives, but purposefully set my puzzlement out of my mind. I felt great today. Nothing was going to wreck that. Nothing.

CHAPTER SEVEN

Later that day, the severe weather system that had been predicted all week arrived with a vengeance. Outbursts of thunder and lightning wreaked havoc even with the surge-protected computers, causing flickering power and lost stories. The editors went to the publisher's well-appointed office in the rear of the second floor for their staff meeting. The rest of us took the disruptions of the storm—and the editors' absence—as an excuse to turn off all the machines and gab.

The meteorological display was energizing for most of the staff, who stared out the windows at the roiling black clouds, debating the possibility of widespread power outages, tremendous auto accidents or even destructive tornadoes. For me, the storm was hell.

Ever since I was a child, I'd been terrified of storms. When lightning and thunder rattled the house, I was normally hiding in a room without windows, where I couldn't see or hear the outside, preferably under a thick set of comforters.

But there wasn't much of a place to hide here, and being new, I didn't want to appear a coward in front of my peers. I compromised by sitting at my desk, which faced away from the windows, but in hearing range of the speculators, where I could —and did—throw in the occasional comment. Dedra sat on her desk next to mine, reading over my shoulder as I leafed through notes downloaded from Internet sites on healing.

"Wait. Let me see that again," she insisted as I passed a piece on Reiki. She skimmed it and nodded. "I saw a bunch of material on this at the clinic. It's for real, too, because I remember a Reiki practitioner came to the P.E. class at Bowling Green once to demonstrate."

I read from the notes, and had to agree that it was a perfectly legitimate technique, recognized in larger circles. I'd found many of the others that the Goldstone Clinic advertised were also widely accepted. That left the possibility that I could blame my perception of the place wholly on the basis of art criticism. Not a very substantial way to form opinions.

Chris Brown, the Yale-educated reporter who constantly protested his independence from the culture of wealth his parents lived in, came to pull up a chair next to my desk. He was a well-built young man with conventional but undistinguished good looks. "So, tell me about the mysterious Doctor Francesca," he said with an arch aspect.

"Why do you want to know?" I asked. A smirk struggled to escape, but I was determined to play this one straight as long as possible, to draw out the burn. I remembered how crass Brown had been the night before about poor dead Lily.

"Oh, come on. A woman in that white coat?" Chris stretched his long legs onto Dedra's desk as he leaned back in the chair, his voice melting into fantasy. "Beautiful, educated, disciplined. What else could you ask for?"

"Disciplined?" Jim O'Neal snickered from his cluttered desk set kitty-corner from mine. "If you're looking for a woman to give you discipline—"

"That's not what I said."

"Oh, I'm sorry. It sure sounded like you had some kind of a fixation going there." The heavy-set crime reporter grinned and drained his coffee cup.

Dedra took pity on Chris. "She's pretty ordinary in person," she said.

"Exactly. Looks like someone's grandmother." I winked at Dedra. "They must have paid someone a heck of a lot to airbrush that brochure."

"Grandmother?" Dismayed, Chris covered his face.

"Well, mother, maybe. You don't have a thing for older women, do you, Brown?" I released the smirk.

"Not unless they can keep up with me," he shot back.

Jim snorted. "Hormones in bloom. Ain't it a lovely sight?"

That provoked a round of laughter, and we heard the editors coming back from their meeting. That spurred everyone to get back to work, Chris getting a ribbing from everyone he passed on the way back to his desk.

Later that afternoon, the rain finally stopped and I felt a little less stressed. Despite the extra tension, I still felt no trace of pain in my back. Maybe all the weirdness at the clinic was just my unfamiliarity with alternative medicine. I had time to find out.

Dedra answered my phone, then handed it to me with an exaggerated grin. "It's a man," she said.

I rolled my eyes. "Thanks so much." I took the receiver. "Sara Woods."

"This is Rick Paulsen. I'd like to get together with you and talk. Soon."

Surprised, I glanced at my Daytimer. "When?"

"Tonight?"

"Sure, I guess." I couldn't help revisiting the thought of his blue eyes. "Where?"

"You know Athena's? It's a Greek restaurant—"

"Yes. Seven o'clock?"

"I'll see you there."

The line went silent. An odd conversation. But no more strange than my visit to his office. Maybe now I'd find out what that was all about.

~*~

As I walked up the block toward the rendezvous, I thought again how strange it was to walk the streets without watching over my shoulder all the time. Only a few cars passed. Traffic didn't drown out my thoughts. I could walk to places I needed to go. There were no muggers, and no ex-husbands waiting to ambush me.

It was warmer today, as often happened in those first spring days, the snow that had covered Lily Kimball melted now that the sun had come out in force. Flocks of crocuses daubed bright color in many yards, over-painting the drab browns and grays of winter detritus. People trimmed old branches and raked up the last of the fall leaves. They waved in greeting as I passed, even though I was a stranger. Another thing that was hard to get used to. God bless small towns.

As I approached the small storefront that held the restaurant, I saw Rick Paulsen coming from the other direction, also on foot. I noticed again his fluid motion. He'd changed into a soft navy blue sweater and khakis for their evening, which made me smile. I'd done the same, gone home to change before our meeting, wearing brown slacks and a smock-like blouse in burnt orange and cream, with gold bangles and earrings. It wasn't a "date". But all the same, I felt compelled to dress like it was.

It must be his eyes.

"Doctor," I said in greeting.

"I thought you were going to call me Rick." He grinned. "I'm glad you came. You look great." He held the door for me. The clatter of pans and dishes from the kitchen punctuated recorded balalaika music, and the air smelled of garlic and lemon. We were effusively greeted by the olive-skinned proprietress, Athena Skouris, who confessed she'd been an adoring patient of Rick's.

"This man, he saved my life. He is a Godsend, a Godsend," she insisted, smiling broadly at us. "Doctor, and you, miss, come this way, come this way."

"Athena, no need to fuss—" Rick tried to catch the woman's arm, but she was unstoppable.

"Nonsense. Without you, I would not be here to make you this wonderful meal. Sit. Sit," she commanded as she seated them at a white-clothed table. "You!" she shouted to one of the dish boys, clearing a table nearby. "Hot bread for this table quick-quick." He nodded and vanished into the kitchen, returning with a basket wrapped in a white cloth napkin, full of crusty country bread.

"Oooh. Heaven," I said, taking a whiff of the fresh baked aroma.

"Wait till you see what's next. Athena will outdo herself now." Rick grinned. "She always nags me about being alone." He nodded toward the table behind the register, where Athena spoke intently to a uniformed server who kept glancing over at their table.

"I can't imagine you're always alone," I said.

His gaze soaked in aching sadness for a moment, then he blinked it away. "It's been awhile," he said.

His pain was so open it shocked me into silence. I knew what that was like. Jesse had caused the same in me, his infidelity and the divorce following on its heels tearing a rip in my heart that had yet to heal. That pain had spurred me to leave Pittsburgh for the first job I could find, even if it meant starting over again. It had chased me all the way to Ralston, and still haunted my dreams.

"I'm sorry," I said. "That's none of my business."

"That's all right. It should be ancient history, three years ago, after all." The doctor's faint smile held regrets like precious treasures. He handed me the bread basket. "This is best warm."

I nodded and helped myself, taking a long whiff of the bread. He took a piece and spread a thin coating of butter on it that melted almost immediately. I did the same and bit into some of the best bread I'd ever tasted. "This is incredible."

"I do love this place," he confessed.

One of Athena's minions appeared with a plate of appetizers, some still sizzling, which he set on the table and disappeared just as quickly. My mouth watered at the spread of olives, black and green, and rolled grape leaves stuffed with rice. Calamari, too, lightly breaded, and other items I'd sampled in other dining adventures in Pittsburgh. Rick pointed out marinated anchovies, which he assured me was a specialty of the house, as well as the fried cheese.

"Does she do this for all her customers?"

"I don't think so." Rick seemed embarrassed. "I try not to come here too often. I don't want to see her go broke."

"Mmmm." I tasted everything, curious, and was grateful I did. All the selections were served at the right temperature and were just crisp enough, the spices tickling the tongue. "Back in Pittsburgh there was a fabulous Indian place we used to hit, especially the lunch buffet. Wonderful food—but you didn't dare ask what it was."

He laughed. "The universe rewards those who keep an open mind."

As we devoured the *mezze*, we also placed a dinner order for souvlaki to share and Greek salad with feta cheese. Once the order was taken, I struggled with words, too many questions to ask, none of them comfortable. I was still baffled by Rick's attitude in his office, mystified by Lily Kimball's death, and reeling from the uncanny experience at the Goldstone Clinic. Maybe something more neutral. I thought back to my earlier observations.

"Did you play sports in college?" I asked.

"What makes you say that?"

"Something in the way you move." After I said it, I realized how loaded the sentence could be. "I mean—"

"Actually I did," he admitted, with a smile. "Football, freshman and sophomore years, since they offered me a scholarship. I escaped with only a broken wrist."

I winced. "Ouch."

"It was what the coach called a 'character-building' experience. You know, that standard drivel about whatever doesn't kill you makes you stronger." He took a long drink of water and leaned back in his chair with a companionable smile. "I decided I might still want to do surgery and I'd better not get killed. So I quit."

I nodded. "I can see that. Although, I've got to say, I hate when people say that, about things making you stronger? Especially when you're feeling like death might be a better alternative."

I could see understanding in his eyes. "Black moments come and go. What counts is retaining the clarity of thought to see through them and move on."

The waiter brought the souvlaki and more bread. After he left, I leaned forward and put my elbows on the table. "So what's going on here? Why did you call me?"

Those blue eyes dissected me. "Because there's something unusual about you."

Oh, please. That was as bad as 'What's your sign, baby?' "Do I seem naïve enough to fall for that line?"

"Not really." He speared a chunk of lamb and dipped it in the creamy cucumber sauce. "That doesn't make it any less true. And I think you really care about Lily Kimball, and what happened to her."

"Then you believe something 'happened.'" Remembering his outburst at the hospital, I added, "You think she was killed by someone. You even know who." I watched his face for reaction.

"I suspect. I don't *know*." He took a long drink of water, as if he were trying to swallow something unpalatable.

"But you haven't gone to the police."

He shook his head.

"Why not?"

He started to answer and then Athena swept over, wanting to make sure everything was to her dear doctor's satisfaction. She effused with grand passion about how wonderful Rick Paulsen was, as a medical professional and as a man, her praise transparently designed to convince me, as his dinner partner and potential life mate, of his worth. He squirmed as she continued, but seemed loath to interrupt her. Once we had assured her that everything was delightful, she withdrew at last, to observe from behind the cash register.

When he didn't answer my last question, I asked again. "Why haven't you gone to the police?"

"You don't understand. The police won't be any help in this matter."

"They're investigating her death—"

"They're not investigating her death! They're just going through the motions until everyone forgets about her and they can toss her file in a cabinet, never to be seen again!" He slapped his fork onto the table, a flush of anger suffusing his face, all the way to the tips of his ears. "Just like the others."

I glanced quickly around to see if his eruption had been noticed, but Athena was, thankfully, out of the room. "What others?" I demanded. "Those three other women? The same people have killed all of them? And no one's noticed except you?"

"No one will. No one will even care." He leaned closer, spoke more softly. "They're careful who they choose. Victims with no close family. Women who won't be missed."

"That Gina had a baby. There must have been someone—"

"Her ex had filed papers to get custody. Once she was dead, he didn't have a worry in the world. He didn't care, as long as she was out of his way. It was the same with the others. Lily's fiancé had broken it off with her, and she was just hiding here with her aunt, letting her ballet practice become her life. Marta was a loner, a waitress who lived by herself. Sandy was a new teacher, she'd just started at the district, and she was so proud of her class." His voice broke with emotion, and he waved away the waiter, who was heading in our direction with a pitcher of ice water.

"You treated them all?" I asked.

"At one time or other. I could sense something not right about them, something in their chemistry, something in their…energy, it just wasn't right."

Energy? That was the second time in two days I'd heard someone talk about a person's energy. Surely he didn't mean… "So who's 'they'? These mysterious bad guys?"

It was almost a whisper. "The Goldstone Clinic."

CHAPTER EIGHT

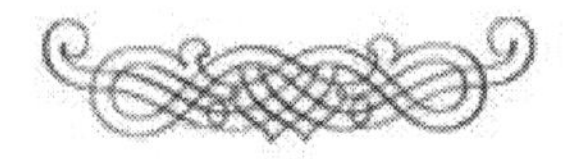

After that, I lost my appetite.Rick somehow set off his pager to cover our agitation. Athena insisted on packing up our food in boxes and sending it with us. "Too skinny," she clucked in my direction, and she shepherded us all the way to the door. Rick walked with me to my car, carrying the overstuffed bags, neither of us saying anything.

At my car, I turned to him, his face shadowed from the street light. "Are you sure all four women were patients at the clinic?"

"Yes. I'd seen each of them in the clinic office."

"What were you doing there?"

He set the bags on the hood of my car. "I used to practice with—" He stopped and restarted. "I've studied a lot of the techniques they use, especially the Eastern medicine derivatives. Because they know me, they've graciously invited me to put in a few hours here or there. Most of what they do is perfectly legitimate, and frankly, superior in some cases, to the practice of most of the doctors at the hospital."

"So you think there's something to this massage stuff? Reiki? Therapeutic touch?" He was confusing me. At the same time he was accusing them, he was praising their work. It made no sense. Were these people villains? I thought back to my single experience, and found that hard to believe. Odd, maybe. Unorthodox. But not killers.

"Absolutely. I'm probably the only doctor in town who prescribes professional massage as often as anti-inflammatories."

He leaned against the fender of the car, turning so the light shone on his face. The soft light gave him an aura of honesty as he stepped onto his soapbox. "Eastern doctors have used alternative therapies for years. It's one of the biggest differences in practice between the East and West. Western medicine focuses on drug development. We have drugs that can radically change the internal chemistry of the body and accomplish great things. But those changes can also engender poor results and side effects.

"Patients don't always see that, though. They see the commercials in the media—no offense," he added, with a flicker of a puckish look. "You know the ones, if you take this medicine, you'll be all better? All the happy, active people with their loving families in the commercial. Everyone wants to be that happy, active person.

So they go to their doctor and demand the quick fix."

"Sure, I've seen those," I said. "But I can't imagine that doctors would really just hand out medicines because patients ask for it by name."

"It happens more than you'd think." He looked off down the street. A dog started to bark, but I couldn't see it. Rick went on, "The drugs may treat a symptom, but not fix the problem. That's where alternative therapies have an edge. Even at Harvard and Yale medical schools, you can take coursework in alternative medicine ranging from herbal remedies to meditation for treatment of all sorts of ailments. The professional journals now say alternative medicine doesn't even exist as a separate entity any more. Whether it's Eastern or Western, chemical-engineered or mind-driven, if it has demonstrable proof of success, it's just part of 'medicine.'"

"I didn't know there were so many legitimate choices," I said. "My doctors always dictated what I was to do, and I did it, not knowing there were alternatives. It's nice to know that some doctors are willing to step down from their god like status." I smiled as he blinked in surprise. "No offense."

He chuckled. "Touché."

"So if the Goldstone Clinic techniques and staff are so wonderful, why do you suspect they killed these four women?"

He rubbed his forehead wearily. "Like I said, I don't know for sure. I'm reluctant to take any further steps until I can pin it down."

I leaned against the car, too, analyzing potential directions to take. The breeze had picked up. It was definitely colder. I thought about standing on the side of the road, and looking at poor frozen Lily. Made me shiver. "Surely the hospital doesn't save all its patients, either, even with traditional medicine. I wonder how many patients the Goldstone treats."

He glanced sidewise at me. "Over the five years it's been open, they've had an average of 250 patients per year. So, nearly 1,300 total." At my raised eyebrow, he produced a small smile. "I checked patient records. Just to get a percentage statistic like that. The hospital loses a lot more patients per capita. But those fatalities take place in a hospital bed, not out wandering in the night."

"That is one of the mystifying parts about this whole thing. It fits with what you said, that the victims all are solitary types who wouldn't be missed." Shivering again, unsure if it was because of Lily or the breeze, I crossed my arms, wishing I'd had the forethought to bring a sweater. "So, you're right. I'm very interested in Lily's story. Are you going to help me tell it?"

His tongue wet his lips as he considered an answer. "I may."

And? The question bounced around inside my mind, but I didn't let it out. Doctors considered their oaths very seriously, in my experience. If Dr. Rick Paulsen was prepared to break all the rules binding him to keep Lily Kimball's life and treatment confidential, we would cross into new territory. I could have a real investigation on my hands, one that could not only win journalistic awards, but perhaps actually be a public service. I could also be putting myself in one hell of a line of fire.

Framing the situation in those terms brought the skin-crawling sensation of suspicious eyes watching me from the shadows of the buildings around us. "All right. I need information then."

"When I can be sure you can be trusted," he said.

That felt like a hit below the belt. "When I can be trusted? What do you mean?"

"Sara, I don't know you well. I meant what I said, that there was something different about you." He suddenly reached for my hand and held it tight in his when I would have pulled it away.

"Why do you keep doing that?" I asked, throat constricted with tension. As powerful as those eyes were, I didn't have any more reason to trust him than he did me—and maybe less, since he seemed irrational some of the time.

"Shhh." He closed his eyes, one hand on top of mine, one underneath. That peculiar buzz of electricity tickled my palm again, but he wouldn't let go. "Open yourself to this, Sara. Relax."

"Like hell." I yanked my hand away. "Maybe it's a flaw in my character, but I actually expect people to tell me what they're up to, especially if they're involving my body in it." Trembling with righteousness, I reached for my car door. "If you're serious about helping me with a story about Lily Kimball and the others, you call me. Otherwise…"

His face twisted with pain when I broke the physical connection between us. "Something's changed," he whispered. "Just between that day at the hospital and now. Your aura is different." He took a step back, staring hard. "You've done something. Increased your power."

"Increased my power? Are you listening to yourself? You've stepped over the edge, I think. I'm just fine. And now I'm going home." I opened the door carefully, watching him every second. "You should take this food with you. You paid for it." I bit my lip. "Thanks for dinner, by the way."

"Sara, please. Don't go." He reached his hand toward me again, and I jumped into the car, closing the door and locking it. His expression was desperate. I nearly reconsidered. Then he turned away and walked north along Adams Street, disappearing around the corner of the Laundromat.

"Oh, my God," I said, now that he was out of sight, my breath finally slowing down. The man was out of control. They let him treat patients? Did they know he was—well, whatever he was? I'm sure he was grieving for his lost patient but… what connection did he have with Lily beyond treating her in the emergency room? Was there something else?

I peered out the windshield at the bags of food he'd left there. No sense in wasting it. Maybe I could persuade Dedra to take some home to her little bit of chaos. She was looking almost scrawny these days. That's it, a good deed. I waited until my hands were steady, then climbed back out of the car to retrieve the brown paper bags.

I'd just stashed them in my back seat when I heard a car pull up behind mine and saw the flash of red lights. Frowning, I straightened and eyed the police patrol car, its bubble gum machine in full radiance. I glanced at the sidewalk next to the car and saw no indication I'd parked in an illegal zone. I clearly wasn't under the influence of anything, except perhaps a nice bit of feta cheese. So what was this about?

I started back toward the vehicle, aware of faces popping into the windows of the buildings around, including the Greek restaurant, all gawking at the flashing lights. What kind of a criminal was on the street? At first I couldn't see through the shaded windshield, but the door opened and Brendon Zale emerged, cocky grin on his face. As I approached him, he leaned on his open car door and looked down at me.

"Do you have business in this neighborhood?" he asked. His tone was much too casual to be a serious inquiry. He was nearly teasing.

"It's a free country, last time I looked," I retorted. "I was just leaving." I stopped, then took a step back toward my car, since he hadn't accused me of anything.

"Wait a minute, now, don't be that way." He stepped away from the car and closed the door, then leaned in the window to douse the red lights. The street went blissfully dark again, and the faces retreated.

"Then don't come on like a Nazi patrol." Embarrassed, my voice reflected the sting to my pride.

"Seriously, what are you doing down here? You live over on Thorn Road. You work on First Street." He studied my face, his steely gaze looking for clues.

A little chill ran up my spine at the thought that Brendon knew where I lived. "Just having dinner." I gestured to the bags in my back seat.

"Alone?" He shone his long black flashlight inside the car, taking in not only the bags but the front seat as well.

This was getting ridiculous. "What do you care, really?"

"I hate to see a pretty girl spending her weekend nights by herself." His expression relaxed into a wide smile.

Idiot. "Right. Well, thanks for your concern." I took another step toward my car door, genuinely ready to head home.

He stepped between me and the door. "You need to be careful. Women shouldn't be out wandering alone after dark. After what happened to Lily Kimball…" He trailed off, his voice thick with meaning.

"What was that, exactly? What happened to her?" As my hackles rose, I went into defensive reporter mode.

"She ended up dead on the side of the road." He scowled.

"Well, I know that. Have you figured out who did it yet?"

"No, I haven't. Bob over at the coroner's office said it was hypothermia when he entered his report this afternoon." Initial temerity faded as he continued to watch my face. "Look, I'm sorry if I scared you. I didn't mean anything by it. I just saw your car and I wanted to get a chance to talk to you again." His stance relaxed into a less-threatening posture. "I don't meet many women that I want to know long-term in this job, you know what I mean?"

That actually sounded honest. He'd seen my car out at the scene on Route

24, so that wasn't incredibly surprising. A little worrisome that he'd pegged it into his memory during that one encounter so he'd remember it on a side street. In the dark. "I could see that. Guess the dead ones aren't much fun. But there's hookers, right?" I eyed him.

He looked like I'd punched him in the gut. His mouth snapped shut and he got in the car, slammed the door. The last look I got at him, his face was cold and closed, as he sped by me. Served him right. I wasn't exactly a hearts and flowers girl, but terrorizing me with a bogus bust was a definite losing strategy.

Still alone after my big night on the town, I headed home to put the leftovers in the refrigerator. I spent the rest of the night on the Internet studying up on energy healing in all its forms, medical and alternative. If it was the Goldstone Clinic that killed Lily Kimball, I wanted to be primed to catch every trick, before it caught me.

If the answers were there, I intended to be there, too.

CHAPTER NINE

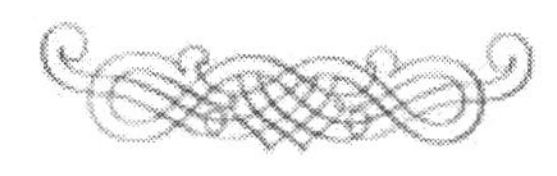

I arranged another visit to the Goldstone at the end of the upcoming week, feeling a little better armed, since I'd gone over their brochure line by line and read about each possible treatment. Confident I had at least a vague familiarity with each of them, enough to recognize the salient points of each, I prepared a list of questions I could ask of the staff or doctor.

Rick Paulsen had said that each of the women were patients at the clinic; I'd have to confirm that. So far it was the only common tie among them. But I had to question as well whether he was a reliable resource at this juncture, after his strange behavior. Maybe Melissa Jones had referred me to him as a source because he'd treated her at the clinic. She might know more about him.

After deadline that following Wednesday, I walked over to her cubicle with some herbal tea in hand. "For you," I said when she looked up from her keyboard.

"How kind." She smiled widely, showing her teeth. My reaction was a shiver that traveled all the way down to my tailbone. I couldn't say exactly what put me off about her smile, because most people showed teeth when they did. Her canine teeth protruded slightly, adding a hint of ferocity. Maybe that was it. I handed her the cup and took the seat next to her.

"You're dragging a little today," she said. Bright bird-like eyes studied me.

"Up reading late last night," I said with an off-putting shrug. "You hate to leave Jack Ryan hanging."

"Tom Clancy? You? I wouldn't have guessed that."

"I try not to be too predictable." I smiled, pleased the lie had come off my tongue so easily, not quite sure who to trust. I hadn't read a thriller in years, except for *The DaVinci Code*, and I'd been sorry about that. Instead, I'd been reading through newspaper clippings and what medical information I'd been able to get from the police about the four women who'd been found dead, as well as several others Jim O'Neal had pulled for me from his files. These other women all fit the profile, less than forty, died of natural causes, most of them without family. But they'd died in the hospital, or elsewhere. Not on an empty strip of frozen road.

"You seemed to do so well after your last visit to the clinic. I hope you're going again." Melissa reached out to pat my knee in a very motherly way. "Dedra's been there a couple of times now."

"It doesn't seem to be doing her much good."

Dedra had avoided me for several days, and I'd wondered why. My guess had been she was embarrassed because I'd seen her house in such bad condition. I would have been mortified, but then I'd been "grown-up" for nearly five years. I'd be willing to admit my college digs had looked like that off and on. Besides, it was her place; who was I to judge?

She'd come to work at least one of the days the week before in dark sweats and a T-shirt, lackluster hair pulled back by a black band. Gloria had gone off on her and she'd pleaded a headache and left the office. She'd lost at least half of the effervescence that had so defined her the first weeks I'd been at the paper. *But maybe she was just having a bad stretch. People did.*

"She told me she's been working with the clinic to try to keep her headaches under control," Melissa said, leaning closer. "After last week's success, she seemed to believe she could just vanquish them forever."

"I wish her luck with that. I've only had a couple of really bad headaches over my life, and I have no idea how she can function feeling like that all the time."

"Poor thing. I hope her situation is resolved soon."

I nodded. "I wanted to ask you about Rick Paulsen."

She smiled again. Another long shiver. "You like him, then? I was hoping you would. A dinner date already!"

Shocked, I sat up straight. "Excuse me? How did you—"

"Oh, honey, it's a small town. Everyone knows everything." She chuckled and tapped her cell phone. "He's been the most eligible for so long that he's on radar all around the county."

"He's a little…" I tried to think of the right word. "Off?"

"What do you mean?"

"Do you know him from the clinic or from somewhere else?"

Her turn to look surprised. "Dr. Paulsen? At the clinic?"

"Yes, he said he did some work there. I figured that's why you referred me to him."

"Oh! Yes, right. I usually see Francesca, but I have seen him there. You're right." Her relief was palpable. Curious.

"Have you had much to do with him? He's a little…erratic, I think. I haven't had the opportunity to verify what he's saying for the most part. He seemed to have good information about the story I was covering for O'Neal."

"The story about the dead girl?" Her demeanor changed. Her eyes followed my lips as though they could devour them. Her fingers twitched on her colored skirt, and I envisioned them lunging in my direction. A chill ran down my neck.

"Yes. He'd apparently seen her before. I don't know. He's just…" Something in the shiver she gave me stopped me from coming right out and discussing Lily. At least the doctor seemed genuinely concerned. Melissa was fascinated in some unhealthy way.

"Really?" Her eyes glittered. "Not reliable, is that what you're saying?"

Best to change the subject, change the sinister vibe I was getting. "Maybe he's coming off a bad love affair or something."

"That would be a shame. He is so handsome. He reminds me of Brad Pitt, the one time I saw him on the street while I was living in Boston. He had one of his children…I don't remember which one. But those eyes. Who could forget them?" She smiled, less vulpine this time, and I smiled back. Boy, did I understand that one.

"Blue eyes. They definitely knock me off my feet."

She seemed to relax at my easy confession, and I hid my satisfaction. I'd been a reporter long enough that I had my little techniques for getting people to open up. Personal details were a biggie. I took advantage of the opening I'd made. "When I was at the clinic, I saw another man there. Very attractive. He seemed to be part of the treating staff. Have you had a chance to treat with him?"

"Chal Talman. Yes, I've worked with him before." Her eyes flicked away to her computer screen as a small ding sounded. An email notification flashed and she slid it away with a few taps of her fingers before I could read the name of the sender.

"What's his specialty? Is he a doctor?"

"He's…an administrator," she answered, with some hesitation. "But he also oversees patient care, so from time to time he sees everyone who's treated there."

Rona's warning to Talman echoed in my head, and I wondered if the man in black would see me sometime. "Oh, thanks. That's good to know." I thought about the brochures I'd seen that featured the female practitioners. "You'd think he'd want to be right out front on the clinic's advertising. You know, bring in the female population looking for that tall, dark, handsome someone."

"He sees the ones he needs to," she said, almost absently, her attention on her computer, where another email had appeared and been quickly hidden. "I'd better attend to this notice." She set her cup down, brow furrowed. "Thank you for the tea."

"My pleasure," I replied, and I left her to whatever emergency awaited. She'd given me some things to consider. First, that she agreed with me about Rick Paulsen's strange behavior, and then that the man who'd treated Dedra was in actuality an administrator who saw only those he "needs" to see. The bottom line was, I was still no closer to answers, just more questions.

One other mystery had presented itself in the wee hours of the morning. When I'd tried to locate information on the Internet about the Goldstone Clinic, I'd found nothing. Considering how much money the clinic had apparently spent on local advertising, décor and office glitz – why wouldn't they have put capital into a web site to attract a wider client base, especially if they offered such unique opportunity for treatment?

Perhaps a website was still in development. That wasn't the only way to find people. Often professionals attempted to be interviewed by the media for free publicity. I'd entered, "Francesca Ruprei."

Nothing.

After using several different search engines and various spellings, I had to conclude there was no trace of this woman on the Internet. Nor the two other women featured at the clinic, or Chal Talman. That was strange, because most professionals could Google themselves and at least find a couple of references from conferences or training or interviews. Rick Paulsen showed up in several stories from here to Cleveland and back, including the one I'd written.

But Dr. Ruprei didn't have a single one.

Even if she'd had bad references, she might have been able to remove some of them, but not usually. If she had good ones, why would she want to?

Another question to ask when I went to the clinic in a few days.

~*~

Gloria kept me on a full round of assignments, though I still didn't have a regular beat. I interviewed farmers, called state legislators on budget talks, and wrote obituaries. But I found that whenever I asked for time to do further investigation about Lily and the others, Gloria bent over backward to make it happen for me.

While I was grateful, I thought it was unlike the hard-bitten editor to allow such devotion to a cause that had been shelved by the police and everyone else. She certainly didn't seem to give others that leeway. After several days, I found myself alone with her by the coffeepot in the hallway between the news and sports departments, a pencil stuck behind one ear, looking very intellectual in the tortoise shell glasses. Her movements were stiff, caused by arthritis, according to newsroom scuttlebutt, but she refused any medication and denied any disability. I asked her about Lily.

"Gloria, I get the feeling you should be telling me to get over this case and move on. But you don't."

"No." She poured a tall mug of black coffee.

I waited for more of an explanation, but she didn't elaborate. I shoved several quarters in the snack machine for some cheesy crackers. "So you think it's worthwhile."

"Yes." Gloria stared out the window, jaw set.

She was as stubborn as I. A little smile inched across my lips. "Because?" I said pointedly.

She looked up and down the hall, and started to speak, but bit her lip instead. "Come to my office," she said, and marched away. After a moment of stunned silence, I followed her. She waited till I was inside, then shut the door. She turned on her radio, loud. National Public Radio's Fresh Air and Terry Gross boomed forth, interviewing a movie director about independent film making. Gloria gestured at the chair next to the desk, and I took it, but she sat on the counter under the window, cranked it open so she could smoke.

She took her time, burning up half the cigarette before she finally turned to me. "I want you to get them."

"Them who?"

"The people who are killing all these women. Because there's more than four. There's more than the ones you pulled from O'Neal's files. By my informal count, there's at least seventeen."

"What?" My voice, tight with surprise, got almost shrill.

She glanced at the radio, then at the door, then at me.

"Sorry," I said, much more softly. "Where does that number come from?"

"Several people have taken notice of the deaths, the pattern, the statistics. We've compared notes and done what we can, but the authorities were less then helpful."

"Good thing that's changed," I said with a heavy helping of sarcasm.

She smiled without warmth. "Cops are cops. They'll never change." She tossed the cigarette butt out the window. "When you're ready, I will give you my contacts. Because I want you to nail the bastards. They killed my baby sister."

CHAPTER TEN

Friday came at last and I went to the clinic.I'd half expected Rick Paulsen to call me, but he hadn't. If I'd told him I was intending to go, perhaps he would have had some opinion about what I should do. But I hadn't told him any more than he'd told me about his specific suspicions.

When I walked in, the girl at the window stood, her face breaking into a smile. "Miss Woods, how nice to see you. I'll let doctor know you're here."

I gave her a brief nod and hesitated near the chairs. Several other women were waiting, the same troubled looks of agitation on their faces as the women who'd been there the first time. Giving them a second look, they could have been the same women. I didn't know. I just knew that the next time I saw them, I didn't want it to be along the road, staring with empty eyes at the sky.

My fingers started to tremble. I crossed my arms, pressing my hands hard against my triceps. I could do this. I knew what to look for, what to expect, from any one of a number of possible treatment techniques, based on my research. If anything was out of line, I should be able to catch it.

If.

That was the big question, of course. Rick Paulsen could be wrong. God knows he seemed crazy enough, all this talk about me changing and that hand-tingling trick he did. Maybe he was just crying wolf here, and Melissa was right, that the clinic was not only harmless, but actually helpful to its patients. I looked at the faces around me again. Those pained expressions could be just that: a representation of those persons' personal suffering.

"Sara?" Rona stood at the door to the inner sanctum, waiting for me.

With a deep breath to jolt my courage into place, I put on a smile and walked inside.

A buzz of activity filled the back area. Several people in gowns and thick white robes were shown into the equipment rooms as we passed them. I found myself focusing on the faces of those we passed, wanting them to become lodged in my memory. Wanting to make sure they mattered.

Rona guided me through the hall, around the nurse's desk and into the rear corridor. "Dr. Ruprei will be with you in a—"

A dark shadow stepped in front of me. When I focused, I found the man in black. "I'll take her with me, Rona. Thank you." He put a hand on my shoulder and steered me away from the nurse, who froze with the protest unspoken. We entered a room, in which he turned on the lights and closed the door, then locked it.

"Please be patient with me a moment, Miss Woods. I'm sure someone will come by to protest my impetuous action." He grinned at me. Blue eyes sparkled with amusement.

Blue eyes? When I'd been here last, he'd had brown eyes. Dark, brown eyes. I know I remembered their smoldering rich look. Or was I losing it altogether?

He held out his hand. "I'm Chal Talman."

"Sara Woods. But apparently you know that." I placed my hand in his, and felt disoriented just a moment before time seemed to stretch out in some direction I'd never gone before. His lips spoke words but I didn't hear them with my ears; they echoed inside my heart.

"We've been waiting for you, Sara. We've been waiting so long." He squeezed my fingers till they pinched a little, then let go as a banging started on the door.

Blood rushed through my veins with a burst of exhilaration. I felt capable of anything. I was only vaguely aware of my surroundings as Talman stepped out of the room and closed the door, leaving me inside. The movement inside my body, my arteries swelling and contracting, the beat of my heart, the air that entered my lungs as golden light, and purified them upon its exit: all these concentrated my attention. Never had I experienced the sensation of being so fully attuned to the smallest movement of my body, every eye blink, each rush of oxygen, every—

The sound of raised voices gradually drew my attention out of myself and back into the room. I don't know how long it had been. The heady feeling of self-knowledge didn't fade, but instead shifted to some internal place to consider and build, while my eyes discerned the silhouettes of three people against the glass of the office door now closed between me and the rest of the world. One was tall, male. The other two were women, the one with her hair done up in a knot surely Dr. Francesca Ruprei. The other I didn't know. They spoke in a language I knew wasn't English, yet I could hear them inside my heart, as I had Talman, and understood their words.

"You must not deplete her. She is vital to the end we all seek. Do you dare jeopardize what we have waited for all these years?"

I recognized the words of Dr. Ruprei by the tinge of her accent, even audible without words, almost like a flavor of some exotic spice.

Talman answered her, his voice knife-like. "You fool. What do you take me for? Do you think I would throw away your hard work? Ulrike's work? Sheila's? Each of you threw in your lot with the next, building our power until each was released from the bonds of earth." He put a hand on her shoulder, then his other hand on the shoulder of the other woman. A long silence followed. "We are one," he said.

"We are one," they intoned, their agitation considerably smoothed.

"I will test her, see if she is ready for the challenge. We are fortunate we were alerted to her potential."

"Yes, fortunate indeed. That one has earned her place at our side." The second woman had warm, motherly vibes to her mental voice.

I couldn't fix on her, though, my mind in some dreamlike place, where I observed from far away. I felt rather than heard Talman turn for the door, down to the friction of his shoe scraping on the floor outside.

"Go back to work," he said to them, and they were gone. He returned to the room, then closed and locked the door again. In my euphoria, I don't know if I really noticed his eyes were brown for just a moment, or if I dreamed it. The next time I looked they were blue. He slipped an arm around my shoulders and guided me to a chair by his desk. "Are you feeling all right?" he asked.

"I feel great." I felt a dumb grin appear on my face. "You're one heck of a doctor."

He smiled. "There are those who do not understand my work. Thank you for your appreciation."

I glanced back at the door, a little dizzy as I turned. "Did you get in trouble?" I asked.

"Me?" He laughed this time. The sound was rich and warm; it filled me with cheer and good humor. "Not at all. Just a misunderstanding." He walked up behind me, put his hands on my shoulders. "Now relax, please. You are safe here."

I wasn't sure what I was feeling, but it surely was akin to being high on some sort of psychedelic drug. My attention constantly wandered inward, to focus on one internal physical response or other, all of them stimulated by whatever Talman was doing. I again lost track of time, and finally became aware of him sitting on the edge of the desk in front of me with a satisfied expression.

"Sorry," I said, pulling wisps of consciousness back together. Easier once he'd stopped touching me. "What was I saying?"

"You were saying how much better you felt after coming to the clinic for your treatments." He nodded encouragement.

A little nervous laugh escaped. I couldn't remember saying that at all. But I certainly did feel good. "You know, Dedra doesn't look like this feels. She looks like she's been dragged home by a one-eyed cat."

"Yes, Miss Rhodes." He sighed. "A very sad case. We have tried so hard to help her, to build her up. She refuses to take care of herself."

My mind struggled to understand what he meant. The sense of the words spoke of deep caring and concern, something shared by Talman and the other clinic workers. "She does?"

"She fights only herself in her desire to be…thin." He looked away, up, over my head, and I got an impression in my heart of a waif, someone turning away from food, rejecting health. "We will continue to try to save her."

"Yes. We must save her," I said.

"You will help us, Sara? You will encourage her to become strong again?" A wave of warmth came from him, and I could swear there was a red aura around the edges of his body.

"Sure. I like Dedra. I don't want to see anything happen to her."

"Very well. Thank you for coming. Come back to see us soon," he said. He slid off the desk and helped me to my feet as well. "Come see us soon," he repeated, and he reached behind me, his hand rubbing very lightly from the base of my skull to my tail bone in one quick movement. I felt the same sort of heat I'd felt when Melissa Jones had done the same. He gave me a little push toward the door. I crossed the room and opened it, and was greeted by several anxious faces at the nurse's desk. The women watched me intently as I walked past them, feeling lighter than air, the hyper-awareness starting to fade, the farther I was from Talman.

By the time I reached my car, the world felt more solid to my feet and to my senses again. I waited several more minutes to make sure I was safe to drive. *Wouldn't want Deputy Zale to catch me driving drunk,* I thought, and dissolved into giggles.

What an odd thought. Drunk? High? Which was it, and what had happened? I tried to pull my memory together and could recall no administration of medication at all, no pills, no needles...so what had happened?

Chal clearly had an extraordinary ability to awaken something in his patients. I felt like I'd had a refreshing nap, charged and ready to go. With a grin I stuck my hand into my purse for my keys, and found the list of questions I'd carefully prepared to ask the practitioner. I'd forgotten all about them. Some kind of reporter I was. I set the list on the dashboard and started the car, driving home at just the speed limit, my gaze flicking frequently to the rear-view mirror, almost expecting a police car to appear there. None did.

The list waited there, accusing me, when I pulled up in the driveway of Thelma McCracken's house. How could I have forgotten this?

I was pretty focused as a reporter. I'd won a PNA Benjamin Franklin award when I worked in Pittsburgh, for heaven's sake. But somehow I'd been sidetracked in the interest of feeling good.

And I did feel good.

I felt so well that I went upstairs and slipped in a Zumba DVD I hadn't been able to get through for months because of lingering back pain. The Latin music filled my mind and my body and I zipped through it, delighted, still feeling fabulous, even better when I came to a heart-racing, hard-breathing stop. As I drank a glass of water afterward, I found myself wondering how long this feeling would last. I wanted it. I wanted it so much.

Now I knew where to get it. And who could give it to me.

CHAPTER ELEVEN

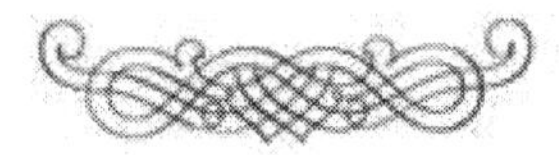

Dedra didn't come to work the following Monday. Gloria paced nervously, speculating to Jim and Chris about the girl's well being, but more irritated that the young woman was unavailable to cover a pre-assigned event that was politically important.

"Maybe we should go to her apartment," Chris said. He lounged against the partition, khakis perfectly ironed. I'd noted that his rather yuppie wardrobe always seemed to be perfectly maintained. Either he had a well-developed female side, or a girl at home we hadn't learned about yet. *Or perhaps he sent his things home to Mother...*

"What did she say when she called in?" Jim asked.

"She didn't. She just never came in. She also won't answer her phone." Gloria fidgeted with her glasses, holding them by one arm, twisting them as she paced. "She's changed over the past several weeks. Sara, you know it's true."

I thought about what Chal had told me. If Dedra had some kind of bulimic or anorexic issues, it could turn out deadly. "Should we really go check on her?"

"If she's just overslept after a late date, it could be a little embarrassing," Chris said, in a tone that sounded like he had experience.

"Damn it. She's an adult." Gloria glowered. "She's supposed to be at Rotary at noon to cover the state representative debate. Mark Stewart's supposed to get some kind of award. Chris, you'll have to go. Take a photographer with you."

Chris, dismayed, protested in vain. "Rotary? Gloria, that's deadly. Grip-and-grin? Are you kidding?"

"Rotary. Noon. Photographer," Gloria said firmly.

Chris walked away, grumbling. Gloria put her glasses on and looked at me. "Someone probably should check on her," Gloria said, her tone laced with a chill I knew was born of fear.

The bad feeling in the pit of my bowels grew as I drove to Dedra's house. The ten minutes seemed to take twice that. I fumbled with a potential excuse in the event everything was all right, a reasonable explanation for my appearance. The girl was an adult, after all, and had a right to her privacy. But something nagged me that everything was not all right. Not at all.

Dedra's car was parked in front of the gray house. I stopped to peek in the windows of the old VW, seeing several half-eaten fast food meals. Two reporter's notebooks and a couple mini-tapes from Dedra's handheld tape recorder lay on the front passenger seat. *Nothing unusual.*

I strolled to the door, nothing in the front giving me a reason to suspect anything untoward. I started to knock, then decided against it. I didn't want to give Dedra a chance to clean up or come up with an excuse. What we saw would be what we got. I took hold of the door handle and twisted, surprised to find it unlocked.

The smell inside was overpowering. Too many scents to identify them all, but definitely rotting food, wet towels and something worse. My nose wrinkled and I instinctively covered it, breathing through my mouth. A glance around showed me all the windows were closed. I hadn't known the Bowling Green senior long, but I was pretty sure Dedra wouldn't be able to tolerate this stench, ants or no.

I left the door open, trying to keep my hastily-gobbled granola bar down as I moved further into the apartment. Clutter reigned. Dirty dishes caked with uneaten food, obviously several days old, towered in the sink. Soiled clothing in small mountains lay piled on the floor, damp, in front of the television and the bathroom. The only sound was a faint hint of music, something Eastern, new age-y, that came from the other room. That "bad news" feeling crawled up into my throat.

"Dedra?" I called. "Dedra!" I glanced in the bathroom to see if she'd fallen in the tub before moving on to the left, to the tiny bedroom, climbing over towels and stacks of boxes in the way. In the bedroom, I found Dedra on the bed, wearing an oversized T shirt, sheets soaked with sweat. She was pale, with deep dark circles under her eyes, and hollows in her cheeks.

"Oh, sweet Lord," I muttered, and laid a hand on her forehead. She wasn't fevered, but she was unresponsive, mumbling to herself and rolling her head from side to side. She was clearly unaware that I was there. I dug in my pocket for my cell and dialed 911, my heart thumping.

The volunteer ambulance dispatcher promised she'd have help there in a few minutes, so I hurried to clear a path for the paramedics to get through. I also opened every window I could get to. The music kept tapping at my brain and I finally turned it off. What the hell had happened? I couldn't tell if anything was missing—in this chaos, how could you?—and there were no signs of injury to Dedra, just that pasty whiteness and the soft, occasional murmur to no one.

The ambulance took forever to arrive. I finally went outside to flag them down as they came around the corner of the block. A young man and an older woman jumped out and hurried inside as I quickly explained the situation, not seeming to notice the smell or the disaster that was Dedra's place. They checked Dedra's vital signs and inserted an intravenous line attached to some clear fluid. After a quick communication with the hospital, the young man went out to the ambulance and brought in a stretcher.

While all this went on, I leaned against the wall, trying to stay out of the way, listening to Dedra's labored breathing, which had started to rattle in her chest. They lifted her easily onto the stretcher, her skinny body looking like it hardly weighed anything. "Can I come?" I asked.

The woman started to shake her head, but the young man, whose name tag said Ted Frantz, agreed. “Sure. Maybe she’ll hang on if she knows she’s got friends close by.”

On the ride, the woman drove, the siren blaring a warning to clear out of our way. Feet planted firmly apart to brace against the jouncing of the emergency vehicle, I felt useless as the male paramedic checked Dedra's blood pressure again. Ted’s face was drawn with urgency as his partner sped us to the hospital. He grabbed an overhead handle as the ambulance swerved around a corner. “Any idea what brought this on? Drug overdose? Some kind of eating disorder?”

“Maybe an eating disorder,” I said cautiously. “I don’t think she’s using drugs. That’s not like her.” I debated mentioning that she was treating at the clinic, but decided to wait on that until a doctor had had a look at her. I didn’t know that this had anything to do with the clinic. Although her skin was certainly as pale as Lily’s had been, and her breathing—

Dedra’s breathing changed to gasps. Ted got hold of an oxygen mask and fastened it to her face. As Dedra struggled, desperation and fear that she wouldn’t even make it as far as the hospital drove me to reach for her hand. If it mattered that someone was there for her, I meant to let her know.

Her cold hand felt dried up and leathery. I rubbed the palm, the fingers, all the acupressure points I’d read about, hoping to stimulate a response. Feeling guilty for my abundant energy, which hadn’t faded since I’d met with Chal, I wished I could pass some of it on to Dedra. Nothing else I could do but pray.

I did that, too.

Lost in my words of comfort and hard wishing, it took a few minutes for me to realize that Dedra's fingers actually warmed up. About that time, the paramedic said, “What are you doing there?”

My eyes snapped open. “Me? I'm just holding her hand, like you said, letting her know I’m here.” His voice held an edge of criticism; I dropped her hand.

He quickly reached for it and put it back in mine. “Whatever it is, don't stop. Her blood pressure's gone up ten points since you started.”

“You’re kidding.” I looked at the equipment, but it was just a jumble of beeps and wavy lines to me. I held on till we arrived at the hospital a few moments later, then the paramedics rolled the gurney through the glass doors as they slid open, and they vanished into the back.

Left suddenly and starkly alone, I leaned against the wall just inside the door, a little puzzled. The paramedic must have been right. Dedra must have realized I was there, supporting her. That knowledge had boosted her consciousness. *That seemed like a good sign, didn’t it?* At loose ends, I reached for my cell to call Gloria.

“Hey, get in here.” Ted popped back through the swinging doors and grabbed my arm.

“Come in here!” he said. “This girl needs you.” He practically dragged me down the hall full of curtained areas and various sounds of pain to the last one, where Dedra lay on a bed. “You stay here a minute.” He disappeared, the curtain swaying behind him.

Shocked, I waited a moment, tried to read the equipment beeping around her. The heart monitor showed a somewhat erratic line and numbers popped up from time to time in the 80s and 90s but I had no idea what they meant. The white sheets and overhead fluorescent lights seemed to leech the remaining color from Dedra's pale face. Muffled voices passed as the ER conducted its grim business around them.

The curtain pulled open again and Ted returned, Rick on his heels. "This is her, doctor."

"Sara," Rick said. His expression changed, eyes widening and his mouth dropped open slightly. "You did this." He moved to Dedra's bedside, checked her hands, fingernails and took her pulse again. "What do you know about her?"

"Dedra and I work together at the *Courier*. She didn't show up at work today so I went to check on her. I found her like this. The place was trashed. I'd guess she hadn't had enough energy to do more than get to work and back for a couple of weeks. We thought she was coming down with something." I looked down at Dedra. "Or maybe...maybe some kind of eating disorder." That mental picture of her turning away from food that I'd experienced at the clinic came back to me, and juxtaposed with the half-eaten food I'd seen in her car and in her apartment, I tended to give it some credence. But with his feeling about the Goldstone clinic, I wasn't sure whether it made sense to tell him she'd been there. He might just go off.

As a lab tech poked her head in, the doctor gestured to her to come take her samples. I winced as the needle slid into Dedra's lean arm and red blood filled the first tube. I hated needles. Always had. "Does she have a regular doctor?" he asked, looking over the mostly-blank admission form on the clipboard in his hand.

A perfect way to approach the subject. "She sees Chal Talman," I said. The startled eyes of the tech flashed up at me and then down at Dedra, though her practiced hands didn't miss a beat.

"Come with me while I call him." Rick took my arm and pulled me out of the treatment area, despite my resistance. I was frankly getting a little tired of people dragging me here and there, but he didn't stop to ask. He gave orders to a passing nurse that no one else should go in or out of that room, then looked at me. "Now it's going to hit the fan."

~*~

He walked quickly to his office, his hand still grasping my arm tightly. Looking both ways first, he closed the door. "How long has she been a patient at the Goldstone?" he demanded.

"About a month now. Maybe a little more."

"How often? Who else did she see? Anyone? Or just Chal?" he asked, intensity hardening his features.

I didn't like where this was going. His near-hostility brought up my defenses. "I think just Chal. Look, is Dedra going to be all right?"

"More than once a week? Did she ever treat with Dr. Ruprei?" Impatient, he snapped. "Come on, Sara, it's important. Give me information."

I shrugged and lounged against the desk, telling him what I knew about Dedra's headaches, and her visits to the clinic, and added a description of Dedra's slow deterioration. "If she's not going to take care of herself, it's not Chal's problem," I said.

"What makes you think she wasn't caring for herself?" His eyes were hard sapphires, cutting me with their scrutiny.

I almost said that Chal had told me so, but I bit that answer back in time. Rick was rabid enough. "What makes *you* think this is the fault of someone at the clinic?"

"It's a direct link. She was healthy enough before she was there, except for the migraines. Within a month after she started treating there, she's on her deathbed."

"Deathbed?" I bit my lip.

He studied me, still closed off. "She's very sick. I don't know if we'll pull her through this. She might already be gone if…" His eyes narrowed.

"If what?"

"Ted told me you revived her in the ambulance, just by laying on hands."

"Well, I don't know about that," I said, embarrassed. "I held her hand, yeah. I wanted her to know she had a friend there." I left out the part about wanting to share my own strength. Surely that wasn't what had happened.

"Let's get back to the room, and I want to see if you can do it again," he said. He stopped short before he opened the door. "And not another word about the clinic. There are eyes and ears everywhere."

Do what again? I wondered. "I didn't *do* anything." It didn't matter. He wasn't listening. When we got back to Dedra, he looked at the machines, and his face clouded with anger. "Whatever you did in the ambulance, try again. Don't argue. Don't think. Just do it," he ordered.

"If you say so." I took Dedra's hand. Nothing happened.

He observed a moment. "You're not trying."

"How do you know?" I glared at him a moment, then he pointed to Dedra. I took a deep breath, then concentrated on Dedra, picturing the girl as she'd been during my first days at the newspaper, bubbly and vivacious. The longer I thought about her, I felt a wave of heat, something like the way I'd heard a hot flash described. It came up from my feet, moved through my midsection with a little sizzle and up into my arms, hands, fingers.

The beeping of the machines quickened, and I could swear Dedra's cheeks turned a little pink. The sound brought my attention back to the room, and I realized I felt weak. My hands slid away from Dedra's and my knees gave way.

Rick stepped up behind me, his arms strong and supportive as he braced me up. I could feel his heart beating where my back rested against his chest, then I felt a rush of blackness.

My eyes opened some time later, and I found myself horizontal on a hospital bed. A blood pressure cuff squeezed my left arm and a sensor of some kind was clipped to my right index finger. Rick came into my field of vision, his face much warmer and welcoming.

"There you are. Just relax. You're fine."

I looked around, and realized I was lying in the cubicle next to Dedra's. The curtains had been drawn back, so he could watch us both at the same time. A nurse fussed with the cuff and then a tray behind her. "IV, doctor?" the nurse asked.

"No!" I snapped.

Rick smiled. "I think she's recovering, thank you." The nurse nodded and left the room.

"What happened?" I persisted.

The doctor shook his head. "I'm not sure. As soon as you touched Dedra, her pulse climbed eight beats a minute, her blood pressure went back up to almost normal. As time passed, she didn't continue to improve. But your touch brought her back up, no question about it."

"Mine. Right." I tried to pick up the scattered parts of my wits. "Now what are you saying? I'm some sort of faith healer? I've got a new career waiting in tent revivals and evangelical circles?"

"That I don't know. But your current weakness suggests you used your own strength to sustain her." He laid a hand on my shoulder before I could protest. He seemed to be doing that thing he did, sensing somehow. "You were stronger before. Much stronger." He left my side and returned to Dedra's bed, cautioning me with a pointed finger not to get up and follow him. "She's much more stable now."

"I should call Gloria," I said. At his puzzled look, I added, "Our editor. She's been very concerned about Dedra."

He waved a finger in my direction. "Don't move from that bed."

"I wasn't, I've got my cell—"

"You can't use that in here." He frowned and waved at a passing nurse and asked for a portable phone. "There. We'll get you hooked up. I've got to check a few things. Stay right there."

If truth were told, I didn't really feel like getting up. I did feel a definite lack of energy. Could I have passed it to Dedra? That wasn't possible. I just didn't believe it. But apparently Rick Paulsen did.

When the phone arrived, I called the *Courier* newsroom. "Gloria, it's Sara. We're at the hospital. Things with Dedra were worse than we thought." I explained what had happened as far as Dedra's apartment was concerned, but didn't share all the hocus-pocus stuff Rick was spouting about energy transfer. That was too far out for me to swallow at the moment.

"So does he think she's going to be all right?"

"I guess so." I looked over at Dedra, who appeared to be sleeping peacefully, her skin no longer white or mottled, her breathing smooth.

"Well, I'm calling her parents anyway. I think they should know what's going on. She can tell them what she wants about the clinic. Are you coming back here?"

"Not just yet. I'd like to make sure she's together before I leave."

"Did you tell Paulsen you're going to the clinic too?"

"No. Trust me, I don't feel anything like she does. I'm fine."

"Maybe," Gloria said darkly. "I don't trust them anyway."

"I know, Gloria. Look, I'll check back in when I can, all right?" I hung up and closed my eyes, taking yogic breaths and trying to relax.

Suddenly the curtain was yanked aside by Dr. Ruprei. Startled, I thought my heart would stop. The monitor started beeping like it was in the Indy 500.

"Sara!" the doctor cried. She came to me, laying her hand on my shoulder. "What is this I hear? Are you all right? I came as soon as I heard." She looked at the monitors, continued to touch me, forehead, solar plexus, even my feet. "We cannot have anything happen to you, my girl."

"It's not me, it's Dedra," I said, with a small gesture toward the second bed.

"Dedra?" She sounded puzzled, and she walked over to study the other girl's face for recognition. As soon as the doctor's back was turned, I scrabbled madly for the nurse call button on the bed and pushed it repeatedly.

Two nurses and Rick swept into the room at the same time. His shocked reaction at finding Dr. Ruprei with his patients kept everyone from asking why they had been summoned in such a peremptory manner.

"Doctor," he said, a little too loudly. "Will you step outside so we may have a word about my patient?" He led the doctor from the space, and I let my eyes slip closed after making sure neither of the nurses had needles in their hands. I could hear them moving about the small area, checking the equipment and checked Dedra and myself to see what had caused the emergency buzzer to sound.

One said, "Does he think Dr. Ruprei would harm a patient?" The voice was indignant. "The doctor is well respected in this community. The woman is a saint."

A Ruprei convert, then. Rick was right. They did have eyes and ears at the hospital.

"I'm sure that's not what he meant," a second voice said. "I didn't think Dr. Ruprei had admitting privileges here." Something rustled close to my ear. "This is the button that went off… Miss Woods? Is there a problem?"

I feigned a weary stretch, adding a little groan that was quite real as I pulled on my back. "I was just trying to sleep."

"It's probably hard for you to do that with all our poking and prodding," the nurse said with a good-natured smile. "We'll be outside if you need something."

"Thanks so much." I glanced over at the other bed. "How's Dedra?"

"She seems to be fine," snapped the Ruprei-ite. "Do you know if she is a drug user? It certainly appears to be an overdose. Nothing that would have happened at the clinic."

"Oh, maybe. Drugs. Hard to know, right?"

I wondered when the issue of drugs had entered the picture. Was the clinic so desperate not to be blamed that they would start rumors and lies? I didn't like that idea. It suggested they had something to hide.

After a few more minutes of fussing, the two nurses finally left. I sat up slowly, testing my head, which seemed clear enough. I unfastened the cuff and the clip, unplugging the things when they started beeping again. My shoes were on the floor beside the bed, and I slipped them on. Ready for a quick getaway, I thought, then I wondered why I would have put it in those terms.

"Dedra?" I asked softly, but there was no response.

Ted, the ambulance attendant, popped in for a moment to study Dedra, then he smiled at me. "She looks a lot better," he said. His eyes scanned the instruments. "Great. Doc talk to you? Did you ever figure out what happened?" His gaze was pointed and curious.

"I'm still not really sure. I'm waiting for him."

"Never saw anything like that," Ted said. "Hope Doc figures it out. Hey—tell her I hope she feels better soon."

"I'll do that. Just as soon as I can. Thanks for your help."

It was several minutes before Rick returned. When he came back, his color was high, and he was agitated.

"We need to talk. Now."

CHAPTER TWELVE

I glanced at Dedra, hesitant to leave her.The doctor nodded approvingly. "I've left orders that only essential personnel are allowed with Dedra until she can be transferred upstairs. She'll be safe."

"She has to stay then?"

"For a few days, I'd think."

I frowned and nodded. "Yes, I think that would be all right." I spoke softly to Dedra, telling her I'd be back soon, and found myself patting her, as the clinic people had often done to me. Disturbed, I pulled my hand back and went with Rick to his office.

Once there, Rick took some dark pink fruit juice out of a small refrigerator behind his desk and poured it into two glasses, cutting me off when I started to speak.

"Replenish yourself first. Talk can wait." He put a CD into a small player behind his desk, and a Mozart score floated from the speakers. He turned it up, and I realized that whatever we said would now be screened from a casual listener outside the door.

I sniffed the juice. "What is it?"

"Pomegranate, acai, some other things. Perfectly natural," he said with a hint of exasperation. He drank his juice, as if to demonstrate its integrity.

Amused, I took a sip. "You're the one skulking around like Fox Mulder warning people to 'trust no one.'" When he failed to smile, I complied with his request and forced myself into a chair, and cocked an eyebrow at him. "Now?"

"Now." He studied me without expression. "Are you seeing someone at the Goldstone as well?"

"Why do you say that?"

Rick frowned. "Don't play games with me. I could tell when I touched you."

"What are you talking about?"

"It's what Ted saw, too. You're charged." He'd been standing, rocking from one foot to the other, and now he came around the desk and sat next to me. "You were holding enough energy to either carry Dedra through until she could get into her own resources, or else to pass energy into her field." He reached for my hand. I jerked back and got up.

"You keep saying that. You keep wanting to touch me. All of you. You all keep putting your hands all over me." I backed away, sure the walls were closing in. "Don't touch me."

He stood up slowly and watched, eyes wide. "You are. You've seen Ruprei and…who else?"

"That's none of your business. I'm not your patient."

"I'd rather you weren't. But if you won't be honest with me, how can I trust you?"

I stared at the floor for several long seconds, finally acknowledging he was probably right. I looked up at him, resigned.

He held out his hand. "Please. It's my best barometer."

I dissolved a grimace as soon as I felt it solidify on my face. "Fine. The last time."

He nodded, and I gave him my hand. The little electric tingle I'd always gotten from him was gone. Its absence bothered me, though I couldn't say why.

Apparently satisfied, he let go and stepped back. "It's not there any more. The excess must have gone to Dedra."

"You're talking crazy, you know. What do you think I am? A battery, charged or not charged or something? That's not possible. Is it?"

"It would explain what happened. Dedra's life force was ebbing and you replenished it."

"Life force. Okay, so we're in *X-Files* territory. Next you'll be talking vampires."

He twitched as if I'd slapped him.

That raised my eyebrow. "No way." I thought about Talman and his charisma.

He walked behind his desk, as if putting the solid wood between us would insulate him. Or was it me he was trying to protect? He studied me, clearly torn about something. Still on the issue of trust?

"What does that have to do with the clinic?" I asked, as the silence went on.

He didn't answer.

"Why did Dr. Ruprei show up so quickly?"

He shook himself and leaned forward, elbows on the desk. He looked so much more tired than he had the first day we'd met. "I don't know why Ruprei was here. I didn't send for her. She didn't hurt you, did she? Or Dedra?"

I shook her head.

"What was it you said? A battery? That's a good analogy. You've been at the clinic recently, haven't you? Within the last twenty-four hours? Within the last week?" He poured another glass of juice for me, disapproval in his voice. As I started to argue with him, he held up a finger. "I know you have. Let's just work this through, all right? Please work with me on this. It's very close to Lily's story. It may be the key."

"All right, fine. I did go, five days ago. But my life force was just fine. In fact, I felt terrific. Better than I had in years."

He rubbed his forehead, lost in thought a moment. "I hadn't thought she would move so soon. Drink the juice."

What use was there arguing at this point? I drank the juice. I had to admit, it seemed to be having a positive effect. "Who's she? Dedra was seeing Talman. But he wasn't doing anything wrong. I told you. I felt great."

"Of course you did. You might have had all your own energy and some of his besides." He leaned back, arms crossed.

"What are you saying, that they put it *into* me?"

"I'm not sure. It's not easily done. Have you ever done any energy work? Studied chakras, tuning meridians, that sort of thing?"

"Speakee English?" I passed an arch look. Had Lily understood any of this, been a willing partner? "I never studied anything like that."

"Amazing," Rick said. "You're a *natural.* I had to study four years with a healer in California to even begin." He blew air through pursed lips. "Tell me about your treatments again, both yours and Dedra's. Whatever you know, even if you don't think it's important."

Thinking of the dead woman, and the near-dead one down the hall, I settled in and told him what he wanted to know, all of it, holding back only the deep smoky attraction I'd felt for Chal. Rick seemed most interested in the first, where we had both felt drained, and the last, when I'd been so charged. When I finished, he read over his notes, then looked at me, speculation written on his face.

"Can I try something?" he asked. Uncertainty must have showed in my face, because he actually laughed. "Nothing bad. It's an experiment. Not dangerous, I promise. I just want to get a feel for your energy field."

"You mean those areas governed by the chakras, the alignment and so on. But you just said I'd given Dedra any power I had." Not that I was buying that. I was guessing if that's really what had happened, that it was one of those miracle emergency adrenaline bursts, like the guy who could lift a car off his child in crisis mode. That made sense. Such events had been documented in the past.

Rick persisted. "I'm not looking for what you've got, just testing your usual state."

"Then will you tell me about Lily and the others? And what this has to do with vampires?"

"Yes. Then I'll share what I know."

Quid pro quo, Clarice... The dark words echoed in my brain. I eyed him. Which of us was Hannibal Lecter?

"This won't hurt a bit," he said with a smile to boost the old doctor's saw. He wheeled his office chair to a stop directly in front of me, then stood up.

"Try to relax. Clear your mind. Feet flat on the floor. Let your arms hang and your head fall forward. If I touch you someplace, it means that place isn't relaxed yet."

Uncomfortable at first, I tried to relax deep into the chair, as he'd asked. He moved around me, poked me lightly several times, my shoulder, my hip, my knee. I tried not to work too hard at releasing those places, finding the effort tended to tense others. Several of the points he touched were those same points I'd seen highlighted on the poster depicting chakras at the clinic.

"Don't *think* about this," he cautioned. "It's not a function of your conscious mind. The energy just is, you don't have to work at it. Close your eyes. Abdominal breathing, like yoga." He came around in front of me and sat in his chair, placing my hands on my thighs, where they were warm against my khakis. He then placed his hands on top of mine.

The room was quiet. I could hear his breathing, my breathing, the ticking of the clock on the wall, the long narrow hand moving one second at a time. His hands, so warm, so big, grew heavier. After a few minutes, I noticed we were breathing in synchronized rhythm. We felt in tune. The trust each of us had been seeking had been found in that moment. Time seemed suspended. It almost felt like Rick and I were not in our bodies, we were moving closer—

after a single staccato knock, the door opened suddenly. "Doctor?" came a female voice from the doorway behind me. My eyes snapped open, and I felt like I'd been wrenched away from someplace warm and safe, somewhere very far away.

Looking at the doctor, I saw a tender light in his eyes. What was he thinking? Had we really crossed some kind of barrier? He appeared to be much more tranquil than I'd ever seen him. His smile held a hint of intimacy. As he turned to the nurse, I could see he was disappointed.

"Yes, Rita?"

"I'm sorry to interrupt —whatever you were doing," she said coolly. "Dedra Rhodes' parents are on the phone and wanted to speak with you."

"Very well. I'll be down in a moment."

The nurse left. I felt like a teenager who'd been caught with her boyfriend *in flagrante* by her parents. I didn't understand exactly what was happening to my life. I had run to Ralston to escape a man—and here I couldn't seem to stay away from them. First Brendon, then Chal…now Rick Paulsen.

Rick stood up, then studied me, shifting his weight from foot to foot. "I felt something there I would like to explore further—you have a very strong energy field. Can we do more of this later?" he asked. "Somewhere else?"

I eyed the door ruefully. "Definitely somewhere else."

"No interruptions would be best." He reached for his white lab coat. "My place is kind of far away. What about yours?"

"You want to come to my apartment? Seriously?" Was this a cheap line? I didn't think so. At the same time, I felt like I'd caught a glimpse inside him in those minutes of contact. I believed he could be trusted. I capitulated. "Sure. How about tomorrow night?"

"I'll be there. I'm off rounds at eight. See you fifteen minutes later." He patted my shoulder, eerily in the manner of Melissa Jones, and hurried out to catch up with the disapproving Rita.

A slow smile came to me. I'd managed to get him right where I wanted him. Now I was going to find out about the vampires.

~*~

By the time I left the hospital that night it was late, and Gloria excused me from work the next day. I imagined Chris's face when she explained that he had to go cover for me as the kindergarten class from the local elementary school visited a nursing home, with their pets. If he'd thought Rotary was bad…

I drove home and found indisputable signs of normalcy, a welcome relief from the past day. After I turned on the CD player, already loaded with five discs, I washed up the few dishes in the sink and spent an hour or so straightening everything, the memory of the chaos in Dedra's apartment leaving me cold. I couldn't live out of boxes like she did, dealing with surface necessities only. My time with Jesse had honed what started out as just a habit of keeping track of projects into a position where he'd often accused me of being a "control freak."

I wondered while I worked if I was so bent on maintaining control, then why did Chal Talman have such an effect on me? I remember going in to see him and then losing myself in the relief he brought. I'd thought his ability was unique, but my experience earlier that evening showed me that other people could connect with me, suspend time, bring me closer to something outside the physical body.

I'd begun meditating back in Pittsburgh when Jesse and I had started having trouble. The stresses of working a big-city paper, combined with his infidelity, had really begun to unravel my ability to keep a grip on my ability to get up and live every day. A friend had steered me to a yoga studio and I'd practiced both yoga and meditation. The yoga had improved the state of my back quite a bit; I really ought to find a local studio.

As for the meditation, I could do that any time. Considering the day I'd had, this seemed like a good time. I paused the CD in the player, and looked around for anything of a New Age nature to facilitate relaxation. The only thing I found nearby was the Goldstone disc. I hesitated, but finally dropped it in. It was a relaxation disc, right? What could it hurt?

I positioned myself comfortably on the floor, sitting with my back straight, leaning just slightly against the couch for support. Breathing deeply into my solar plexus, I listened to the violins in the music and let myself go, slipping easily into a meditative state.

For the first while—I never knew how long the sessions lasted, mostly until I felt refreshed—everything was as it always was. I listened to my breath, saw it as golden light, not as clearly as Chal had showed me, but in a similar manner.

As I continued, though, it felt like dark clouds came near, cutting off the sun, cutting off the light. As the crepuscule grew, the air thickened with a scent of acrid smoke, like burning fall leaves. Thunder rumbled overhead. I struggled to catch my breath through an atmosphere increasingly like corn syrup, my heart thudding as it vainly attempted to serve my body. I gasped for air—

--and woke abruptly, pulse racing and in a cold sweat.

At first my legs wouldn't work, but I finally gained control over them and pushed myself up, the very act of walking and breathing normally restoring my calm to some extent. The only image I could reconstruct from my panicked mind was that of the Goldstone clinic. Its windows were all dark except the wide window in the front, and in that window, one shadow watched the passing world with glowing crimson eyes.

After that, it took me a long time to allow myself to fall asleep, but with a hot toddy and a healthy dose of Fox News babble, I managed.

CHAPTER THIRTEEN

The next day I decided to go to work anyway. I wasn't surprised when Melissa, a florid long skirt flowing around her ankles, cornered me as soon as I arrived.

"You went to the hospital?" she asked, blocking my entrance to the newsroom.

"I went with Dedra," I said. Peculiar question when Dedra had clearly been much more ill.

"What did they think was wrong with you?"

Okay, I could play this game. "Maybe they thought Dedra had something contagious. I mean, I'd just gone to her house, so I'd have been exposed."

"Was anything said about the clinic?" Melissa demanded.

"I told them she'd been going there. It was the only thing I knew about her medical history," I lied smoothly. "I figured if they needed more information, the clinic records might have it."

"Well, that's unfortunate," Melissa said. Seeing my speculative eye on her, she added quickly, "It's unfortunate Dedra is feeling so ill. Will she survive?"

Survive? What an odd choice of words! "I'm sure. She was better even before I left, once they gave her fluids, and so on."

"Oh?" Melissa asked. Her face was carefully controlled. I couldn't read her emotions.

"Probably just the flu. But I'll let you know if I start throwing up, okay?" I smiled brightly and reached for the stack of messages that had piled up. Only when she walked away did I stop to notice the furious beating of my heart. I was outraged that both Melissa and Dr. Ruprei had ignored poor Dedra's condition. Why didn't she matter to them?

Something was obviously wrong. Both Rick's and Melissa's reactions seemed to confirm it. Only further investigation would reveal what it was.

Jim O'Neal bopped over after deadline passed to hand me a name and number. His note indicated that I could find Ben Fosdick at the Fosdick and Stearns Funeral Home out on Route 24. He walked me out to my car.

"You're not trying to steal my beat, are you?" he said. "Bodies are my livelihood. Thou shalt not steal other people's bodies." A weak smile showed his insecurity as a middle-aged man in a young person's business.

I opened the car door and looked at him in a way I hoped was reassuring. "I'm not going to lie, it's a great beat. I loved it when I had it from time to time in Pittsburgh. But this is something special, something different." I looked him in the eye. "Something personal."

"Gloria thinks that what happened to Dedra might be a part of this." He studied me curiously.

"It might."

"My wife Kim goes there. To that clinic. Is she going to be all right?" His hands had clenched into fists. "Is she?"

"I'm sure she'll be just fine." I got in the car and started out of the lot toward the funeral home. I also prayed like hell I knew what I was talking about.

Ben Fosdick was a spare, graying man who still cultivated his sideburns from the 1970s. He seemed well aware of the reason I was there; I should have known Gloria would have prepared the road for me.

"Gloria called me about you," he said, drawing me down a back hall into a small musty office, closing the door with a quiet click. "You're investigating the clinic."

I shrugged. "Gloria seems to think there's something to uncover."

"Oh, there is, there is." He showed me to a battered leather chair and took a seat at a card table next to me. Yellowed certificates hung on the walls in dusty frames and the floor looked like it hadn't been swept in a month. A couple dozen cardboard file boxes were stacked against the far wall, words in jagged black marker showing dates for twenty years earlier.

I'd done my best not to spend much time in funeral homes over the years, but all of them I'd seen had been very proper and immaculate. Not like this. "You bring families…in here?"

Fosdick smiled, that so-sincere-but-not-quite-warm smile. Oh yes, he was a funeral director. "This isn't my Ethan Allen office. That's up the hall. What we're talking about isn't 'public' business." The smile vanished.

I settled into the chair and set my notebook on the table, glancing over the files spread out next to it. "I still don't understand why the newspaper's investigating this. Why haven't the police done anything? Why haven't the families called for a public hearing or something?"

"Many reasons." As I reached for a pen, he shook his head. "This isn't for the record. I'll tell you the background, so you know who to talk to and what to ask. You see, my daughter Barbara was the first to die." At my look of surprise, he seemed a little smug. "Gloria didn't tell you?"

"She's played pretty close to the chest on this," I said. "Not everyone is convinced the clinic is at fault." I didn't tell him one of those people was me.

He smiled wistfully. "Barbara died five years ago. She was a cheerleader at the high school, very active. She was even in line for a softball scholarship at the end of her senior year. Here's her picture."

He reached across the table to show me a beautifully framed senior portrait of a dark haired girl in a cheerleading sweater, eyes sparkling and vivacious. Her smile was wide and genuine.

"She's very pretty."

"Oh, yes. Her mother and I were very proud of her." He gazed at the picture in silence for a few moments, then returned it to its place.

"The fall of her senior year, she fell from the top of a cheerleading pyramid and injured her neck. One of my wife's friends insisted we take her to the Goldstone clinic for treatment. She said she'd achieved wonderful results. But after several treatments, Barbara began to lose interest in everything. She didn't take care of herself, didn't keep up with her schoolwork. She looked like hell."

I nodded, thinking of Dedra.

"Finally, we took her to her regular family doctor, who gave a whole battery of tests to see what was wrong. Tests proved nothing." He shrugged. "He gave her some iron pills. He was baffled."

He went on, "After she went to see Dr. Fry, she started getting better. We just figured her condition was improving and were grateful. We started going out as a family again and she went back to the team, even though she was still seeing the therapist at the clinic once a week to keep her neck healthy.

"But a month or so later, she fell again. Our doctor recommended physical therapy at the hospital. Barbara wouldn't agree. She said she wanted the woman at the clinic, so we gave in to her. Three weeks later, she was dead."

"What did they determine to be the cause of death?"

"She had a heart attack. The doctor theorized the repeated injuries had caused some blood clots, which blocked a valve." His eyes grew fierce. "But that kid was an athlete. Her heart was in prime condition. It was *no* heart attack."

"Didn't you have an autopsy?"

"Her mother wouldn't let us. Barbara was our only child. She couldn't bear the thought of any more damage to that girl's body. Dr. Fry found a reason. That was good enough for her." He sighed and leaned back in his chair, staring at the ceiling.

"So this is one of the ones who died at the hospital, not out in the field." I thought about Rick's theory. Certainly this would back it up. I wondered why he hadn't come to Ben for support months before.

"Yes. But like I said, she was the first. I began noticing others in the funeral parlors all around town, previously healthy young women who suddenly began a downward slide to hell."

"After they went to the clinic?"

"That I don't know. If the doctor who signed the death certificate was on staff at the hospital, there might not be any obvious connection to the clinic."

"It would seem to be the crucial bit of information. You've got it for your daughter. Were there any others?"

Fosdick started to answer, then stopped, getting up to listen at the door as footsteps approached, then faded away. "Never can be too careful." He lifted up two of the boxes in the stack closest to him, flipping one over on top of the card table. Taped to the bottom of it was a large manila envelope.

He certainly was maintaining the cloak and dagger atmosphere in this. I watched, foot tapping impatiently, as he peeled the envelope off, opened it, slid out a set of documents.

"Three I know of my own personal knowledge." He set the three death certificates on the table before me. "One was a friend of Barbara's. My wife and I didn't know she was a patient at the clinic until it was too late. Two others were students at the college, their parents located in some distant city."

"We suspect several more were patients because they fit the profile and because they'd been injured in the recent past, according to court documents filed because of automobile accidents or injuries on the job." Fosdick set out several more.

"But what about the deaths out in the open, like Lily Kimball? Some official investigation had to take place, a formal determination. The coroner—"

"The coroner refuses to classify any of the deaths as mysterious, no matter what the families say. Each of the women could be pegged with a death from natural causes, as legitimately certified by their own doctors —heart failure, pneumonia, or other illness. Like Lily Kimball and her hypothermia. So no one's willing to go any further."

I studied the death certificates. They were what he said, apparent final evidence of a reason each had died without any need for further examination. I tried to commit the names to memory, in case I ever got a chance to scope out files at Goldstone. "And the others are just typecast," I said, looking over the remainder.

"Exactly."

"You said the coroner wouldn't even make the leap to the next level?" While it could be coincidence, I could certainly see a pattern. Just for argument's sake, wouldn't they have followed it?

"Jim Reed, the coroner, is tied up with them somehow, I don't know if he's a patient, or if he's an investor? He'd always listen to my theories, then pooh pooh them as overactive imagination or flights of fantasy. 'You're just too sensitive about this,' he'd say, 'because of Barbara.' No one would ever listen to my suspicions. Or Gloria's."

"Because of her sister."

"You can understand why people would think we were biased."

"Sure. But women like Lily—they don't have any reason to be dead. Someone has to find out what drove her into the blizzard in the middle of the night. We owe her that."

"We owe them all peace, Miss Woods."

~*~

After I left the funeral home, I stopped at the convenience store for some coffee while I decided my next move. As I passed the *Courier* rack, I noticed I had no stories above the fold and frowned. That's what happened when you spent the days wrapped up in Nancy Drew crap, instead of working at your chosen vocation. I knew my feature on the newspaper-sponsored cooking competition and annual recipe book was inside somewhere.

Yippee.

I paid for a large cup, then retreated to the center island, the one with the condiments, feeling the need for comfort in my coffee. I surveyed the flavored additives available and settled for hazelnut. Impulse drove me to add chocolate. Then vanilla. I considered the amaretto for a minute.

"You don't want to do that," came a male voice from behind me.

"Is it against the law to have mixed drinks?" I asked, tone heavy with sarcasm.

"Hey, I'm all for mixed drinks," said Brendon Zale, leaning one elbow on the counter. "I prefer Jack with about anything. Or even Southern Comfort. I'll buy you one, if you're interested." He studied my face, searching for a sign of hope. "Are you?"

I held up the steaming paper cup. "Coffee. I'm all set, thanks."

"That's a shame." He didn't look so bad, dressed down and off duty. Well-fitting jeans over brown leather-tooled boots, a plain black T-shirt under a blue and gray plaid flannel shirt that complimented his steely eyes; it screamed "All-American Boy."

I walked over to one of the cheaply-constructed little vinyl booths and slid in to the side away from the window. Setting the cup down, I reached in my purse for my cell. I went to dial, then became aware of Brendon standing behind me. I looked over my shoulder. "Do you mind?"

He grinned. "Sorry. I just can't seem to tear myself away. Can I at least have a rain check? Please?"

I really didn't need any more male companionship, particularly from someone who I saw as kind of a stalker. On the other hand, who knew when I might need a friend in the police department?

"Fine. If I can get back to what I'm doing, I'll promise you a rain check." I smiled as warmly as I could.

He beamed. "Hey, thanks! I'll hold you to that. You just let me know when. Or I'll pester you." He chuckled and started for the door, then turned back. "Tell Dedra I'm glad she's feeling better." He left the store. I watched him cross the parking lot and climb into a black Chevy pickup that looked considerably used. He waved as he pulled away.

I found my smile stayed. He seemed like a nice kid. Well, not a kid. He probably wasn't much younger than I was, five years, maybe. I remembered back to when I was that age, 21 or 22, just finishing journalism school at Kent State, thinking I knew damn near everything. Talk about self-delusion…

I picked up the phone again and dialed the hospital, wanting to find out how Dedra was doing. The front desk operator waved HIPPA at me, but I managed to get put through to Rick Paulsen's office.

"How are you feeling, Sara?" he asked.

"No worries, thanks. I called to see about Dedra."

"She's much better. I think she was demanding cheeseburgers a little while ago. She also wanted to know if I'd seen you." There was a pregnant pause. "She seems to think you might have some inclination to be with me."

"What? I didn't tell her that."

He sounded amused. "Oh. Must have been when she was feverish, then. Are you coming by the hospital or will I see you tonight?"

"Ton—oh. Right. Probably tonight."

"All right. See you then." He hung up and I chewed myself out for forgetting. A lot on my mind, I guess, what with all the information Fosdick had given me. And the lack of sleep. I tucked the phone away, grabbed the coffee and headed home to get ready.

CHAPTER FOURTEEN

Rick arrived at precisely the appointed hour. When I answered the door, I noticed details about him, the exact amount of hair that lay against his collar, irrepressibly wavy; the shade of his powder blue polo shirt and khakis; the scuffs on his well-worn Doc Martens. The way he studied me, I got the feeling he was doing the same.

"Come in," I said finally, glad I'd picked a simple knit shirt and slacks in a dark green shade. Nothing dressy. Awkward, I stepped aside.

He handed me a bottle of Chardonnay. "Thanks," he said, and he walked in to take a long look around. More details. He nodded with approval. "What did Ben Fosdick have to say?"

"Ben? How did you—" I uncorked the wine, set it aside to breathe a moment, eyes narrowing with curiosity, or perhaps even suspicion.

He laughed, very much at ease. "It's not a big town, you know. I was out for errands this afternoon, and I saw your car in his lot."

I wondered a moment who else might have seen my car there, and what they might have thought of it. I wasn't as paranoid as Ben Fosdick, of course, but the fact he was so concerned tended to make me a little twitchy.

"He has some interesting theories about the Goldstone, and the dead women." I reached for two tulip-shaped stemmed glasses, setting them gently on the tiny counter. My six Ravenscroft crystal wine glasses were a shower gift from my wedding to Jesse Stewart, a treasure I'd wanted since I was a teenager. To make myself worthy of them, I'd studied wines and the science of glassware designed for them, and these were deemed appropriate for white wines. I didn't imagine Rick would appreciate what had gone into them; but I appreciated him bringing wine. My nerves could use a little chemical relaxation.

"He agrees with me." Rick nodded and walked over to glance out the front window, then he turned to face me.

"It would seem that way. Have you discussed this with him?"

"Briefly. He's been reluctant to be obvious about it. You've got a much easier in at the hospital. Funeral directors hanging around the ER tend to give hospital administrators the willies." He smiled.

"The patients, too, I'd imagine." I watched him. He seemed comfortable, even though he was a stranger here. He walked along my bookcase, reading the titles, touching a few of them. I smiled to see he noted my favorites.

Judging the wine was ready, I poured two half-glasses and carried one over to him. "I would have pegged you as a Merlot man."

"It is better for your heart. But I wasn't sure what you'd drink. Chardonnay seemed safe." His cheeks flushed. "Or that's what the guy at the store said."

"Ah-ha, the truth comes out." I chuckled. "Who'd have thought they'd hire a sommelier at the 7-Eleven?"

"But it's okay?"

I took a sip, rolled it around my tongue judiciously. "Far superior to Mad Dog."

He laughed again. "Well, I'll hope so!"

That past, we didn't have anything else to say. We filled the uncomfortable silence with the wine, and gradually drifted over to the small gold couch, really a love seat. I sat at one end, consciously sitting against the small arm so he could sit at the other end, careful not to make any move that invited him to think this was a romantic moment.

"So," I said. "The one link that seems to be missing in the investigative process is the person who has access to the clinic records. You said you practice there. Does that make that person you?"

He shrugged. "Maybe. They've been accepting of me so far, though they keep much of their data private. They know I've trained with a healer, and have dabbled in energy work. I understand they've all studied for certifications and licensure in a number of genuine treatment areas, like Feldenkrais and Reiki, so it will take some time before I'd be able to prove anything. At least by myself."

"One deep, dark conspiracy leads to another? The good guys battle the evil guys?"

His smile faded. "Sara, what do you want to do?"

"I want to find out why these young women died. Something's very wrong about it. But I don't necessarily believe it has anything to do with—"

"When will you? When you find yourself in a ditch?" He'd tensed up, and he set the glass down on the coffee table, pulling his hand back quickly, as if he thought he'd snap the stem. "Cat and mouse is a dangerous game to play with these people!"

"I have no intention of 'playing'. But with enough information, we should be able to bring it to the attention of people who can do something about it. If it's true that the local police and the local coroner are ignoring this, or are even complicit in this, then outside authorities might be pulled in. State police. Attorney General's office. Hell, if it's true they came here from Boston after operating a clinic there—"

"It's true." His gaze intensified, and I felt drawn to him again.

I looked away, wanting to keep my thoughts clear. "If it is, then it's interstate commerce and the FBI can get involved. But we're going to have to be sure we know what we're talking about, not just working on guesses and theories."

Rick seemed to search for words. "We'll have that case. When we're finished."

"What about your theory the other day? The 'vampires'? Tell me about that."

He fidgeted a moment. "That was hyperbole. Vampires don't exist, not in the shadowy ways of literature, skulking around with black capes and pointy teeth." He shifted, straightening his posture. "What's more important for you and I to discuss is what happens until we have that case put together. I advise that you don't continue to see them for treatment. The first whiff they get that you're investigating them, it puts you at risk for the same fate as Lily."

"Perhaps. On the other hand, if I suddenly pull out, I think that's more of a red flag, don't you think?"

As the words fell from my lips, I knew they were a bland excuse. I had no intention of ending my treatment at the clinic. I'd felt so wonderful after meeting with Talman, I was counting the days until I could make another appointment to see him. If the Ruprei woman thought she was getting her hands on me again, she was deluded. The more I thought about it, I actually reached for the phone on the coffee table and flipped it open.

"Who are you calling?" he asked, furrows dividing his brow.

"What? No one." I put the phone down. It was nearly nine p.m. on a weeknight. No one would have been there. Why had I done that?

"You know, I can understand what you're saying. The clinic might well think it's a red flag if you quit showing up altogether. If you're going to insist on remaining a patient there, I think you need my help. I can show you how to resist the kind of compulsions I believe they are giving their patients, compulsions like...that."

His gaze trailed to the phone, then back to my face. "It wouldn't be easy work. Certainly not the kind of work you're used to, solving puzzles with your brain, planning strategies. It's deep, emotional, feeling work. Sometimes you run up against barriers you've constructed inside yourself to protect you from pain. This puts some people off, if they're not brave enough to deal with the potential consequences."

"So now you're a psychologist, too?"

He shook his head. "It's not psychology, exactly. That's what I'm trying to explain to you. We won't process history using words and thoughts. Your spiritual energy is very strong. You have reserves of strength in you that are very powerful, and I believe you've only dipped shallowly into them, except to help construct walls to keep your pain hidden away." He spread his hands, relaxing. "And to help Dedra Rhodes."

"Right." He was starting to sound like one of the Lone Gunmen again. "This is more of your battery theory, hmm?"

"That's a good point in the explanation where we can begin. If we both understand what is meant by that, then the rest will come. If you're sure you want to try."

I touched the cool glass to my lips, letting it block a quick retort. "I'm not sure at all. I don't think it's fair to say I'm working against the clinic at this point, Rick. I'm just trying to discover what's going on. Especially after what we've just been through with Dedra."

"The open mind. Where all things begin. If you want to discover what's happening, you'll need to embrace that concept."

I was starting to get weird vibes about this. All the New Age rhetoric didn't really serve me. On the other hand, I was a little curious if we could recreate that suspension of time and place we'd shared in Rick's office. If I were to get his cooperation, he'd made it clear I'd have to do things his way. "All right. How do we begin?"

His expression changed to one of relief and delight. "I'm glad you asked." He stood up and pushed the coffee table aside, creating a space about seven feet square. He turned off the overhead light, leaving only the one on the small TV set, the room now dim and mysterious.

Taking one of the sofa cushions, he set it on the floor directly in front of the sofa. "Sit here," he said. "This will support your back."

Finding it odd that he'd choose exactly the place I meditated, I complied with his directive, the position more comfortable with the cushion than without. He moved himself into a cross legged position mirroring mine, on the cushion I'd vacated, scooting close until he was directly in front of me, knees touching mine. My heart gave a little thud-thud as he moved into my personal space, but he must have sensed my discomfort.

"Don't worry, Sara. This will open you to your full self. You're entitled to know." He took a deep breath, a cleansing breath, and I mimicked him. "Now, breathe. Relax. Listen, and let me guide you."

I purposefully put my knee-jerk rebellion aside, and soon we were breathing once again in perfect synchronization, just as we had in his office. He allowed this to continue for some time. One part of me aware of physical surroundings, making sure he didn't make any sudden moves, the rest I let go into a mental haze, letting myself escape.

After awhile, he spoke softly. "You're relaxed, deep inside. Breathe in, out. Feel your abdomen expand, air reaching to every cell and vessel in your body. Don't open your eyes."

My head felt heavy. The last thing I wanted to do was open my eyes. If he'd stopped talking, I'd bet I would have fallen right to sleep.

"I'm going to take your hands. It will facilitate the next step. Is that all right with you?"

"Yes," I replied, my tongue sluggish. I was very relaxed, as he'd said. He hadn't attempted to invade my space, my mind, or my perception. I felt he wouldn't hurt me.

"I want you to remain in the place you are now, relaxed and deep inside yourself, the place where you feel safe and whole. But I want you to expand that place from inside, to outside. The space we're looking for is the space your energy occupies. This is not contained by your skin. Your whole life, your senses have been trained to recognize that boundary, using the sense of touch. The energy field which accompanies your physical self is larger than your body, though centered within it."

He stopped talking for a few moments as we continued to breathe together in harmony. The sounds out the open window faded into the distance, the only sound I focused on was the soft whisper of breath. *In, out...in, out...*

"Sometimes the expanded energy field is described as an aura, a visible colored light which surrounds you. But it's there, seen or unseen. You must learn to sense your energy levels, so you can be alert to changes which might result from any treatment."

He waited in silence again for a few moments, breathing into relaxation.

"What I want you to try now is to expand your awareness into your full energetic space." He paused to let that sink in. "I'll do the same. Our ultimate goal will be to include each other inside our expanded energy circles."

Rick's voice was husky as he finished, and he took my hands. I was aware of our knees touching, the warmth of fingers and palms touching. In a near-whisper, he invited me to open my eyes.

At first, seeing him so near, I went to pull back, but something in his eyes warned me not to. The longer I looked into those eyes, I felt he was totally unguarded, baring his soul. An intimacy welcomed me, made me aware of him in some way other than physical. A completely Zen moment, experienced totally in the Now.

When his lips moved to speak, it seemed to come from far away, although I saw it happening right in front of me. I kept breathing in the long, slow, deep way that had become second nature.

"Think about the core of your being, in the area of the heart or solar plexus. That's where the strongest chakras reside," Rick murmured. "Test its boundaries."

Funny, I always found the core of my being in my head, where my consciousness emanated. That's the place from which I usually operated. Not what he was looking for, apparently. I tried to sense something near my heart, as he'd suggested. *Breathe, breathe...* It was hard to concentrate while he stared into my eyes.

I let go of the effort to search, and discovered a sudden tiny warmth in the center of my chest. I imagined myself cupping my hands around that space and blowing on it softly, like a new flame. It grew within a few moments to be fist-sized. The more I connected with it, the more focused it became.

"When you've found it, expand that place to the limits of your skin," Rick said, never wavering from his intent stare.

This took longer, as no matter how well I envisioned the light inside, whenever I tried to control it, it would fold away from me.

"Let go," he whispered.

Was the struggle so obvious? My breathing tripped over itself for several seconds as my conscious mind became re-engaged. I had to start again. Rick was patient with me, and I got the feeling he was facilitating, somehow, though I never felt he had intruded in any way.

After several attempts, I breathed into the process, and finally felt the warmth grow from inside, from the area of my heart to the edges of my body, gentle as the flutter of butterfly wings. "I did it!" I whispered, trying to remain relaxed despite my excitement. It was a novel experience, a vibration throughout my entire body, blood pumping to the tips of fingers and toes, sensation spreading along my skin from shoulder to trunk to thigh, but different from the rush of microsensation I'd received from Talman. This wasn't a runaway train without control; this I had done myself. It felt safe.

"Good," Rick said, warm approval in his eyes. "Hold here for a few minutes."

When I was ready, he went on quietly, "Now, imagine there's a globe of light around you, and expand the energy you've just opened to fill that place."

Imagining the globe was easy. My mental picture came from the clinic brochure Melissa had given me, the one with the chakras marked—the egg-shaped space which the brochure said surrounded and protected me.

"Slowly," Rick prompted. "It takes practice."

I started over again, taking deep breaths to ground myself, beginning at the bottom of my spine, where it touched the worn cushion, moving my focus upward slowly, past the areas that so often ached but at the moment were quiescent, through that warm bright area of the heart chakra up to the top of my head.

After a few minutes, I envisioned the globe again, pictured it around myself, some four feet in diameter, maybe a little more. The globe glistened, vibrated, waxed iridescent. It was beautiful. When I was secure in the globe's existence, I let my thoughts go and put my feelings in the driver's seat, letting them flow into my center of light. From there it didn't take much to release, to let the light move outward into the globe I'd created. The light filled the globe, warm like sunlight on bare skin. It felt like love, the first stirring when every touch, every word brought a thrill. It was wonderful.

"I can't believe how naturally you do this. It's...amazing," Rick said. "Now, let's just hold this for a few minutes."

We continued to breathe until we were once again in harmony, attuned to each other. I'd totally lost track of time, and the clock was behind me. It could have been fifteen minutes, it could be nearly dawn. This exercise had practically suspended time.

"Are you ready for more?" he asked.

"I don't know." I was awed I had accomplished this, and feared losing the peace I felt at that moment.

"When you're ready, I'll expand my space to include you. Just for a few moments, so you can see how it feels. You'll just have to let it happen."

How was I going to do that? I had no idea. Blissful in my safe space, I sensed the edges of the globe area and let them fray to mist. "All right. I think."

"Tell me if this gets to be too much." Rick took a deep breath and re-established eye contact. "I'm beginning now."

I hadn't been able to see any sort of globe/space/circle evident around the doctor, but I definitely felt something as he squeezed my hands and gazed into my eyes. A presence, reassuring, comforting, so different from the disturbed, almost flaky appearance he'd put forth in the first few times we'd met. I held back, I know I did, but a few moments later, when he pulled away, let go of my hands, and I knew we'd become separate again, he didn't seem to blame me.

"How do you feel?" he asked.

"Good," I had to admit. "Whole. If that makes sense."

"Believe me, it does." He leaned forward and hugged me. "You were awesome."

"Awesome? In the medical meaning?" I didn't pull away. It felt good to be held. I laid my head on his shoulder, and he continued to hold me, hands moving up and down my back, pausing at the site of my injury. I wondered for a second how he'd known where it was, but was distracted by his actions, as he laid his hand flat over the area, then took deep breaths, relaxing. His hand felt warm against my spine. The discomfort I usually experienced after sitting for long periods faded away.

I felt perfectly grounded and settled, more so than any time since my headlong rush from Pittsburgh. The impression of well being filled me, and the sensation of release continued to grow as I leaned on Rick, eyes closed, thinking Jesse hadn't often made her feel this safe, or content...

I suddenly remembered one of our last arguments, after I'd discovered his affair, the two of us standing in the small bedroom of the apartment. I'd told him to get out, but he was convinced the marriage could be saved.

Jesse had run his fingers through his hair, as he often did when frustrated. "Sara, please, it's over with Beth Ann. I just want to work it out with you. I love you!" He'd reached out to me, but I'd jerked away, knocking several perfume bottles off the nightstand. They'd shattered, a vivid metaphor for my life, the blended odor of their scents overpowering. I'd never been able to wear my favorite perfume after that. It brought back too many memories.

The same memories flooded over me now, the rejection, betrayal and the utter despair of those days. Uncontrollable tears welled up in my eyes. The wave of pain was followed by the wish for withdrawal. I pulled away from Rick, and he let me go after a gentle caress to my tear streaked face.

"Opening yourself to someone means opening to yourself as well," he said.

I wasn't so sure. That might be the "healthy" attitude, but the wound reopened was not a pleasant thing to bear. "Some things may be better left hidden," I said, and I went for some tissues.

He shrugged. "That's for you to decide." He stood up and stretched. "Another glass of wine?"

"Sure. Sounds like a fabulous idea." I ducked into the bathroom to wash my face, and found a new softness in the eyes that looked back at me. I had to admit, this had been a good experience, even with the flashback.

When I returned, Rick stood by the window, watching the street below. He had his glass, and I saw he'd poured mine as well. I walked over to see what fascinated him outside.

It was dark, much of the activity passed in shadows except for the area directly under the streetlight opposite. A group of older children with a basketball jumped and shoved down the sidewalk, followed by a man in a short jacket and a baseball cap strolling with a big furry dog. As we watched, a familiar person in a long, flowing skirt shuffled under the light. Melissa Jones stopped and cocked her white haired head, looking directly at the window where Rick and I stood.

I frowned, stepping back out of sight from the ground. "What's she doing here?"

"Isn't that Melissa?" Rick didn't seem particularly rattled. "Does she live around here?" He turned back to the window, but I could see Melissa had gone.

I shook my head. "I don't think so." *So much for secrecy.* I wondered what people would think, if anything, that Rick and I had been seen together. If he were considered a friend of the clinic, maybe that would allay suspicions. Maybe this was a good thing. On the other hand, if they suspected him of working against them…

"Hey, don't worry," Rick said. He slipped an arm around me. His strong presence gave me support, and my energy keyed up at his touch, almost like static electricity made hair stand up on my arm. "You've done a lot for one day," he said. "I'm really pleased."

I blushed a little and concentrated on drinking the wine. "Thanks. All that open mind stuff, you know."

"We work well together. I think we'll be a successful team." He held me at arms' length and studied my face. "I've brought you a list of books which might be helpful to understand more of the theory of what we're doing."

"Sure, for my spare three minutes a day," I said. "No, really, thanks. I'll try to get that done."

"Good. Everything we can do for safety's sake is important. You should drink water, several glasses. Your system has likely let loose some toxins that need to be washed away. And you should get some rest." He set a piece of paper on the table by the window.

I hadn't realized how tired I was. I went to sit down, and nearly lost my footing, catching myself on the back of the couch.

"Told you so. Are you sure you can get yourself to bed all right?" he asked.

I nodded. Boy, was that ever a line. "No problem."

"Good night, then." He kissed me on the forehead and left the apartment, locking the door as he went out.

I carried the glasses and the nearly empty bottle of wine to the kitchen area and set them all in the sink. The clock showed it was after midnight, and I was beat. As Scarlett had said, tomorrow was another day. I checked the door, and looked out the window at the empty sidewalk across the street, still suspicious of Melissa's appearance there, then I dragged myself into my room.

Too tired to even change clothes, I flopped down on the bed and fell asleep almost immediately. With me feeling safe in my body, the bad dreams stayed away, and I had the best night's sleep I'd had in months.

CHAPTER FIFTEEN

Dedra stayed in the hospital nearly a week. We in the newsroom took turns visiting, once her parents went home to their jobs. I knew that Gloria had met with them several times, reassuring them someone was looking out for their little girl, and in fact Dedra was a little more natural and animated. But something about her still worried me.

She'd gone in on a Friday; the Tuesday after she'd been admitted, I came to visit her. As I passed through the hospital's ER doors, I saw Ted, the paramedic who'd been with us on the mad ride to the hospital talking with a police officer. When Ted waved at me, the officer turned; it was Brendon Zale. He gave me a little nod of the head, then glanced down at the pad he had in his hand. "All right, man, thanks. I'll catch up with you if I've got more questions," he said, then he walked off toward the door I'd just entered. Ted was called into the treatment area, and I continued on upstairs, wondering what new developments the two of them might be discussing.

In her hospital room, Dedra sat in a little nest of white blankets on the hospital bed, its back rolled up as straight as it would go, a thin hospital gown much too big for her bagging over her shoulders. She was restless, and not particularly entertained with my stories of the newsroom, the tea the nurses brought for the two of us, or even discussion of the world outside. Suddenly she just started talking, her tone one of urgency.

"Sara, I think I'm going crazy."

"Deed, you're not. You're just sick. Hasn't Rick found the reason yet? The flu? Some kind of 'female trouble'?" I mugged, showing her I was half-teasing. Damned 'female trouble' was blamed for half the things male doctors just didn't want to be bothered with.

"He keeps telling me he doesn't know yet. He's doing tests all the time. Look at my arm." She held it out to display a whole line of bruises. "I've given blood till I don't think there's anything left." A lone tear ran down her cheek. She wiped it away with an angry gesture.

"What did you tell him? About how you got to that condition?" A fleeting memory of the stench in her apartment made me shove the tea away to the other side of the tray.

"I didn't tell him anything—I don't remember anything after the night before." She recounted coming home from a full day at work, exhausted. She'd washed up, dried with a towel that she'd dropped on the floor and thought she'd made something to eat. She'd turned on the CD player just after the television news was over, hoping it would help her shake off the weariness.

"It worked, actually. The first CD was pretty hot—dance music, you know, and I thought maybe I'd have the energy to clean up the sink. I mean, oh my God, I know it looks like hell in there, Sara. But I was always going to do it, like, in the morning. You know, get up the next morning half an hour early and clean up."

"But you were too tired."

Dedra nodded. "I could hardly drag myself out of bed even after I'd hit the snooze a couple of times." Her hands twisted together in her lap, atop the white hospital blanket. "But then the next CD in the player flipped in, the one from the clinic. Wow, that one always relaxes me right away. So I laid down, just for a minute, I thought."

"Guess that was an underestimate."

The fact she'd stayed home, not wandered out to the clinic, certainly put holes in Rick's theory. If Dedra hadn't gone to the clinic, how could they have sucked her dry? "You didn't leave your house?"

"No." Dedra looked troubled. "It was dark outside, and I was just so sleepy. Then I had a dream. Well, I—I think it was a dream. I was at the clinic. It didn't look the same, it was all hidden in shadows, except for these candles, and some kind of chanting. It was dark. I felt…lost. I couldn't get out. And then there were scary things there." She shuddered, covering her face with her hands. "I don't want to think about it any more."

"Then don't. You probably had a fever. People get delusional when there's a fever, if it's bad enough. You're not crazy. You just need to get better." I stood up and hugged the blonde girl. "That's what's important now." I concentrated on just holding her for comfort, not attempting any sort of interchange. She held on, it seemed, for dear life.

"It's just so confusing," Dedra cried. "I don't know who to trust. Did your Dr. Rick really forbid anyone from the clinic to come in this room?"

"Who told you that?" I frowned. "And he's not 'my' Dr. Rick."

She ignored my irritation. "I heard the nurses talking about it outside this morning. The doctor apparently entered the orders right on my chart."

I thought about Rick's reaction when I'd let them know Dr. Ruprei was there, that first night. "It wouldn't surprise me. I'm not sure he's keen on everything they do at the Goldstone. Even if he's got patients there too." Dedra looked surprised and I nodded. "He apparently agrees with their therapy modalities, the massage and other energetic treatments. He said sometimes they were more useful than drugs and traditional Western medicine."

"Huh. I thought he was a regular doctor."

I laughed. "He is a 'regular' doctor. He just has an open mind." His words echoed in my head. He'd appreciate me trying to make a new convert, I was sure.

"Even so. Melissa didn't seem to like him, though."

"Melissa? What makes you say that?"

"She's been here a couple of times in the evenings," Dedra said. "She brought me a plant and a candy bar." She pointed to the thriving philodendron on the windowsill.

Melissa popping up at the hospital concerned me a little. "What didn't Melissa like about Dr. Paulsen?" *Except for the fact he saved you, apparently. Or the fact that he's seeing me.* I was still disturbed by Melissa's spying on me, or spying on Rick, one or the other. What possible purpose could there be in her keeping tabs on us?

"She didn't say exactly. She just questioned every step of the hospital treatment and wanted to know what tests had been done. She was ticked when she found out Dr. Ruprei wasn't allowed here!" Dedra made a face. "When the nurse came in, they were all over the clinic staff and how fab everyone was there. The nurse acted like she thought I was malingering or something."

I tried the tea again, wanting something to do with my hands. I knew Dedra had been very sick indeed. Why would someone want to minimize it that way?

"A nurse in the emergency room the day you came sounded just like that. Maybe it's the same one."

I also wondered about Melissa's sudden interest in Dedra. When I'd come to the newsroom, I'd been the one she'd focused on. But now… It could be innocent. That was the problem with so much of this whole situation. It might be innocent, the treatments, the doctors, everything that had gone on. People died. It was part of life. It could all be a coincidence. So it would be understandable why no one else wanted to investigate the deaths. *It could be…*

The more I heard, though, I didn't know for sure. If it hadn't been for my own experience, I might be on the bandwagon one hundred percent.

Meanwhile, I couldn't think of a diplomatic way to stop Melissa from coming.

"That Dr. Paulsen keeps asking about you, though. You know, he's kind of cute, for an old guy."

"Dedra!"

"What? He's got to be like, wow, nearly forty."

"That doesn't make him old." My cheeks got hot. "What does he ask?"

She grinned, knowing she had my full attention now. "He wanted to know about your background, you know, about the divorce and your family being gone and all. What you liked, what you didn't like. He said you were a good friend to me."

"I'm not sure I want you telling him all about me." Besides, with the intimacy they'd achieved at her apartment, she felt like they knew quite a lot about each other. They'd merged their energy, after all. "I don't know if I want a relationship right now."

"Hey, I've got to do something so that you quit mooning over my man Chal." Dedra smirked.

I looked away a moment, the name bringing his darkly handsome face back to my consciousness. I should see him again. Tearing my attention away from the thought of him, I reached out to pat Dedra's hand. The contact gave us both a slight tingle.

Dedra smiled shyly. “The paramedic said you saved my life.”

“No, I didn't. Rick did that.”

“Ted was adamant about this,” she said. “He said this happened before we even got to the hospital.”

Well, damn. I hope the supposedly helpful Ted hadn’t gone around sharing this story with too many other people. I thought of him speaking to Brendon in the ER. “When did you talk to him?”

“He came to see me yesterday, just to see how I was doing. Small towns are so nice like that,” Dedra said with a warm smile and a flush of color in her cheeks.

“A-ha!” The flush had exposed Dedra's feelings. “And you were happy to see him. He sure was concerned after they brought you in, He asked me to pass on his best wishes.”

“He says maybe we can get together after I get out. Finally, a social life.”

“Yeah, that would be a nice thing, hmm?” I finished the tea, thought about all the files that awaited me back at the office. “So what are you going to do now? I mean, after you get out and back home?”

Dedra's mouth tightened just a moment. “I guess I’ll come back to work.” She sighed. “My parents want me to come home to Cleveland. I can’t believe Gloria called them. They’re determined to rescue me. They’ll be here in about an hour.”

“You almost died,” I reminded her gently.

“But they're treating me like such a baby.” Dedra sighed, picking at the light blanket across her knees.

“They don’t mean anything bad by it,” Sara said. “What about the clinic? Are you done there?”

Dedra shrugged. “I don't know.”

“Dedra!”

“Hey, no one's proved the clinic made me ill. I didn’t go there the day this all happened. I mean, I think it really was just the flu. Or maybe that super staph bug they’ve been talking about.” She ran her fingers nervously along her arm. “The clinic’s done for me what they promised. I haven't had a migraine in a month. That's a record for me!”

I thought about my own experience, and understood the power of freedom from pain. You felt like a whole new person, one who could do anything. The pain was just starting to return, over a week later. I’d obsessed about the clinic all week, thinking about my last session and its results. In the face of Dedra's decline, and Rick’s concern, I’d resisted the temptation so far. “I know. I do.”

“As for home, I’ve got some work to do there.” She sighed and leaned back against the pillows.

“Boy, do you. Maybe Gloria and I—“

Dedra rolled her eyes. “No, my mother’s already been there. I heard about it for half an hour on the phone. You know how they say you can’t go home again?

There's a good reason for that. I could never live with my mother again." Her smile wavered. "You want to stay till they come? Maybe distract them? Save me?"

I shook my head. "I've got too much to do at the office. Someone's got to pick up your slack." The mock scolding was fine, but that wasn't the real reason. Once I'd started thinking about the clinic, I couldn't get the place out of my mind. "I've got to go, Deed. I'll come back—I promise."

"Bring me something from McDonald's," Dedra said hopefully.

That made me laugh. "I'm sure the hospital food is just fine. Nutritious and flavorless, too." I bent down to hug Dedra and felt the tingle again.

"I believe Ted," Dedra said near my ear. "There's something when we touch. Don't tell me you can't feel it."

"See you later," I said, and left the room. As I hurried around the corner of the pale green hallway toward the exit, I found Rick heading in the direction of Dedra's room.

"A pleasant surprise," he said. "Come from visiting Dedra?"

"Yes. She looks better today."

His smile was warm, and reminded her of the warm energetic light we'd shared. "You have a few minutes? We could grab coffee in the cafeteria."

I was about to agree, when twinges of pain shot across my back. The muscles were tightening. I bit my lip.

"Coffee?" he asked again, when I didn't answer.

I wanted to say yes, but shook my head. I needed to get to the clinic. Now. "I've got to go," I said, inching toward the door.

He eyed me with a good dose of skepticism. "I'll call you later, then," he said.

"Sure, that's fine." I skittered away from him, tension spreading down through my legs and fingers. Hurrying across the parking lot, all I could see was my car. In the car, I fastened my seatbelt, taking a deep breath, something nagging in a small voice that I really would have liked to have coffee with Rick, to debrief the experience of the evening we had together, now that we'd had time to digest it.

What was the rush to get to Dr. Ruprei?

I couldn't explain it. I started the car and grabbed my cell, tapping down through the phone book for the number—

Or maybe they'd just fit me in, if I came right away.

They surely seemed willing to accommodate me otherwise. Heck, the practitioners were in competition to get to see me. Yes. I'd just go straight over. I'd go over now, and nothing would stop me.

CHAPTER SIXTEEN

I found myself driving to the clinic's landscaped lot, almost on autopilot. I wasn't focused on the road, but on the sky. Since I'd entered the hospital to visit Dedra that afternoon, the weather had gone from a heavy gray layer of clouds as far as you could see, to openly stormy. Thunder rolled, and I cringed as lightning cracked somewhere nearby. I wanted more than anything to go home and hide from the storm, but my focus didn't change. Something stronger than my own will drove me onward.

I reached the clinic as the clouds burst, and had to run to the lobby, though I still got drenched. The receptionist's smile skewed sideways with puzzlement.

"Do you have an appointment, Sara?"

"I need to see someone," I said. The air conditioning was on, and I shivered as the cool air hit my wet skin. My white cotton blouse was practically see-through, now that it was soaked. Rain had even bounced up from the pavement to wet the knee-length skirt, which hung against my knees.

"I'm sure we can accommodate you. Just a moment, please." She disappeared into the back, returning with a bright smile and an open door. "Dr. Ruprei says you're welcome any time."

She walked down the hall with me to the room I'd been in the first time, and she rummaged in a closet, coming out with two hospital gowns and a thick white towel. "Here. Why don't you get out of those wet things and I'll run them in our dryer for a few minutes?" Her smile widened.

"Oh, you don't have to do that. I'll just—" I felt myself shiver again. The cold dampness aggravated my tight muscles. I sighed my defeat. "All right. But just for a few minutes, all right? I won't be here that long, I'm sure."

"Of course. Take your time changing. Doctor will let me know when you're ready." She nodded and slipped out.

I took off my blouse and skirt, laid them on the end of the table, and dried off with the towel. It was much more luxurious than anything I had at home, and I felt like wrapping up in it instead. I slipped into the gowns, one frontward and one backward, so I wouldn't be exposed. Taking a seat on the table next to my clothes, I relaxed, feeling more at home, as if this was the only place on earth I needed to be. Without windows in the room, I didn't need to worry about the weather. The hiss of the air conditioner overhead even dampened the sound of the thunder. I looked forward to the relief of my tension and pain.

Dr. Ruprei was delayed, but warm when she entered the room. She handed the clothes to the waiting receptionist, then came in and closed the door. "Sara, I'm surprised to see you, but I'm glad you're here. How is Dedra?" She held her hand out and ran it the length of my back, then frowned and got the little electronic reader, doing the same. "What has happened?"
I tried to sit still, not to think about the pain. I'd been rid of the worst of it for a couple of weeks, and it had seemed like paradise. The volatile weather in spring and fall, changes in barometric pressure, all these impacted how I felt, I knew that. Stormy days were horrible, for more than one reason.

"Nothing really happened," I said. "I didn't do anything in particular that hurt it."

She continued to check readings. "And Dedra?"

"She's much better. I think they'll let her go home soon."

"That's good to hear. Poor child." Her sympathy certainly sounded genuine. "I don't feel anything out of place," she said after her examination. "Were you in pain?"

"It was starting. As soon as it began, I just—had to come." That sounded crazy. Kind of like what Dedra had said. What was going on?

"You had to come? You were drawn here?" Her eyes held a hint of wariness.

I nodded. "Once I started thinking about it, I just knew I had to come."

"I see." The two words were clipped and tight. "Excuse me just a moment. I want to ask for a consult on this." She took the meter and stepped out of the room.

Now what was all this about? Cold fingers spread in my gut. I didn't like feeling out of control, and this felt that way, for sure. I slid off the table, and I would have dressed if my clothes had been there. But they weren't. I was trapped.

A few minutes later, Dr. Ruprei came in with the Amazon-looking woman from the brochure cover. The tall blonde towered over the doctor, with an overwhelming presence, well muscled and powerful, yet undeniably feminine. Her eyes were hard an anomaly here at the clinic, where everyone else warmly welcomed and reassured.

The doctor's face had relaxed, and she shared a warm smile. "Little Sara," she said, patting my leg. "I'm very glad you came."

She took paper from the drawer under the counter, red ink a slash on the page as she made notes. I thought it odd that she wasn't using the laptop electronic notepad the nurses usually used, but maybe it had something to do with the storm. "You are wise to head off any major problems. This is Ulrike von Dorn. I've asked her to give you a massage. I think that will put your symptoms at ease."

"Sara," von Dorn said, by way of greeting. "Please lie on your stomach."

Dr. Ruprei waited until I was lying comfortably on the table, then excused herself. "You're in good hands now," she said. "I'll be back to check on you."

Without further explanation, von Dorn began. For such a large woman, she was surprisingly gentle. She lightly ran her fingers across my back, then as we became accustomed to each other, she settled into a pattern, kneading and smoothing the taut muscles. She seemed to be checking out all the musculature as she rubbed and squeezed and sometimes just held a warm hand over a particular area. It felt so good. I felt cared for, tended to. Despite von Dorn's off-putting attitude, she obviously knew what she was doing.

After awhile, I lost conscious observation of her actions, lulled by the rhythm. It was only a massage. What could a massage hurt? I stopped worrying and drifted away in the lovely sensations.

Some time later, I didn't know how long, something brought me to sharp awareness. My body felt sluggish, lethargic, and I couldn't move. As my mind came into focus, though, I felt a red heat of danger above me. When I turned a mental eye to that heat, I received a vision of huge pointed teeth hovering over me. von Dorn was standing beside me, muttering, one hand over my midback, the other just behind my head, lightly touching.

I tried to get up, but only managed a jerk and twist. She jerked as well, perhaps startled, and turned to rubbing a small spot on my shoulder blade with her nearest hand. Then she stepped back from the table and invited me to sit up, actually helping me upright, since I felt like I was moving through gelatin.

I evaluated myself as I came upright, not sure I could do anything if I found something wrong. My muscles felt very relaxed. I was a little vague, like at the conclusion of meditation, that feeling of having traveled from a long way to come back to Now. I detected no drain or burst of energy, just a dragging lassitude.

"I hope you feel better," von Dorn said, without any trace of irritation or surprise at my reaction. "You had some deep muscle tightness. That's probably why you couldn't pinpoint exactly what was off. But your body knew to come here to have that healed." The masseuse actually smiled.

That seemed like a logical explanation. Really, it did. But I still couldn't push that mental picture from my mind. *Hungry teeth in a gigantic mouth, inches from me...* I shuddered.

Ulrike was looking at me, eyebrow raised. "Sara? Did you hear me?"

"Yes, I did. Thank you. Where are my clothes?"

I will check on that for you." She gave me a jerky little bow and disappeared out the door.

As soon as she was gone, I slipped off the end of the table, pacing along the side of the table, willing my legs to work, my brain to kick into a more useful gear.

But the pain was gone.

The receptionist knocked and came in, my clothing perfectly dry. "Here you are, Sara," she said brightly. "I hope you feel better."

"Thanks," I said, just wanting her to get out. When she was gone, I dressed myself, feeling a little stronger as I went along. I steeled myself to walk out the door erect, though I felt a little woozy after the effort of remaining upright.

As I approached the reception desk, I spied Talman and Ulrike in what appeared to be a bitter argument in the middle of a back hall. As I saw him, he turned and stared at me, his eyes hot and liquid. He took a step toward me, but Ulrike said something I couldn't hear. He drew back like she'd slapped him.

My attention was distracted as Dr. Ruprei came up behind me and took my arm, leading me toward the front. "Sara, dear, that's much better," the doctor said, touching my shoulder and passing her hand down my arm. "Much better. Your body knows when to come, even if your head doesn't know why, yes?"

"I guess so," I said. Little bugs of apprehension tickled under my skin, despite the fact that the massage had seemed to do its work. I was definitely relaxed, perhaps overly so. I didn't feel drained, though, despite my sluggishness. And the teeth… I shivered as that image returned, haunting me. Where had that come from? Had Rick so poisoned my thoughts against the clinic that I was determined to find something evil here? *Sometimes a massage was just a massage...*

"Come back soon," the doctor said.

"I will." I left the building, fresh air acting like a tonic upon my escape. The clouds were dissipating, that sudden clearing that often happened after a rain. The drag disappeared, and I believed I could feel blood surging through my veins. Each step felt like a warm jolt of energy rising from my feet to my head. It was delightful.

As I pulled out of the parking lot, I caught a glimpse of the doctor and Ulrike in the front window, watching me go. Their eyes were perfectly normal. The picture, somehow, was not comforting. It seemed wrong —*felt* wrong.

I was definitely getting paranoid.

CHAPTER SEVENTEEN

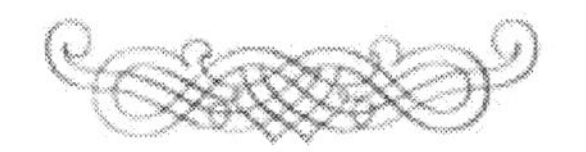

Dedra was discharged and came back to work. I continued to feel well. Life went on. Rick pushed me to get together with him again, but I put him off, wanting just to have a normal life for a little while. Days passed and spring came into full swing. The sun tried to establish a firm hold on the season, and we all spent time walking, admiring the tulips and daffodils that everyone seemed to have planted in their yards.

People were starting to recognize me now, three months after I'd begun working at the *Courier*. They'd say hello at the library, in the courthouse, or mostly at the IGA. While there was a Meijer store out on the highway, I often chose the independent grocer just to experience that small-town recognition. It's an ego thing. Reporters like it.

One late afternoon in early April I stopped into the IGA to pick up some yogurt and fruit on my walk home. Thelma's friend with the oxfords greeted me genially as I came in. I made my way to the back of the store, to the dairy case. As I pulled open the glass door, I caught a glimpse of Brendon Zale out of the corner of my eye. Cool air floated out of the case as I watched him not watching me for a change. His attention was firmly centered on Ulrike von Dorn, who was selecting some items from the meat counter.

"You need something, Miss Woods?" asked a voice from inside the case. Startled, I came back to the present and squinted into the shadowed darkness within. "You been standing there with the door open awhile. Something you can't find?"

"Ralph, is that you?" Embarrassed, I grinned at the store owner, who I'd interviewed for a story on the economy not long before. "I'm sorry! I've got what I need right here."

"Just wanting to make sure you're satisfied," he said. "You have a good day, now."

"You too." I reached for a couple cartons of fat-free yogurt and closed the door. When I looked for Brendon again, he was gone.

As I headed for the fresh fruit area, I didn't know whether to be flattered or disappointed that Brendon had found a new target for his affections. And Ulrike, of all people. She looked like she could break a man in two with those muscular legs.

Or suck them dry.

A frown pulled my facial muscles down as I recalled the image of those teeth. I couldn't shake it, no matter how I'd tried. Maybe it was the end product of an overactive imagination, but it had felt so real…

I heard a large crash, then several women screamed in the next aisle. Alarmed, I set the yogurt down and ran around the end cap to see Ulrike lying on the floor in the canned goods aisle, a cart next to her, buried in a display of tomato puree cans. A woman I recognized from the library was dialing furiously on her cell, and got through to 911 before I could. She practically shrieked that there was a woman having a seizure at the IGA and would someone come *right now*!

Brendon Zale was there, bent over Ulrike, feeling for a pulse at her neck. He seemed to be having a difficult time finding it. As I came to a stop, he looked up at me and his eyes widened. He pulled his hand back and stuck it in his jacket pocket. Uncomfortable for a moment, he studied me, then straightened, putting on his game face.

He stood up. "All right, everyone step back, please. The paramedics will be here in a few minutes."

Ralph came out of the back. "Anything you need me to do, officer?"

"No, sir. I think the situation is under control." His jaw was set, and his eyes as hard as I'd ever seen them.

I glanced down at Ulrike. She hadn't moved. As I studied her further, I realized she wasn't even breathing. Her man-style shirt was open several buttons at the neck, and I could see a deep purple mottling spreading from her chest up toward her neck and then across her jaw to the bottom of her cheek. "What happened?" I said.

The woman I knew held her closed cell phone, trembling. "She was just standing there. She had a can of Del Monte in her hand. She was reading the label. Then she just fell. She just fell."

Brendon concentrated on keeping the aisle clear of people. He'd done nothing else for Ulrike after checking her pulse. He must have known she was dead. Curious that he hadn't tried to revive her. He seemed the 'hero' type to me, the one who would go above and beyond for that bit of recognition. I watched him, going about his work with a professional attitude, no emotion showing in his expression.

The paramedics arrived several minutes later, siren blaring. Brendon's voice tightened, his words coming out a little strained, as he made us all step back. I talked to several of the other witnesses while we were waiting, and they confirmed the first story. The Amazon had just dropped dead.

As the paramedics wheeled her out, a white sheet covering her from head to toe, the gurney jolted when it hit one of the fallen cans on the floor. An arm dropped off the edge of the gurney, swinging a little from the impact. Its skin was puckered and mottled as her neck had been. A silver ring in a snake motif flashed on the third finger of her hand.

What the hell?

I followed them out, but they didn't know me, and they loaded their burden into the truck and sped away without answering any of my questions. Irritated, I turned and went back into the store to ask Brendon about the strange event, but he was nowhere to be found.

"Did you see where the officer went?" I asked Thelma's friend at her register, but she just shook her head. Ralph, restacking the cans with help from his young son, said the same. I walked up and down the aisles, even peeking into the rear storeroom, but they were right. He was gone. Frustrated, I retrieved my yogurt and a small pack of berries, paid for them and walked out to my car. I called the office to tell Gloria I'd been here in person and had some interview notes for Jim O'Neal.

"She's dead? You're sure?" Gloria asked. I could hear the squeak of the crank of her window.

"She looked real dead to me. Purple, too."

"What?" I heard her puff on a cigarette, then just the slightest susurration of breath as she blew out the smoke.

I explained what I had seen, adding I wasn't sure what it meant. "Do you want me to go to the hospital?"

A dry laugh. "Are you kidding? As soon as O'Neal heard 'body,' he left skid marks on the newsroom floor. I'll let him know you've got something to add."

"All right. Thanks, Gloria." I tucked the phone into my purse, thinking the auspicious streak of normal we'd enjoyed had come to an end.

~*~

While I was in the shower the next morning, the phone rang. Uttering a blasphemous curse, I shut off the water, grabbed a thin towel and dripped my way out to the small bedside table to answer it. "Hello?"

"Sara. It's Ben Fosdick."

Goosebumps formed all along my skin at his ominous tone. I didn't think it was because I was still wet. "Has there been another one?"

"Not exactly. How quickly can you get here?"

I glanced down at the pool around my feet. "I don't know, fifteen minutes?"

"Make it ten. I can't hold them off much longer. Come in the back." He hung up.

Stunned, I stared at the phone for a few seconds, then sprinted back to the shower to wash the apricot-scented shampoo from my hair. As soon as I was clean, I picked up the jeans and turquoise embroidered smock I'd thrown on top of the hamper the night before and pulled them back on as fast as I could. Making sure I had a pad and pen in my purse, I grabbed it and ran out the door, comb in hand. My hair would have to air dry on the way there.

As the lights on the dash came on, the clock announced it was six-forty-five a.m. I whipped the comb through my hair and spun the tires as I came out of the driveway, spraying gravel across Thelma's yard. Promising I'd clean it up later, I opened the windows and let the wind blow full speed, Tori Amos blasting on the car stereo as I sped up the highway.

Unsure who "they" were and what the situation was, I parked two blocks from the funeral home in the parking lot of an optical store and walked up through the yards to the back door of the funeral home, as Ben had directed. The sun had risen enough to invite the birds to share their morning song. I waved at a couple of kids who were waiting at the bus stop, surely wondering why some woman with frazzled hair was sneaking around through their roses.

As I approached the building, I could see several large dark vehicles parked off to the side, empty. I knocked a couple of times, softly, and the door flew open. Ben barely had time to recognize it was me before he seized my arm and yanked me inside, closing the door in the same breath.

"What's going on?" I gasped.

"You've got to see this." He was pale, shaken. I followed him down the hall to what must be the cooled embalming room, where a body lay on the table amid trays of long metal tools and other things I just didn't want to think about someone using on me. He closed that door and locked it when we were inside. The damp chill in the air made me shiver. His hands were shaking, and I could swear I saw tears in his eyes.

"Ben, are you all right? You don't look good."

"Look!" He pulled the sheet back to reveal an elderly, wrinkled woman, her hair silver-white, skin age-spotted.

I raised an eyebrow. "It's a dead body. An old woman." He'd called me here for this?

He chewed his lip a moment, staring down at the corpse. "This is Ulrike von Dorn."

CHAPTER EIGHTEEN

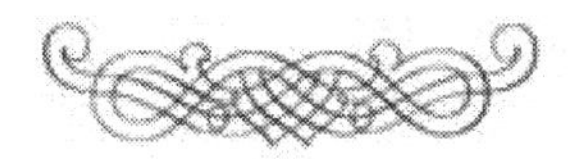

If I'd been drinking coffee, I would have done a major spit take. "She—what?" I stared, then inched closer, a sick feeling on my tongue. "That can't be. I was there. She was maybe…thirty. Maybe. I mean, she could have dyed her hair, maybe. But —"

My throat choked up at the thought of being close to Ulrike's dead body, especially under these circumstances. Inside my stomach, butterflies tried wildly to escape at the thought of getting near her, half expecting her mouth to open, and those thin, dried lips to pull back, and the horrible, sharp teeth of my vision would fasten on my arm and—

A little scream slipped from my mouth, and I slapped a hand over it, with a guilty look at the funeral director.

"Are you all right?" he asked, coming to my side, his professional solicitude in evidence. "I know it's shocking, but I didn't think you'd come unglued about it."

"Sorry." I cleared what felt like spider webs from my throat and shook myself thoroughly. When I'd done that, I felt more able to cope. "Now. Let's try this again. You were saying this is Ulrike von Dorn. The therapist from the Goldstone clinic. The one who died at the IGA yesterday."

At his surprised look, I nodded. "I was there, actually. I saw her, dead. She didn't look anything like this." Sucking it up, I walked over to the table and pulled the sheet down quickly enough for a glance at what was clearly an aged carcass, then covered her back up. The bad taste in my mouth hadn't gone away. "Nothing like this. Except for those purple marks.

"I remember she had—'' I lifted up just the corner of the sheet, looked for Ulrike's hand. The silver snake. It was her.

Ben's expression perked up with interest. "I wondered about those." He returned to the table and pulled the sheet down again, exposing desiccated breasts and shriveled, taut skin across her ribs. But what drew the eye was the mottling across the base of the throat, the color of ripe mulberries. The size of dimes, the individual marks trailed up across Ulrike's left shoulder and disappeared at her shoulder blade. A larger circle sat square on the cap of her shoulder, just where epaulets would lay on a jacket, its shade darker, almost black.

"She looked like a young woman when they brought her in last evening, except for the usual signs of death. But those markings seemed to start the process. I came back after dinner, and the skin around the marks was puckering, changing somehow, I didn't know how then. I could see it spreading across her chest and face, though. It haunted me all night." He rubbed his hands together as if they were freezing. "When I came back at five a.m., the transformation, for lack of a better word, was complete. I was stunned."

"I can imagine." I leaned closer to examine the blotch, thinking at first it was a bruise, but it wasn't. Markings and letters in a language other than English were legible, but I couldn't tell what they said. "What's this—"

Before I could finish, there was an urgent knock at the door. A male voice called through from the other side. "Ben? The doctor is out here wanting to take the body. She's pretty insistent."

The funeral director paled, then straightened his shoulders. "I'll be ready for them in a minute!" he called back. "Just ask them to be patient."

"It's been forty-five minutes."

"I know. I'm trying to make her presentable. Please."

Muttering on the far side of the door dwindled away and we were alone again.

"They've come from the clinic?" I asked.

He nodded. "I'm sure they don't want anyone to know about this."

"Can't you get an order? Some kind of a court injunction?" My mind raced. This would prove there was something going on. Maybe it didn't address Lily's case, or Dedra's, but certainly there was something odd going on. If there was one odd thing, it would be easier to convince the authorities that something else was going on, too. I turned, expecting hope on his face, but found none.

"The only one who could legitimately ask for that would be the coroner. I told you, Jim Reed's hooked up with these people. It'll never happen."

Disappointed, I looked around the room. "Do you at least have a camera?"

He nodded and crossed to a glass-fronted cupboard. He took out an old Nikon, the kind that had regular film in it. I raised an eyebrow.

"You're kidding me. No digital?"

His eyes revealed a decidedly weary man. "This is what I have."

"It'll do." With an exasperated sigh, I checked the settings and started shooting until I ran out of film, including a couple of close-ups of that mark on her shoulder. Then I took out my cell and shot a dozen more. The knocking on the door startled us both.

"Ben!"

"All right. Two minutes. Let me cover her up." Ben eyed me as I started to rewind the film to take it out of the camera. "No time for that. You'd best go along. Take it. Don't show anyone."

"I'm way ahead of you," I assured him. I tucked the camera and the cell in my purse.

"Don't let them see you on the way out. And don't tell anyone. Anyone! Or else all this is for nothing." He tottered a little, and I realized he was not a young man.

"Are you going to be all right?"

"I didn't sleep much. I imagine they'll take her and then this will pass." He smiled faintly. "Maybe I'll call it an early day and go home before dark for a change."

I smiled, hoping it was encouraging. "That sounds like a plan. I'll let you know about the photos."

"Go out the back way," he warned. "Here's a shortcut." He opened a door off the embalming room and let me into a darkened hallway. I could hear a babble of agitated voices down the hall to the left, so I went the other direction, and came out at the door where I'd come in. Very carefully I opened the door, taking a rapid look in both directions before slipping outside and closing it after me.

No one was in sight.

I counted to three in my head and then bolted across the back parking lot into the maple trees that lined the yard across from the funeral home. Hunkering down behind a pile of split logs, I waited sixty long seconds to see if anyone had followed me, my heart rate accelerated till it pounded in my ears.

I saw no trace that someone was coming after me.

With a long sigh of relief, I snaked a path through the yards back to my car, peeking over my shoulder occasionally to make sure the trail was clear. I jumped in the driver's seat, happy to hear the locks click shut as I started the engine. I set aside the impulse to review the photos on my cell right then, strong as it was. Safer places awaited. I headed in the opposite direction from the funeral home, debating what to do next.

One thing was true: this evidence was dynamite.

What to do with it?

Surely Rick would be pleased to have such evidence. Gloria and Ben as well. I wondered what Brendon would think about the metamorphosis in the woman we'd watched die less than twenty-four hours before. Maybe then he'd finally be able to see that the guys in his department were wrong, that something unseemly was going on at the clinic, the place that claimed to be about 'wellness' and 'healing.'

Maybe this had convinced me of the same thing.

I parked behind a dry cleaning store and pulled out my cell phone. I paged slowly through the photos, once again overwhelmed by the graphic reality. I would have expected my natural skepticism to reject the possibility that a dead woman could age almost seventy years in fifteen hours. But when the news came from Ben Fosdick, the mottled markings matched what I'd seen the day before, the ring.... This time I'd seen it with my own eyes. It was hard to argue with that.

I turned off the small screen and leaned back in the seat, my breath slipping away as stark awareness set in. I felt like a weight pressed me into the seat, keeping the air out, starving my lungs, suffocating me.

This was real.

The Dorian Gray reference seemed too facile, but it was the only explanation that made sense. I remembered Dedra and I joking, after that first time, about how young and beautiful everyone seemed at the clinic. Thick, shiny hair. Perfect skin. Perfect.

My chest eased a little, but I was still shaky. Where did that good health come from? Sucking the energy from others? Perpetuating their lives at the expense of all these other women? All the women…including Dedra? Including me? I swallowed hard, horrified.

Was there any reason to believe that Ulrike was the only one? Of course not. How many of the rest of them were in on it? Dr. Ruprei? Chal Talman? The nurses? The receptionist? The effing janitor?

My breaths came in halting gasps. Tears filled my burning eyes, spilled over, ran down my cheeks. I could feel each heartbeat; it echoed in my ears. I'd been betrayed before, but it had been nothing like this. Nothing.

I couldn't stand by and watch this happen.

They were going down.

All of them.

I gunned the engine and burned rubber, heading back to the office.

~*~

When I came into the newsroom, I could see Melissa was designated "out" on the tote board. Perhaps she'd been one of those waiting at the funeral home to claim Ulrike's body. If Ulrike had been so old, and looked so young, I wondered how old Melissa might be. She looked to be sixty already; was she 100? 150? Older?

The thought gave me serious chills.

Gloria gave me a nod as she passed through to check her pages in composing, and I tried to remain nondescript, so I wouldn't catch her interest. Something in the way Ben Fosdick had implored me not to share his shocking discovery with anyone struck fear into my core. The fact the clinic personnel had banded together so quickly and moved on the funeral home didn't make me feel any more secure, either. I decided I'd give Ben a call in the afternoon and see if everything had gone well.

The other conclusion that had settled into my bones was that I was done treating at the clinic. Those people could not be trusted. It was impossible to know at this point if they were even people—

That echoed into the conversation I'd had with Rick Paulsen in his office about the *X-Files*, about the possibility of…vampires. He'd sloughed me off when we'd met at my apartment, claiming that's not what he'd really meant. But considering the logical inferences of what I'd seen that morning, wasn't that something like what we had in Ralston? Was there even such a thing, vampires who didn't suck blood, *per se*, but stole something more precious, something that couldn't be as easily replenished, from their victims: life force?

Giving a quick glance around to find everyone busy working on something, I sat down at my computer and did a quick and dirty internet search for "vampire energy." The first title that popped up was "Energy Vampires Drain Your Spirit; 11 Ways to Protect Yourself."

In disbelief, I paged through that one and then page after page more, even videos on Youtube. The more correct term was "psychic vampire," I discovered, but the concept was the same. People existed who could drain the life force, the energy, from one spirit and take it into their own. The Goldstone staff must have raised the practice to an art, not only giving themselves a temporary boost, but in fact prolonging their own lives at the cost of their victims.

I read on to find a webpage that pointed out while some were energy thieves, there were also those whose personal qi, or life energy, tended to leak away from them. The author of the page seemed particularly concerned that those people might be perceived as healers, as they would make those they came in contact with feel better—but that they needed to guard against depletion of their own resources.

What if the Goldstone doctors had not only strengthened their own abilities to steal energy from others, but had somehow identified a way to find those who were unable to stop "bleeding" their own energy away? Those who were unable to replenish themselves, by interaction with family, friends, a loving spouse, did they give off some sign that would set them up as potential prey?

I froze a moment, recalling several potential signs that had seemed odd, but not portentous. Is that why the initial intake forms wanted to know about parents and siblings? And that woman, Gina, the one with the child and the vicious ex-husband, had she broadcast her lack of support as well?

"Psychic vampires?" Dedra read aloud over my shoulder. "What is that about?"

I could feel other eyes in the newsroom heating up the attention grid. I minimized that screen and pushed back from the desk, forcing a laugh. "Nothing. I've been bored a lot lately, and I've been trying to find a subject to write a novel about. Vampires are all the rage now, you know, what with all that Stephanie Meyer stuff!"

"I *love Twilight*," Dedra said with a little wistful smile.

"See? So many people do." I checked off staffers with a glance. Brown had returned to whatever was giving him furious fits of typing. Melissa was thankfully now in evidence; the same for Gloria. Dedra was off on a roll now about Meyer's book and its progeny. Only O'Neal watched me, a speculative look on his face.

Gloria marched back through, glasses perched on her head, and snipped, "I think you all have work to do, ladies and gentlemen." She stopped at her door, looked around once more and cocked her head at Chris Brown, who was the only one working. "Maybe Yale does have its advantages." She disappeared into her office and closed the door. A date with the Marlboro Man.

Dedra wandered off, in conversation with one of the clerical typists about the appeal of romance. She was looking better. I knew she was seeing Ted the ambulance guy from time to time. Certainly quite a difference from a couple of weeks before. Now all I had to do was make sure she stayed that way.

CHAPTER NINETEEN

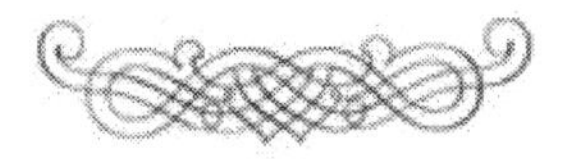

The days passed, and the knowledge I'd shared with Ben Fosdick seemed to swell until I was ready to burst. I had said nothing. No one had, apparently. Nothing about Ulrike's strange death and metamorphosis had shown up in the media or in any word on the street. The Goldstone people had been able to make the whole eerie phenomenon vanish without a trace.

The lack of developments seemed to get on Gloria's nerves. She was moody, and for awhile she seemed to avoid me. My assignments often came by email or in a phone message, and they piled up to the point I nearly couldn't meet the deadlines she'd set. I could barely stay ahead of them. I was beginning to wonder if she regretted hiring me and was trying to drive me out.

The Internet became my teacher as well, as I read anything I could find on vampires, all flavors, from both the fact and fiction perspectives. I knew that in order for them to get inside a house, they had to be invited in. I knew that methods of protection against vampires included iron or silver as a barrier, and hawthorn, whatever that was. Fire was the only universally understood method of destroying vampires. Otherwise, they were pretty much invincible.

Fine, I thought. *All I have to do is get all of them into the clinic and light a match.* Piece of cake, right?

I met Rick several times very casually, as he was busy at the hospital, and I had way too much to do. Nothing similar to our intense session at my apartment occurred. We managed a couple of quick lunches at the hospital cafeteria and coffee and lemon meringue pie at the local diner twice. The place had pie to die for, we both firmly agreed on that point. Both times someone from the police department watched us with exceptional interest, the first time Brendon Zale, the second time the officer named Tom who had given me such a hard time at the first crime scene. I was getting used to it by then. I tried to ignore it.

I mentioned my troubles with my editor to the doctor over coffee, and he countered by inviting the two of us to dinner.

"Are you serious?" I was surprised he would take my problems so personally, but it was touching at the same time. "You know, it might work. If we meet in a neutral place, really good food, maybe a glass of wine? Maybe she'll loosen up enough to tell me what's wrong."

"Leave it to me," he grinned.

Later that afternoon , Gloria called me into her office. I instinctively closed the door behind me, half expecting a pink slip. She sat behind her desk, a curious smile on her face. "Your doctor friend just invited me to dinner. With you. Is something going on?"

I shook my head. "You know, we're all thinking about the clinic in the same way. Maybe he believes sitting down and brainstorming will help move us off center."

She nodded judiciously, and leaned back, crossed her legs. "True that nothing has happened. But you and Dedra have been safe. I've made sure."

"How's that?"

"You've been too busy to think about the place. Haven't you?" Her little dry laugh punctuated her challenge.

"Busy—that's what this has been about?!" Partly relieved, partly annoyed as hell, I sank into a chair as my knees went weak. "Keeping us busy and healthy?"

"What did you think? You girls are like my daughters. I have to take care of you if I can." Her brow screwed into a close approximation of a question mark. Then she waved an officious hand. "Never mind. I like the man. We both serve on the board of Big Brothers. I told him yes. But we're meeting up in Toledo. I thought it best if we might get on dangerous subjects, not to be on dangerous ground."

"All right. Did he say where?"

"He said he'd pick us up. Here. Four p.m. "

I glanced at the clock. That gave us two hours. "I guess I'd better get the farming story in then." I grinned. "Thanks, Gloria."

"I'm looking forward to it."

At four p.m. precisely, Rick pulled up outside in a sedate silver BMW sedan. Gloria waved at me from the door, where she'd been watching out the window. I tucked my bag under my arm and headed for the door. Melissa stopped in her trek back to her desk to study us, nose twitching with interest.

"Where are you two off to?" she asked. Her tone was light and friendly, but I thought I heard a barely-lined edge to it underneath.

"Rubber chicken dinner," Gloria snapped in a "don't-ask" voice. "Figured Sara might as well get used to the routine."

She hurried me outside and took the back seat, leaving the front passenger seat to me. Rick smiled in warm greeting.

"You look like you're feeling great," he said.

"Thanks. I am," I assured him.

"Nice to see a girl with natural color in her cheeks, isn't it?" Gloria's comment was tart, and after she said it, she settled into her seat to look out the window. Rick gave me a wink, and we headed off to the Beirut, a Lebanese-Italian restaurant of some repute. Gloria mentioned that Jamie Farr of *M.A.S.H.* fame had visited the place on a couple of occasions when she'd been there. I tried to remember who that was.

Gloria insisted that we be seated at the table in the farthest corner from the door, where she could see who came in.

"Are you kidding?" I asked.

"What?" Gloria said. "You're only paranoid if they're not after you."

Rick laughed and escorted us to our table, putting his back to the door so Gloria could watch the door for enemies, imagined or real. The two of them seemed to hit it off. I was a little surprised that she allowed him inside her usually prickly personal space, but Rick played up to the hard edge of Gloria's persona, seeming deliberately out to win her over.

Dinner proceeded without any troubling talk, but after some post-dinner coffee, Gloria's face grew serious. "Sara tells me you've been tracking this string of deaths," she said to Rick.

"Yes. Several ER patients died, but I'd never seen them prior. It didn't seem particularly strange to me. Patients die in the ER all too often, despite what you see on television about young doctors doing complete cancer cures in sixty minutes less commercial time." He pursed his lips and looked away, collecting himself. "But then I lost one of my own patients, a young woman I knew had been healthy. Only after her death did her mother tell me she'd treated at Goldstone for persistent headaches."

Gloria looked up sharply. "Like Dedra."

"She never asked you to treat them?" I asked.

"No," Rick said. "I reviewed her records after she died, and all I found was a brief mention of headache with her monthly cycle. She'd agreed to modify her diet and drink more water. I'd given her yoga-based exercises too, for strength and relaxation. They should have helped cut down on the headaches. It *should* have," he finished with a nervous tapping of one finger on the red tablecloth.

"It wasn't your fault," Gloria said. "We all feel like there's more we should have done." She chewed her lip, fighting tears. "My personal cross was that I didn't keep Marnie away from Melissa Jones. That woman's insidious voice pulled my sister down that path." She shuddered and looked at me. "Then I let you and Dedra get sucked in just the same way. How could I?"

"In all fairness, the clinic does some good work," Rick said. "I've seen some remarkable therapies used there to heal people. We can't condemn every treatment or doctor there just because it isn't traditional medicine."

I bit my lip hard to keep a sharp retort inside about exactly what kind of untraditional medicine might be going on there. I was a little surprised to hear Rick defending the clinic after all his earlier concerns. I knew from what he said that he subscribed to some of the same healing theories as practitioners at the Goldstone, but really! Maybe he was being misled into thinking that he and Ruprei shared the same end goals.

"We can be concerned about the way people drop dead after they've been there," I snapped.

"Of course we should," he said agreeably.

Something rang false in his tone, but Gloria didn't seem to notice. "I'm glad you're helping Sara with this," she said.

"Believe me, I find it very important to watch out for her. I'd hate for her to be in over her head and not have anyone she can ask for help."

"Thank you." Gloria finished her coffee and set down her cup.

"It's late," Rick said. "I should take you ladies home. Gloria? It's been a pleasure."

I was getting bad vibes with every word that passed his lips. *Why was he shutting this discussion down?*

"I enjoyed it very much." Gloria said, setting enough on the table to cover dinner for the three of us. When Rick started to protest, Gloria insisted. "You drove up here," she said by way of explanation. "At what gas costs, I think we're about even."

I let them argue about it, torn about revealing what I knew. I even had my cell in my hand to show them the pictures when it rang. I excused myself and stepped outside to take the call from the *Courier* newsroom. The night sky was cloud-free, and the faint light of stars could be seen out to the west, dimmed by the bright streetlights on Monroe.

Not sure how long I'd be alone, I skipped the usual pleasantries. O'Neal was a newsman, he'd understand. "What is it, Jim?"

"Weren't you dealing with Ben Fosdick on your story about the dead woman?" he asked.

"I was," I replied with some suspicion.

"When's the last time you saw him?"

I frowned and counted back. "About two weeks ago. Why? What's going on?"

"His wife reported him missing this morning. She said he hadn't been home for three days. Have you heard from him?"

My mouth had dried up. "I haven't," I finally got out.

"All right. Cops want to know. I expect someone'll be calling you. Heads up." He hung up, annoying me that he sounded amused.

"Everything all right?" Gloria said as she exited the restaurant, companionably holding Rick's arm. Rick smiled and went around the corner to get his car.

"Yeah. Everything's fine." I didn't feel like sharing right then. Rick would be back before we could talk all about it, and frankly, I was a little disturbed that she and Rick were buddy-buddy all of a sudden when they appeared to have such different views. I put the phone away.

Rick carried the conversation on the way back, telling funny stories about his work and talking a little bit about his own history, some of his training in the energy fields. I managed to advance comments at the appropriate moments, but my growing trepidation about Jim O'Neal's news soon overshadowed any possibility of light conversation. Rick took us back to the newspaper office, where we exchanged thanks once again and each headed home, alone.

I took the route along Route 24, where they'd found Lily Kimball, half afraid to find a police work site and another dead body, and the other half more worried that Ben hadn't been located.

There were worse things that could happen in this town than just being found dead.

CHAPTER TWENTY

Sure enough, the next morning I got a call from Brendon Zale as I was driving to the *Courier* office. “Miss Woods? “ He hesitated. “Can I call you Sara? I mean, we’re practically on standby for a date, right?”

If I hadn’t been so tense about the subject of his call, I might have laughed. “Sure. Why not?”

“Okay.” The grin came right through the phone.

I imagined his smiling face, added a tail wagging happily behind him, and then I did laugh. I pulled over into the Meijer parking lot, paranoid about driving and talking on the phone at the same time. The way things were going, it seemed a good idea to be as focused as possible, not distracted by too much multi-tasking. “Is that all you needed, officer?” I asked.

“Oh! No, actually, I wanted to talk with you about Ben Fosdick. When’s the last time you saw him?”

A small stab of fear pierced my chest. I’d prayed late into the night that sometime before dawn the lanky funeral director would turn up, the perpetrator of a marital indiscretion or other fairly innocent activity. Anything other than seeing him as I’d seen Lily.

“I haven’t seen him for a couple of weeks.”

“When exactly? And where? And you should call me Bren. Only fair.”

“I…ah—” The last time I’d seen the man appeared in my mind, very fresh, and the circumstances, and the body… I took a deep breath. “You know, I don’t know. I think it was a Tuesday. I met him over at his office.”

“To talk about the clinic deaths?”

That shocked me into a couple of blinks. What did he mean by that? Did he know? Was he in on it? I swallowed hard, pushing indecision down deeper into myself. I was glad we were doing this on the phone, instead of face to face. “Clinic deaths?” I asked.

His turn to pause, flustered. “I heard he was looking into some, um, irregularities.”

Where was that damned snappy comeback when I needed it? I scrambled for words. “Irregularities? Now that’s something I’d like to hear about,” I finally said.

"Where are you?" he asked. "Perhaps we could meet up and discuss this."

Like hell. "I'm on the road, on the way to an assignment. Look, I hope you find him. He's a very nice guy."

"It wouldn't take long," he said.

Talking to someone who knew about "irregularities" at the clinic was the last thing I wanted to do. I resorted to a cheap trick. "Hello? Hello?" I said, feigning bad reception. "Brendon? Hello? You're—up—can't—er." I hung up. One of the few redeeming qualities of cell phones. Every once in awhile you got out of talking to someone you just didn't want to talk with.

I quickly got back on the road and headed out of town instead of going to work. I had a feeling Brendon would be staked out, waiting to pounce on me when I arrived. From the first time I'd met him, I'd felt he was a young system wannabe, part of the up and coming generation. I certainly wouldn't put it past him to be part of the cover-up, eager little beaver that he was.

I bet he even called the clinic from the IGA the day Ulrike died.

With a little shudder, I kept going. As I passed the city limits, I called Gloria and left her a message that something had come up and I'd be in later that afternoon. I reached into the glove compartment and took out the camera I'd been given by Ben Fosdick. If someone wanted to prove any "irregularities," the pictures on this roll of film would have done it.

I decided I'd take the time to get the film developed, then get the camera back somehow before it was missed. The police would probably be crawling all over the funeral home for clues. Where had I seen a drug store or something else with a one-hour photo studio? I rolled the windows down, letting in the air of late May, the sun warm on my arm as I propped it on the car door. I reached into the CD case I kept in the car without looking, just pulled one and slipped it into the player. 'Black Water' by the Doobie Brothers. Perfect.

I sang along as I continued out 24. The louder I sang, the more I could shut out worries that nibbled at my heels with razor sharp teeth. Ben Fosdick. What could have happened to him? Did the clinic people know he'd seen Ulrike von Dorn in her true form? Did that mark him for disposal? Had they taken him? When? Apparently not the day I'd left him there to face the crowd. Why had they waited?

What was going on?

I cruised into Napoleon and came across a Rite Aid that advertised a one-hour shop in the window. Now that's what I was talking about. I parked around the far side, some distance from the door, but blocked from easy view of the road, and headed inside. I couldn't stop looking over my shoulder, half expecting Brendon or someone from the clinic to appear, eyes full of dark purpose.

Inside, I forced myself to walk nonchalantly to the photo counter, where a weary-faced middle-aged woman asked me for my name and address as she filled out the photo order on her computer. I nearly told her 'Brenda Starr' but I had second thoughts, wondering if that might not even flag me. In the end I gave her a fake name and address in Cleveland.

"I'm just in town for my grandmother's funeral," I said. "My mother couldn't come. She asked me to take some pictures, like before and after." I added a faint smile. "They're kind of creepy, at the home? But she gave me real specific instructions. I need double prints. And the CD," I added.

The woman eyed me in that, "are you kidding me?' way. "Do you have a reward card?" she asked.

I nearly said I did, until I remembered at the last micro-second that it certainly bore a different name, one I did not want associated with those photos. "No. No, I don't." I said.

"Want to apply for one?" Her voice showed she'd asked the same question hundreds of times. It didn't get any more exciting with time, apparently.

"No, thanks." I smiled as she printed out the receipt and handed it to me. An hour to wait. What's the chance there was a decent donut shop in town with coffee?

Not so good, apparently, since there was no such thing up any of the main streets. I did find a small used book store, however, always a good excuse for a time-killer. I smiled at the woman in the hippie-style denim jumper and tights behind the cash register and perused the shelves for anything of interest.

The book that seemed to leap out at me was a book on "women's medicine," drawing heavily on the Native American tradition. The main theories the book seemed to be based on were the importance of being in touch with natural things and welcoming contact with the unknown, the spirits of the things around one. I'd never been much for religion. My parents had belonged to a country church which was firmly non denominational Protestant, and served as much for a social gathering place as spiritual guidance. I was guided more by the minister's son when I was 15, and after a tempestuous fling that was decidedly not in keeping with the teachings of his father, my parents had agreed we wouldn't go back.

As an adult, organized religion hadn't made much sense. Jesse was unchurched as well, so we spent Sunday mornings sleeping late, reading the paper over breakfast on trays in bed listening to jazz tunes on local public radio.

Reading the text about good and evil, heaven vs. hell, I didn't think I agreed that my fight against the clinic fell into such grand categories. I'd have to fashion my own base from which to attack these strange life-suckers with weapons of my own choosing.

I read on and discovered rituals to prepare the warrior in any woman for the conflicts of life, ceremonies which would help her feel in control of herself and her path. These I liked very much. Anything that might provide an edge when confronting Francesca Ruprei and the others at the clinic, I needed in my arsenal.

"Finding everything?" the woman asked, suddenly at my elbow.

A little yelp escaped me. "Don't sneak up on people like that!" I fought to reclaim my breath.

"I'm so sorry. If you need any help, please ask." She smiled wide and walked back to the counter.

When I'd settled myself again, I decided the book might be better read over a cup of blackberry sage tea with some relaxing music. I bought it, then headed back to the drug store. A few minutes later, my photos were ready. The woman gave me a decidedly peculiar look.

Sheepish grin ready, I paid her and took the envelope, tucked it into my purse. "My mother. I mean, she's my mother. What are you going to do?"

"Right." She continued to look at me that same way until I got through the door, and may have continued to stare after me even past that moment. I didn't blame her. I would have sent them off if I could have trusted anyone at the post office. This way I dropped them off and picked them up myself. That had to be better.

Mission accomplished, I drove back to Ralston. As I pulled into the *Courier* lot, I spied Dedra and Ted in a hot clinch behind her VW. I beeped my horn at them, startling them into mock fist-brandishing. They got into his car and drove away. I tucked the camera, film and one set of the photos into an old lunch bag and then into the glove compartment. I zipped the CD and the other set of photos into a compartment of my purse. One thing for sure, I didn't want them all to be able to disappear at once. Then, halfway through the afternoon, I went inside to begin my assignments for the day.

~*~

I worked late, until after nine p.m., my only company the sports guys coming in to file their reports on the high school games. Half expecting Brendon or some other officer to stop in to continue the interrogation I'd avoided that morning, I flinched each time the door to the newsroom opened. But they never came.

Maybe Ben had gone home. I mean, I couldn't blame the guy. Already considered a gadfly on the subject, he was a prime target for those at the clinic. A quiet month or two somewhere else until the hubbub quieted down might be exactly what could save his life.

On the way home, my cell rang. I turned down Pat Benatar's *Love is a Battlefield* and answered it. "Hello? Sara Woods."

"Hello, Sara Woods." The voice was smoky, dark, and unmistakably belonged to Chal Talman. "Are you free for coffee? Or perhaps a glass of wine somewhere?"

I blinked and nearly drove off the road. "I…ah…" Stalling for time for my shock to subside, I let my inner rabid journalist take over. "Sure, why not? How about the lounge out at the Holiday Inn on the highway?"

"Delightful. I'll meet you there in twenty minutes." The line went dead.

Thinking of the man's enigmatic eyes, his sleek build, I practically put the car on auto-pilot for the destination. A brief thought about going home to change was quickly quashed in favor of arriving sooner. Dedra had teasingly warned me that Chal was for her, but I'd seen she'd moved on. He was free and clear, fair game, and a most eligible bachelor. All the maneuvering and banter I'd exchanged with Rick and Brendon over the past couple of months seemed like playground games compared to the way Chal made me feel when I looked in his eyes.

The inner voice that warned me about having any traffic with clinic staff in any form wailed briefly, a signal flashing red for danger in my mind's eye, but my desire to see the man took over. The warning was compacted and shut down and shoved away in some internal closet, locked up and then left to perish.

CHAPTER TWENTY-ONE

Hotel lounges all tend to look the same. Even the same as they did thirty years before—well, except for the smoke. The habit was banned in public places now, like it was most places, and made it actually tolerable for non-smokers like me to patronize the facility.

The lights were dimmed by this time of night, and small globes with a flame within sat on some of the tables as a function of ambiance. I scanned the room for the mysterious Talman, but didn't see him. Perhaps, dressed all in black as I'd always seen him, he would just fade to life from one of the shadows and—

A tap on my shoulder startled me. "There you are," came a soft, welcoming voice.

I turned around, a little tingle passing from my shoulder all the way down to my toes. "Here I am," I said, with a momentary irritation at the way I sounded, like some lovesick teen.

He smiled, warming the reserved distance of aquamarine eyes. He'd changed from his usual black to a red polo shirt and dark slacks. His arms were muscular, and he slipped one around me, guiding me inside to a table, one of those without a candle. "You look wonderful," he said, taking the chair to my immediate right instead of the one across the tiny table.

I glanced down ruefully at what I'd worn to work, a drab green blouse and jeans. "I should have stopped by the house," I said.

"Not at all." As the short-skirted waitress came over to the table, he turned his charm on her. She practically melted. After a compliment that I thought pressed the edges of good taste but seemed to please her immensely, he asked her for a bottle of wine and two glasses. "A Napa Valley Merlot. 2005, if you've got it."

Her smile never fading, she backed away, nearly tripping a man in a light blue jacket trying to get past her, and she disappeared into the back.

"You have a lot of faith, thinking this place actually carries a real vintage," I said with a small laugh.

"I have faith," he confirmed. He took my hand, held it inside his on the table. "You have been feeling well? We have not seen you at the clinic. I begin to worry."

I watched the clasped hands, remembering what had happened last time we'd met. It wasn't happening now. "The pain has been manageable." I shrugged, the look in his eyes making me feel like I'd cheated on him somehow. "I've gone back to some of what I did before I moved here—yoga, home exercise, meditation for stress relief. Pain pills now and again."

My uncomfortable little laugh drew a look of concern onto his face. "But you have not felt well. Not as you did when you left my office. Is that not so?" His expression softened to that of a wise old teacher or mentor, kindly scolding. His voice had also picked up just the slightest edge of an accent. Something European.

"No, that's true enough." With gentle pressure, I pulled my hand from his, dropped it into my lap. He didn't even blink.

"You are well, though. I can see this." He thanked the server with a smile as she brought the wine and glasses, watching as she expertly removed the cork. I caught a glimpse of the label. Damned if it wasn't a Napa Valley 2005.

"I must say I am a fan of your work," Chal said as he poured wine into the glasses. I noted he held the bottle up away from the glass while he poured, giving the wine a chance to breathe.

"You read my work? Really?" *Well, of course he does, you idiot. It's the only local paper. Most people here read it before they tear it up for the bottom of their bird cages.* When even I could make myself feel stupid, it had to be good times. I just hoped he wouldn't compound my embarrassment.

"In a small town, one never knows whose path one will cross," he said, continuing on in that Mr. Miyagi way. "Young Dedra also contributes, and I follow her writing as well."

I seized on the change of topic. "She's doing better, isn't she? I think she looks good."

"Yes. You have done well to direct her along a less destructive way." He handed me one of the glasses, swirling it gently before releasing it to my fingers. "We heard about what happened at the hospital."

"About—what happened?" My brow wrinkled, and the glass waited halfway to my lips. Was he going to hold me responsible for Rick refusing the clinic staff entrance? Or was this about my summoning help when Dr. Ruprei showed up?

"About how you brought Dedra back from the edge of death." He studied my face intently.

"Me?" I shook my head. "I'm sure you heard wrong. I'm no medical woman." Besides, I hadn't yet come to terms with whatever I had done that day. I was satisfied that, for whatever reason, Dedra made it. Survived, to use Melissa's creepy expression.

"Yet the medical workers know. A toast to Sara and her humble gifts." He raised his glass and waited for me to do the same before touching his to mine with a gratifying 'ting.'

I pondered for several seconds, tasting the wine on my tongue, then, invited by something in his absorbed gaze, I asked, "You think I have gifts?"

"Very much so," he assured me. "We all do."

His meaning wasn't clear, but I didn't ask for more. Did he mean everyone had gifts, or that everyone believed I had them? He'd made it clear in the few times I'd seen him that he thought I held something special. Had he sensed whatever Rick Paulsen called "natural" within me, that ability that he said allowed me to hold or transfer power? I wasn't sure I believed that at all, but if practitioners of that sort of alternative medicine could tell it was there, was it valuable other than to be able to jump start a dying friend in an ambulance? Even my mental ruminations held a heavy dose of sarcasm. As if…anyone could do such a thing.

But why were they all so interested?

Ill at ease, I fished around for a way to turn the conversation away from me. "So, what is it you do there, at the clinic? You're not a doctor?"

He ran the edge of the wine glass along his lip, just hard enough to show an indentation, before he answered. "No."

I had to admit, the man knew his wines. This merlot was delicious. I waited for an answer. When one didn't come, I glanced around the murky interior of the lounge to see who else had let boredom or the desire for company drag them out on a weekday evening. A couple of over-dressed women with earrings much too young and too much hairspray sat at the middle of the bar with tall frozen drinks, alternately watching the door in chatty desperation and glaring at me for sitting with a handsome man. One man in a rumpled suit sat in a booth alone with a beer, staring into it with a mournful expression. Another talked on his cell phone by the window, leaning against the wall with a drink in hand. I was about to ask Chal the question again when I caught a watchful pair of eyes in the shadows at the far end of the bar.

Brendon Zale.

When he realized I'd seen him, he smiled and raised his glass. I bit my lip, not happy to find him here, but at least he hadn't imposed upon my meeting. Chal noticed my interest and followed my gaze.

"A friend of yours?" he asked.

"Not at all." I didn't add that I was actually somewhat disturbed to find the officer here.

Brendon eyed Chal a moment, no doubt sizing up his ability to compete against the movie-star good looks, then emptied his glass down his throat. Exchanging words I couldn't hear and a smile with the bartender, he stood up. His boots thudded heavily along the floor as he came around the bar toward us on his way to the door. He didn't even look at me as he passed. Then he was gone.

"He doesn't seem good enough for you," Chal mused.

The comment astonished me. Maybe I'd heard him wrong. Certainly he had no right to comment on my potential suitors. If that's what Bren was. "Excuse me?"

"That man. You have the ear of others more powerful, more…appropriate. He should not waste his time." Chal took a long drink of the blood-red liquid.

I laughed softly. "I don't give him much time, trust me. He's likely to be handy some time, though, since he's a cop. I might need him, you know?"

He studied me a moment, then nodded. "I know exactly what you mean."

I fidgeted with the wine, uncomfortable, and finally went back to my question. "So what do you do at the clinic, really? If you're not a doctor. Clearly you've trained. You're a…therapist?"

He considered that term, filling both glasses again. "Yes. That is an accurate assessment. I am also—how do you say…? A facilitator. I bring people together with what they need."

Those words echoed what Melissa had said. "So, administrator would be correct then?"

"Yes. I direct the purpose and actions of the other staff." He nodded, pleased.

"Rick Paulsen? He's part of your staff?"

A definite hesitation. "Rick is…special."

I searched his face for clues to his real meaning, not easy in the bar's half-light. I'd hoped for a definitive line on whether Rick was accepted or not, to see whether he'd be able to really help with what I might need in the investigation. After all, it was his investigation, too. He'd implied the clinic staff were murderers, and attempted murderers as well. I tried again. "As in he rides the short bus?" I asked, coming at the subject from what I hoped would be a humorous angle.

"I'm sorry?" Chal frowned. "I do not know that reference. I meant that he is given privileges an ordinary doctor would not be given. Because of—"

"Because of his training?" I finished for him.

Chal seemed relieved. "Yes. Because of his training. He understands our work. He supports our work, unlike others in the medical community."

I nodded. "I can see that."

"He is a good man. Do you like him?"

"He's all right. I mean, he seemed to care well for Dedra." I obviously didn't want to mention Lily and the others. "He and I have talked about energetic work. He seems very knowledgeable."

Chal stared into his glass a moment, then regarded me quite seriously. He took my hand again, I supposed to emphasize his intent. "He is a good man. Rick Paulsen will help to find your potential, your center. You should trust him."

I felt just a little whirl of that earlier effect he'd had on me at the clinic, a sharpening, a buzz in my ears, then he let go, and it stopped. "I should do that," I said. "You're never too old to learn, isn't that right?"

He finished the wine in his glass. "That is right. You are a wise woman, Sara Woods." He checked his watch. "I am sorry, I have another meeting. But this has been delightful. I trust you will allow me to meet you another time?"

The women at the bar shot me another jealous look, and I couldn't help a small triumphant smile. "I'd love to."

He took my hand and kissed it, just like the heroes from those old movies. "Don't rush," he said. "Stay to finish your wine, please. I am so sorry I have to leave you."

At my half-hearted nod, he walked to the bar to hand the waitress a couple of bills. She seemed delighted, and I saw him stop to give her a business card as well.

"Good night," he said, his voice almost a husky whisper as he passed the table. "Come to the clinic and see us soon, will you?"

After he'd gone, I thought about the clinic. Couldn't stop thinking about the clinic. At the same time, I began to formulate a theory. If these practitioners could tell by the touch of a hand whether a person was well, or ill, wouldn't they turn away someone who didn't need help? Maybe there was a way to test what they were really after. If I was brave enough.

CHAPTER TWENTY-TWO

When I came into the *Courier* office the next afternoon, I faked a slow, twisted gait, a grimace of pain across my face. The switchboard operator rose quickly to help me, but I waved her back into her seat. She wasn't the one whose attention I was out to get.

I lumbered instead to my desk, and was gratified (but careful not to show it) that Melissa followed me as if pulled by a charged magnet.

"Sara? What's happened?" Melissa hurried to lay her hand on my back.

I winced and pulled away from her, not sure if she was capable of determining there was nothing really wrong. "Coming down the steps at Thelma's house," I said by way of explanation. I swear her eyes lit up like a starving woman standing before a Christmas banquet. I sat down gingerly in my chair.

"You'd best call Francesca." Melissa's eyes met mine, hard and determined, as if she anticipated an argument.

I waited a long moment, not wanting to appear too eager. "Please call for me. I don't know how long I can stand this." I relived some old memories, sat arched in the chair, arms bracing the desk for support. I could almost believe my sciatic nerve was screaming in pain.

Word had apparently infiltrated the newsroom, and the other reporters filtered up to see what was happening. Gloria came down the hall, briskly brushing past the rest.

"Sara, what's all this?" she snapped. Only her eyes betrayed her concern; the overwhelming impression she put out was pure agitation at a slacker.

"The situation's being handled, Gloria," Melissa soothed, turning as she waited for her phone call to be answered.

"What were you doing?" Gloria studied me, and I tried to stand firm.

"Just pulled something coming down the steps." I hoped Gloria's interest didn't dissuade Melissa. I'd thought long and hard on this, and I was sure the best way to get myself into the clinic without suspicion was for one of them to set it up. Now that I had decided to try this route, I wanted a chance to finish it.

As someone answered the phone Melissa was holding, everyone stopped to listen, like in those old stockbroker commercials.

"Rona, this is Melissa Jones. Sara Woods needs an appointment immediately."

As Melissa glanced away to get a pen, Gloria shot me a look. I thought she had guessed what I was up to—and didn't like it. "Well, I expect you back here this afternoon to finish your assignments. No lollygagging around at the doctor's office." As she turned to go, she was muttering something about worker's compensation.

"I'll send her right down," Melissa said.

Dedra watched from the edge of the carpet. "Melissa, I'd be glad to take her." Melissa stopped her preparations and eyed her. "It's no trouble," she said.

I considered the options, and decided Dedra was a better choice. "I really appreciate your offer, Melissa, but I know how busy you are. Dedra can just drop me at home afterward."

"Are you sure Gloria will—" Dedra interrupted.

"*I'll* handle Gloria," Melissa said firmly. "You get to the clinic." She helped me up from the chair, and handed my arm to Dedra.

"You look like you're really hurting," Dedra said as she waited for me to get in the passenger door of her Volkswagen.

"Good," I said, half under my breath. As Dedra raised an eyebrow, I added a ragged smile. "'Cause I really am."

Dedra hurried around and started the car, then drove out of the lot, slowing her shifts between gears to avoid jolting me.

"I can't believe you're going to the clinic," Dedra said, her eyes on the road ahead. "After all you complained about them when I was sick. It's really not such a bad place, you know."

"They just almost killed you," I said with a bit of acid in my voice.

"Why are you going then?"

I shifted with a groan, careful to keep up the ruse. "Because they know how to fix my back like no one else does."

"That's what I don't understand," Dedra said. "How they can keep my headaches away. Because no one else can. Your Dr. Paulsen gave me some kind of drugs, but they didn't work."

"So what have you been doing for the headaches?"

Dedra looked away again. "I've been going to the clinic."

"What?" I nearly came across the seat at her, but belatedly remembered my "injury," and slumped down a little. "Dedra, you can't do that."

"Sara, I really don't know about Dr. Paulsen," Dedra said. "He seemed more interested in finding out what I knew about the clinic."

That provoked my curiosity, recalling Rick's sudden distance the other night. "Because of the treatments?"

Dedra shrugged. "Not sure. Just what I knew about them."

"That's crazy," I said. "Rick wants to help you get well. We all do!"

"Maybe," Dedra said. "Or maybe he's working with them, trying to keep them in business. I've seen him there, many times, but when he sees me, he just fades down the hall."

"Are you seeing Chal?"

"Yeah." She relaxed into the seat with a smile. "He's so wonderful. Him and Dr. Ruprei both."

We drove in silence the rest of the way to the clinic. Dedra pulled up to the door to let me off. The crabapple trees along the walk were in full fragrant bloom, beautiful against the blue sky. The weather had warmed, the air was full of fresh scents, and what I'd really like to have done was take a long walk in the woods. But I was here now.

Two women rushed out with a wheelchair, soft nurses' shoes hardly making a sound on the freshly-swept sidewalk.

"Good Lord," I said. "I don't think that's necessary."

"Nonsense," Rona said. "If you're as bad off as Melissa said, we'd better take care that no damage takes place."

Yes, I certainly don't want to be damaged, I thought as they bundled me into the chair and inside.

Francesca Ruprei met us in the hall going toward an examining room. "Sara!" she cried. "What has happened?"

Dedra gave her a quick rundown. The women who had brought me in buzzed away down the hallway like busy bees, and other heads peeked around corners to take a look. I saw Chal come out a door and stare.

Dr. Ruprei saw it too, and I saw her head snap around before she pushed the chair into an exam room and closed the door. Did I detect relief on her face that she'd gotten to me first? As she relaxed, I noticed she looked as beautiful and forbidding as before, her brown eyes shot with hint of gold, and not a hair out of place. She asked if I was able to lift myself onto the table.

When I was there, she asked me to show her where it hurt. I tried to remember exactly how the last flareup I'd had felt. I winced when Dr. Ruprei palpated the area with two fingers.

"This needs some therapy," the doctor confirmed. "Come with me."

Trying not to smirk, I slid off the table, wondering what kind of "therapy" was appropriate when nothing was wrong. She led the way deeper into the maze of rooms to one with a standard massage table as well as other equipment, physical therapy machines, a large metal whirlpool, some ultrasound equipment, and a couple of oversized exercise balls and mats; nothing ominous.

Dr. Ruprei asked me to lie face-down on the massage table, then took a hot towel out of a warmer and laid it across my back. "I'll send someone in to give you a treatment in a few minutes," she promised, and she left the room.

Whether I was broken or not, the warm towel felt wonderful in any case. A quick look around at the other equipment in the room reassured me. Certainly nothing I hadn't seen during my post-accident medical and physical therapy adventures.

Nothing that was scary on the surface.

Soon afterward, a slight woman in a white coat came in. "I'm Sheila Morgan. Doctor Ruprei asked me to take a look at you. Tell me what happened?"

I mumbled my way through an explanation, suddenly grateful I wouldn't be exposed to Ulrike and that awful impression of teeth.

Sheila smiled. “Please, just relax. We’ll have you back to normal in no time.” She helped me turn over, then she slowly pushed my left leg across my body to the right, stretching my lower back until my lower back bones actually popped into place.

Holy cow. I thought I was faking that. Maybe something really needed to be fixed.

Sheila came around to the other side and did the same thing, pushing to the left to stretch the right side. There was a corresponding release of tension and an audible 'crack' as the bones went back into alignment.

“There, that should have released the sciatic nerve. Let me work for a moment on those deep back muscles.” She helped me turn over once again to my stomach, keeping her hands on me at all times to steady me. It was impossible not to relax. Her hands felt so wonderful. I melted into the rubdown, and, pleased, she began to hum in deep alto tones, some sort of tune with no recurring pattern. The song hit some chord deep within me. My consciousness receded into the music, and the surroundings got fuzzy as the massage blended with the melody, the rhythms of both working together…

When my thoughts coalesced again, I was lying on the table, deeply relaxed, so far gone I could hardly summon the control to direct my brain. Soft, urgent women's voices spoke just out of my sight, back by the whirlpool. I heard my name several times. And Rick Paulsen's.

I tried to focus, coming to realize the conversation was between Sheila and Dr. Ruprei. My limbs felt motionless and heavy, as if I’d been in a deep sleep. My breathing was deep, rhythmic and I couldn’t change it. I realized I was altered. I couldn’t change it. I’d lost control.

How had Sheila been able to hypnotize me that way?

As I contemplated my state, I heard them move toward me. I couldn’t move without such an effort that it would have been obvious I knew *something* had happened. Best perhaps, to wait and watch, see what I could learn. That was why I’d come, after all.

Dr. Ruprei ran her hand along my body from my head to my hip. “Sara?” the doctor said softly. I tried to let go, not to reveal I was awake. I was relieved when the doctor continued to stroke my back, more insistently. “Sara, are you awake?”

I made no move in response.

The doctor seemed satisfied. “I think she's ready.”

“She is so full of delicious strength,” Sheila said. “I don't know how she stores it, but she is so readily tapped.”

“No doubt why Paulsen is so interested in her,” the doctor said, a bitter tone in her voice. “You know, he has been trying to discover more about her.” A speculative pause stretched out, during which I could hardly breathe for fear of giving myself away. Ruprei continued, “I have no worries about being able to control him. His great energetic strength will be very useful to us. He and I have…an understanding.”

"But is he cooperative? He does not seem to believe we can re-animate the dead."

What? Re-animate the dead? What nonsense was this? As they stood, one on each side of me, I felt pressed down, almost restrained in some way. The words continued to dangle in front of my disbelieving conscious mind like bait on fish hooks floating in the water.

"This remains to be seen. I will certainly encourage his interest. His help will be of great use, as he can be quite persuasive," the doctor said, smile inherent in her voice.

"His interest has been constant," Sheila agreed.

"I warned him what would happen if he opposed us," the doctor said. "He knows what reward will come to all who join us. He would not lightly set that aside. Certainly not for the mere slip of a girl, untrained, weak and unsure."

Sheila touched me lightly. "Melissa insists this one is the repository of the strength we will need, when we meet at the end of the cycle for the Quickening. Whether we give or take her strength, she is still full of power. Perhaps his work with her is enhancing her gifts."

"None of the others have had the enduring fortitude of Sara," Ruprei said in an almost-loving whisper. "They withered before we could fully use them. We have worked many years to become attuned so we might achieve the Quickening. Sara's gifts will be the final edge we need. Such power." Ruprei caressed my back. A twitch skipped across my skin like electric current. "All here for the taking."

I'd felt my body returning slowly to my control as they'd been distracted by their conversation. I managed to make a finger move, but it went unremarked by the two women. They moved closer, each placing a hand on one of my shoulder blades. I heard, rather than saw, both women breathe in deeply, as if forcing the air into their lungs. As they continued to breathe, I felt a wave of weakness. I saw yellow before my eyes, then red, then green, in a psychedelic progression which left me numb.

"For the Quickening," the doctor said in a monotone.

"When we shall come together to give life to those who have gone before," Sheila said, like a mantra or a holy chant.

"This cycle has come to the end. We have taken life force from the weak, passing the strength from one to another, until we have gathered enough to break the barrier of death."

"We will become one spirit and Quicken our Master," Sheila said.

I barely followed this, my world folding in on itself as I felt utter fatigue, then a giddiness with no substance. One final voice of reason in the back of my head screamed out, and I realized I was in trouble.

CHAPTER TWENTY-THREE

*Desperate measures.*I reached down mentally to center myself, contacting that core of energy Rick had helped me find. The colors continued to float before me. I moved before I felt I was truly ready, but I had no choice. I raised myself upright with a shove which required most of my remaining strength. The women were jarred, and withdrew their hands quickly as I overbalanced and nearly fell off the table.

"Sara? Are you all right?" Ruprei's voice was forced calm, but she was clearly shocked. She reached out to me, but I pulled back and grabbed the table instead. I had to buy time. "Need—water," I gasped.

Sheila stared at me curiously. Dr. Ruprei sent her from the room. The doctor had recovered from her initial surprise, and I could see she was trying to regain control of the situation.

"What's the matter, Sara?" the doctor persisted. "What are you feeling?" Her hand hung in the air between us, and I knew she wanted to touch me. I couldn't let that happen. I concentrated on the doctor's face.

"I'm sorry, I must have dozed off. That was a great massage. I have to get back to finish a story for this afternoon!" I said, with as confident a smile as I could manage. I had to get out of there while I still could. And write down everything I'd heard before it frayed away.

I swung my legs off the table. The simple action hit me with a wave of vertigo. My jaw clenched with the effort to keep the beauty queen smile glued to my face. Even though I felt like I was moving through gelatin, I had to get out of there without showing another sign of weakness. "Working too hard at the office, I guess. Sheila is very good. My back feels wonderful."

Dr. Ruprei reached out to hold me in place on the table. "Don't get up too fast, dear. Your energy fields may have been realigned. You should take some deep breaths, relax until you feel you can move."

Panic started to set in as the implications of what I'd overheard began to gel. I stood up and swayed dizzily. I stumbled and reached out for something, grabbed Dr. Ruprei's shoulder before I fell and—

—felt a jolt as vitality seemed to return, hot, sweet syrup running through fingers and hand to my arm, through my arm into my body, where the warmth and strength flowed to my feet. My smile became more genuine as I felt the power come to me. I saw the doctor's face, very close to mine, and saw shock and surprise again in Ruprei's eyes.

"I think it's catching up," I said, trying not to be flip or arrogant. That wasn't how I felt, though. I felt wildly superior.

I'd obviously pulled energy from the doctor's body to replenish what had been taken. And from the doctor's look, it hadn't been expected. Did that make me more valuable to them? Or more of a threat?

As Sheila came in with the water, she froze at the tension between the doctor and myself. I forced myself to let go and walked steadily to Sheila, plucking the cup from her hand. "Thanks for everything," I said, sipping the cool water reflectively, poised to bolt if either of them took a step toward me.

"Of c course," the masseuse stammered.

The doctor, in the meantime, had again recovered her presence. She smiled and opened the door for me. Her jaw was tight, and her eyes had lost their warm friendliness. She walked me out to the waiting room, stopping to talk with Dedra a moment about how she was feeling, then watched, her arms crossed with displeasure, as we left the building.

"You look better," Dedra said. Her tone sounded more like it was a question. "Do you want to go back to the office? You could get your car then and go home when you're finished."

I tried to get a good sense of my body, but as the adrenaline rush was fading, so was my energy. Fast. I saw on her dashboard clock that we'd been at the Goldstone nearly two hours. I'd lost so much time… "I'd better go home."

Some tune came on the radio Dedra liked, and her attention switched to that, as it would for most girls her age. She sang along, keeping rhythm on the steering wheel with the heel of her hand. I was just as glad not to talk. I wasn't sure she could be trusted with the truth if she was still an active client at the clinic. Better to keep it to myself.

When we arrived at Thelma's house, Dedra turned off the car. "Shall I come in and help you up?" she asked.

"No, really. I feel incredible," I lied. "I may take the stairs two at a time." I grabbed my bag and headed up the steps, stopping at the door to wave at Dedra.

Once I was out of sight, I leaned against the door, bravado starting to waver. Delighted about the result of the face-off with Dr. Ruprei, I couldn't help the other thought that kept running through my mind.

You could have been dead.

It was like ice water splashing over me as I entered my apartment. The silent air carried the faint reminder of the fresh orange I'd cut for breakfast. How long ago had that been? It felt like days.

As the thought sank in, I felt my knees wobble. I sat down on the couch just in time. Remembering the feeling I'd experienced just before I broke away from the pair of women, like a person freezing to death—the realization something was very wrong but a disinclination to do anything about it, I felt the fear I'd shut away. The delayed reaction caused chills and shivering which made my teeth chatter. My fingers scrabbled along the top of the couch for the blue knitted comforter my grandmother had made. I wrapped it around me, but it didn't stop the shivering.

Like a person freezing to death. Like Lily Kimball.

As the feeling was getting totally out of control, my cell vibrated in my pocket. I reached for it, dropping it from weakened fingers the first time I got it open. "Hello?" I said shakily.

"Sara?" It was Rick Paulsen. "Are you all right?"

"I'm all right."

"You sound terrible," he said. "Why don't you come over to my office?"

"I don't think I could do that right now."

"I could come there if you like," he said.

Strange that he'd known I was at home. I should have been at the paper for another couple of hours at least. "No, I think I'm just going to get some sleep."

"I was really concerned," he said. "I called the paper to see if you had time to meet this evening, and Gloria said you'd been rushed out of there to the clinic. Sara, I thought we agreed you were going to stay away from that place!"

A perfectly reasonable excuse. Everything was making me paranoid at this juncture. "I was in a lot of pain," I lied, betting it made sense to keeping my story consistent. Besides, I didn't want to admit I'd been foolish enough to almost get killed.

"You don't sound like it helped."

"No, I'm okay." My eyelids closed of their own accord, and I realized I was dog tired. "Can't we talk about this later?"

After a pause, he relented. "Sure. No problem."

"Kay. See you." After I clicked the phone shut, I reached for the remote control and flipped on the television, finding an early news report a welcome alternative to talk shows. I felt a bit guilty about not going back to work, but I hoped Dedra had gone back and made the proper excuses.

The pleasant monotone of the news anchor blurred in my mind as the fear crept in again, making me shiver despite the blanket. I shouldn't have let them lull me into a vulnerable position like that again. Even without Ulrike. I could never let that happen again.

At the same time, now I had some clue about what was going on, those odd murmurings about Quickening and raising the dead, and energy. I'd have to think about it for awhile, sort it out, because I wasn't at my best when I'd taken in the information.

And I'd been able to marshal my waning resources when they'd tried to what—suck me dry? Perhaps it had left me at a disadvantage now that Ruprei and the others knew I had the power to resist them, even to recharge from one of them. But what had they been thinking? Didn't they need me to be alive for the ritual? Just a snack for the troops, maybe, I thought with morbid humor. A little psychic popcorn before the upcoming feast.

That was too depressing by far.

I also had to admit that at this point, the matter had quit being just a story for the paper, just an investigation that individually touched me, as it had so many others. This had moved into something much more personal, much more dangerous. The book I'd bought in Napoleon sat on the coffee table, ready for use, and I believed now I would use it.

Soldiers didn't go to war without proper training; this was giving every indication it could come down to war. It was time to begin training in earnest. The next time I faced Francesca Ruprei, I would be ready.

CHAPTER TWENTY-FOUR

I awoke in the dark, wrapped tight in the comforter, TV still babbling, to the sound of heavy banging on the door. Wisps of awareness floated just outside my grasp, and before I could form thought and follow it with action, the knocking stopped. My eyelids closed again.

A few moments later, the door burst open. Rick Paulsen rushed in. As my eyes flickered open, I saw Mrs. McCracken silhouetted in the doorway, hands twisting anxiously.

"Sara!" Rick shook me. My head rolled loosely as he held my shoulders. "Come out of it!"

He slapped my face once, hard, and the shock of that contact brought me to the surface, as did the sudden brightness of the overhead light, flicked on by the landlady. "Is she all right?" Thelma demanded. "Should I call an ambulance?"

He reached for my wrist, squeezed his fingers tight to locate a pulse. After silently counting for ten seconds, he dropped my hand into my lap and took my chin in his hand, searching for something in my eyes. Finally, he turned to Thelma.

"No. She's coming around. Thank you for letting me in. I'll stay to monitor her awhile."

"Shall I come make tea, Doctor?" Her gaze sparkled, inquisitive, as she leaned around Rick to peer at me.

"I think I can handle it," Rick assured her. She looked to me for permission, and I told her I'd be fine. A disappointed look on her face, she stepped out and closed the door. Rick straightened and went straight to the kitchen. "Tea would be just the thing," he said, as if everything was perfectly normal.

I knew I should get up, help him, since it was my kitchen, but my movements felt like I'd been partially anesthetized. What the hell was the matter with me? Lethargy threatened to drag my eyelids shut again, and I laid my head against the back of the sofa, for what I intended would be just a moment, just until I could stir myself.

"Sara? Sara!" Another slap stung me into awareness. Rick was sitting next to me on the sofa, holding a cup to my lips. "Drink this," he urged.

An aroma I couldn't identify filled my nose, and I swallowed instinctively as he filled my mouth with the warm brew. The sweet taste was vaguely appealing.

He urged repeated sips, then set the cup down and waited. My mind slowly emerged from its fog.

"That's not my tea."

"Correct again!" Rick said with a game show host smile. "I brought it with me. It's a ginseng blend tea, supposed to have healing powers. It's got natural honey, peppermint and other good things." He eyed me. "Now suppose you tell me what really happened today. Start with the part about how you went to the clinic, even after we'd talked about all the bad things happening there—even after Dedra."

I looked away. Why should I account to him? On the other hand, it had been very clear that both Dr. Ruprei and Sheila believed that Rick could pose a strong force against them. With a sigh, I closed my eyes and he immediately shook me again.

"Oh, no, you don't." He forced some more of the tea down me.

Sputtering, I pushed his arm away. "All right, all right," I wiped off what had spilled and straightened up, moving away from the sofa back that was so comfortable. "I wanted to get back inside the clinic, to see what I could find out. I don't know, to see what they were up to." I didn't need to see Rick's facial expression to remind myself how stupid that had been. But he didn't interrupt.

"I didn't really feel like anything was wrong, not until I got there. When I was lying on that table, it was a regular massage table. I had no idea anything would happen. Sheila released something in the lower back, then she started singing and..."

As I came closer to the memory of the conversation the women had shared across my body, I fumbled over what to reveal and what not to. Finally, I told him about the weird ritual touch, and the commentary about the raising of the dead. Nothing about what they'd said on the subject of him.

"They were touching me, and I realized I was in danger." I crossed my arms tighter as I relived those moments, hugging myself. He made the gesture to slip an arm around my shoulders and I surrendered to it, grateful for anyone to provide support. As soon as he touched me, I felt stronger, safer. "I just knew I had to fight to live. I did what you said, I found a center and pulled strength from it. I just shoved away. Scared them about as much as it scared me."

"They didn't try to keep you then?" he said, eyes narrowing.

"Keep me? No. Why would they do that?"

"They must not think you are a threat, then." He nodded, considering what I'd said.

"Well, I don't know." I reached for the tea again, and he put it in my hands, waited until I'd emptied the cup. "Something happened."

"What happened?"

What *had* happened? I wasn't sure. I'd been weak, weaker than I was now, but I'd recovered, somehow. "I got up to leave and stumbled into Dr. Ruprei. I got a huge jolt of energy. Incredible," I remembered so vividly the expression on the doctor's face, the shock, the horror, the—fear? "It looked like she was afraid of me."

"Dr. Ruprei? Afraid of you?" He set his cup on the coffee table and stood up, walking across the room and back, brow furrowed in thought. "No doubt she would be. She considers herself the pinnacle of ability. No one should be able to take energy from her without her permission. You should have been drained... No. You shouldn't have been there at all."

He whirled to face me, clearly frustrated. "What if you had ended up like Dedra? You could have died." He returned to sit next to me, again waiting for permission before he slipped his arm around my shoulders for comfort. I wasn't sure which of us got the maximum benefit.

"I guess I see that now," I said, a little sheepish. "If I hadn't been able to draw on what you've taught me, I don't know what would have happened."

"I'm so glad," he said. He gathered me into his arms. I wanted to rest there, safe and warm, but I had too many questions.

"Am I all right, then? Was any of that permanent?"

"I think you're fine. Your pulse and color are good. I honestly don't know what they did, but it was obviously something intended to take energy. Your energy reserves have been depleted, which is what I would expect is affecting you now."

"But the burst I received?"

"Some of it was probably from Ruprei's own energetic store, or else she wouldn't have reacted in that way." He held my hand as if he were afraid I'd slip away as he watched. "Which explains why it's worn off. A burst of neurotransmitters gave you the force you needed to survive, but the crisis is past. They've been re-absorbed into the system." He handed her another cup of ginseng. "Or…in layman's terms, you crashed."

"It sure feels like it."

"You'll be back to normal within several days, I'd think. I had a similar experience while I was in training in California, and it took me some time. But you've got to stay away from that place." He studied my face. "Now, at least, I think you're scared enough to be more cautious."

I muttered and pulled the comforter closer, feeling cold seep in.

"Have you eaten?"

I tried to remember, but most of the day was a blur. "I don't think so."

"Well, then, point me in the right direction, and I'll make us a feast."

"I should do that. It's my house."

"You can come with me." He half led, half carried me into the kitchen, and set me on one of its narrow vinyl chairs, so I could direct his search for sustenance. I didn't have much; he eventually settled for cheese omelette and crisp toast with raspberry jam. Rick made me more of the foreign-tasting tea, and it did rejuvenate me.

He tried to distract me while we ate with more of the light-hearted stories he'd shared on the ride home from the dinner with Gloria, but my thoughts kept ricocheting to the frightening words between the clinic women.

"Rick, what are we up against? You put me off last time we talked, but today they were particularly interested in you. And me. And something about dead people. Re-animating the dead. They said you didn't believe it was possible."

Rick raised an eyebrow. "I see."

From his facial expression, I couldn't tell what he really thought. "They kept referring to me as a repository of power they could use to do this Quickening thing." I shivered, recalling the hunger in their voices as they spoke.

The doctor nodded. "I knew they had plans for you." He put the teakettle back on to boil. "You're in a different category from Dedra, from Lily, and some of the other women. Dr. Ruprei is very interested because of the potential power you hold. She knows if you are not joined with them, you will work against them."

"Because I won't just let them sacrifice me for their ceremony," I said bitterly.

He didn't reply, but stared at the tabletop, biting his lip.

"I thought you were supposed to be some kind of hero to the community—I can't believe you'd be a part of this."

"It's not like that. It's—it's like what you intended when you went there today. Outsiders can't discover anything. You have to be inside to get anything to work with."

I studied him with hard eyes. Maybe he was telling the truth. Maybe he wasn't. If he really wanted my help, and to help me, he'd best lay all his cards on the table. I told him so.

He sighed and rubbed his forehead wearily. "As you wish. The Goldstone practitioners are pooling energy. They were once all together, the master and his followers, but someone hunted them. About seventy years ago, this hunter managed somehow to break the bonds of the group by killing the master. The others were flung to far ends of the country, banished there until they could be energetically brought back into harmony."

I thought about what Talman had said, about each of them being released in some manner over the years. All right, that made some sense then. "Where is this master?"

"They haven't seen fit to give me that information at my current level. He's apparently not buried in the traditional fashion, and the talk is that a large burst of psychic energy will jump-start him back to life."

I tried to remember through the haze that surrounded that time period, lying there on that massage table, what I'd heard. "*...we shall... take the life force from the weak, passing the strength from one to another, until we break through the barrier of death... by becoming one spirit and Quickening with our Master.*"

"That sounds like what they were saying. But it's laughable. You can't bring dead people back to life."

"Have you learned nothing of Dr. Ruprei? She has powers you haven't even imagined. She has been training all her life to create this miracle."

"Even if it's possible, how could she do this without someone catching on? The police, the coroner, the elected officials who zoned the place? This is one hell of a small, small town. People talk. People know."

He looked at me with pity, as if I were a child who just couldn't understand. "Think of our culture, Sara. Places of power go to those who are young, who appear strong and virile, striking and beautiful. People you'd never suspect go to the clinic and receive their gifts of youth, in exchange for protection from the outside world."

"So Ben's right. People are in on it. It's a conspiracy."

"It most certainly is. The way to fight them is to build up, get strong and band together. Ben, Gloria, you, me…and I'm sure there's others."

"And the cycle they were talking about? I'm sure they said it was coming to an end."

Rick shrugged. "They preserve themselves by taking energy from others. Each of them may have lived several normal lifetimes by now. But you're right, Francesca certainly seems to be escalating preparations. Whatever's going to happen, it's going to be soon. You shouldn't be alone. I'll stay with you."

I bit my lip, undecided. *What man comes over to a woman's house, cares for her, cooks her dinner, lectures her AND does the dishes?* That was something special. All the same, I didn't know him that well, and now he'd invited himself to stay? I started to object, and he shook his head.

"What you need is some bed rest. Doctor's orders. Get ready for bed, and I'll bring you some more tea."

Stubbornly, I didn't move. He whisked the kettle from the burner, then hauled me to my feet, rubbing my shoulder gently. "I'll clean up the dishes and come tuck you in," he said. "Go on." He shoved me in the direction of the bedroom.

My objections melting away, I slipped on the white baby doll nightgown I'd left out that morning. The short blue lamp on the nightstand illuminated the worn crocheted doily my grandmother had made, the small gold clock left to me by my mother, and my latest library acquisition.

I climbed under the sheet and listened to the noise of Rick's progress through the kitchen, as he alternatively ran water and clanked dishes. Those small domestic sounds comforted me; I suddenly realized how quiet it would be when he left. *You shouldn't be alone*, Rick had said. *You shouldn't be alone.* The words echoed in my head. My heart beat a little faster, and I fought off panic. What if Ruprei came here to finish me off, now that she knew I could hurt her? I was in no condition to take them on.

Rick appeared a few minutes later with a steaming cup, and immediately sensed my unease. "What is it?"

I grabbed his hand and pulled him down on the bed next to me, struck with a sudden feeling of dread. All the nightmare images I had accumulated, those red glowing eyes and shadowy figures appeared in my over-stimulated imagination. "Don't leave me alone, don't leave me," I begged. "They'll come to get me, please don't go, please—"

"All right, I won't go," he said, taking me in his arms. "They won't come here. They're much stronger on their own territory. This is still your ground." His smile seemed satisfied. "Sara, I'll stay with you. I can protect you."

He let go only long enough to slip off his loafers and come around the other side of the bed, where he sat atop the covers, arm around me, cradling my head on his shoulder while he rubbed my back. I stayed close, craving safety.

As I breathed deeply, trying to release the fear, I smelled the faint tangy smell of Rick's cologne. I felt his inhalations as I lay on his chest. It had been months since I had been in bed with a man, I realized with a tingle.

His hand smoothed my hair as though I were a frightened child. I had been sleepy, but something inside me had awakened. He was a good man. A special man. Some internal mantra told me I could trust him.

"You're glad I'm here, aren't you, Sara?" His smile was tender.

"Thank you for staying."

"I'll always watch over you." His hand stopped, fastened onto my hair, and pulled gently, tipping my head up so I looked at him. His eyes were warm, deep, full of emotion. My hand remained on his chest, so I felt when his breath quickened. He leaned down. His lips brushed mine with an almost electrical tension. My instinct was to pull away, but he wouldn't allow it, hand tightening on my hair.

"No, Sara. Don't stop this. We'll grow closer." He brushed my lips again, his hand sliding delicately up my cheek in a caress. "Think how good we'll be together."

My uncertainty faded into mist as a need intensified within. He touched me, kissed me, but so lightly that his fingers would be gone by the time the heat they left behind would register in my mind.

And there *was* heat.

The heat didn't fade as his touch left me, but accumulated and built and swelled inside the space the two of us shared. I was aware of where our bodies touched, each contact prickling with energy. I unbuttoned his shirt, ran my fingers lightly down his bare chest, feeling the exchange, a buzz that went from his skin to mine and back again. His heartbeat thudded faster, keeping up with mine. His mouth grew more insistent, and we finally connected in a kiss that was an explosion of electrical tension.

He let those searing lips move down my neck, the heat spreading through my body. A whisper at my ear. "Sara, give yourself to me."

I wanted him more than I'd wanted anyone in my life, but I couldn't have formed a coherent thought to say so, the raw emotion he'd awakened taking over my will. All I could do was nod.

In a matter of seconds, he had stripped off his clothing, had pulled the hem of my nightgown, lifted it over my head in one smooth movement. My body pulsed in one cohesive movement as he slipped beneath the sheets and made contact. Our hands moved over each other, each bringing sounds of pleasure from the other, pulling that sphere of energy closer, making each sensation more intense.

We clung to each other, as physically close as we had been energetically close in our earlier encounter. The heat grew, doubled, exploded. My long-dry well of emotion filled and overflowed as the fire of passion fortified and reinforced us both.

CHAPTER TWENTY-FIVE

Sometime that night, a patrol found Ben Fosdick dead in a ravine on the west side of town. His face had been eaten off.

Fortunately O'Neal was in town and he covered that corpse.

While hearing about poor Ben on the morning news sickened me, I had my own issues. When I'd woken up, I was alone. At first I'd thought maybe I imagined that incendiary session with Rick Paulsen. Except I was naked. And there was a note from him on the table apologizing for leaving early to make rounds.

What had I done?

I'd been open to the idea of further study with Rick, perfecting what was apparently a natural ability to channel energy, or at least manifest it somehow. What had happened the night before was way past "study," and it sure as hell wasn't a "teacher, I need an A" moment.

In all honesty, it was probably the best sex I'd ever had. But I wasn't at all sure I had really wanted it.

After a hot shower and a few cups of coffee, I felt more like myself. I re-examined the night. Granted, I'd been shaken and vulnerable after that stunt at the clinic. Stupid. I knew it was stupid. Well, now I did. At the time, I really had been trying to do something good, but in that twenty-twenty hindsight, I realized this was one of those things heroes did in the movies when they had a cohort outside waiting to burst in and rescue them. Definitely not something to try without a safety net.

With Ben dead, that left…me.

I still had that damned camera, too. I had to get it back to the funeral home. Without Ben there it was going to be a lot harder.

Considering what I knew, the stakes for the dead girls, my live friend, and now myself, I had a lot to do, and not many tools with which to do it. I thought seriously about just getting back in bed and pulling the covers over my head. Call it a day. Let the rest of the world deal with the mess for awhile.

Then I thought about the impulses I had, the urges to go to the clinic, the very real and personal intentions of the people there to harm me. It wasn't going to happen. I'd see to it.

I got dressed and drove to the office, figuring the freshest news would be there, and I was right. O'Neal had a book full of notes, details on Ben's body, most of which I didn't want to know.

"What about motive?" I asked. "Has anyone gotten to that?"

The crime reporter leaned back in his chair, with a familiar groan of the springs underneath as he tested its limits. "Police haven't found any. They're not even calling it a murder. Accidental death—out hiking, feral dogs got him, etc." He eyed me. "Unless someone knows something different."

Accidental death? Who were they kidding? I knew right then who was responsible, and why. Ben had seen something he shouldn't have seen, and they wanted to make sure no one else saw it, either.

He wasn't the only one who'd seen Ulrike's body, though. Did they know about me?

O'Neal cleared his throat, and I realized he was waiting for an answer. The only thing that came to me was a lame response. "He didn't seem like the hiking type to me."

"Funny. That's what his wife said." O'Neal snapped his book shut and headed out to the parking lot.

I worked on my stories the rest of the day from the comfort of my desk, a little paranoid about going out into the open. Bad enough to have Melissa coming by every hour or so, her eye on me long enough just to check on me, even though she only spoke once. Who'd sent her to keep tabs?

I was damned tired of looking over my shoulder all the time. I needed protection. And not the kind some doctor wanted to provide. In my reading, I'd found a couple of things I thought were kind of ridiculous at the time, but I was ready to try them. After I'd filed everything Gloria needed for the day, I left the *Courier* for a small shop downtown owned by a woman who specialized in jewelry-making and semi-precious stones. On the way there, I tried to come up with a reasonable explanation for asking her for what I wanted.

I couldn't think of one.

Judy Hunt was quite the artist when it came to combinations of metal and stone. I took my time admiring many of her creations while she waited on another customer. When the slight woman with salt and pepper hair and multi-colored caftan came to greet me, I smiled.

"Is there something special you're looking for today?" she asked.

"Actually, there is. I didn't know where to buy supplies to make jewelry anywhere around here. I thought maybe you'd know. Or have some."

"You need a particular kind of piece? I'd be glad to take an order."

"No," I said quickly. "I need to make it. Myself." I fidgeted as I leaned against her glass display case.

"I see." She studied me a moment. "You could order from a catalog online —"

"I really need it soon. For protection." I kicked myself as that slipped out and her face changed. Was this woman part of the cabal at the clinic? I waited for her to dash into the back and call someone to warn them.

She appeared just as uncomfortable for several seconds, then her tongue flicked across her lips. Her hands clenched into fists for a moment. She looked away, then back at me. "You want to safeguard your…energy," she said cautiously.

That raised an eyebrow. I studied her face, getting the feeling I could trust her. "Exactly."

"Silver," she said, moving along the cabinets to her little workspace. "Garnet. Quartz crystal."

I followed her, a little stunned that she'd known precisely what I was going to ask for. "I'm not the first person who's come looking for this?" I asked.

She hesitated, her gaze flicking away, then to the counter, then to me again. Her fingers trembled a little. "I've recommended it to several women," she said. "After what's happened."

She dug in the drawer and extracted some thin silver wire. "Do you know how to use it?"

"I think so. Wrap the wire around the stones, hang them from a chain."

"With intent." Her eyes burned with fervor. "You have to keep your intent in mind at every twist, every turn, every time you put on the amulet. *Every* time."

I nodded slowly. "I will."

She chose a small dark red stone and a small clear one from black velvet bags in her drawer, and cut a length of the wire, then wrapped them all in white tissue paper and put them in a bag. We didn't speak further of the meaning or purpose of the purchase, bonded in a special sisterhood of some sort. I wanted to tell her there was hope that the deaths would come to an end soon, but I was afraid.

I was tired of being afraid.

As she handed me the bag, she reached across the counter with her other hand and took mine. "I'll pray for you," she said.

That floored me. I wasn't sure how to respond, since that route hadn't worked much for me. "Um, thanks," I finally said, and I squeezed her hand back. As I left the store, she watched after me with a worried expression on her face.

I took the bag home and spent a good part of the evening constructing the amulet, with each bend of wire, each tap of the stone, bearing in mind the purpose of the item: to protect me from the psychic vampires and to keep my own energy firm and whole.

When I'd finished, I had a small lumpy pendant, mostly wire along the outside like a cage, the stones inside. If I'd had more time or training, I may well have made something more aesthetically beautiful, but this would do. I strung it on an old silver chain I'd carried in my small jewelry box for years and put it around my neck.

Feeling a little stronger after I'd done that, I made myself some tea to give myself a few minutes to decide what to do next. On the counter was a plastic sandwich bag with several tea bags in it; they didn't belong to me. Rick must have left them, the ginseng brew he'd given me the night before. I thought about the tea, how much stronger I'd felt, but also how I'd acted in a way that was not natural to me.

Better safe than sorry. I threw them in the trash and drank good old orange pekoe.

Fortified with tea and amulet, I slipped in a yoga DVD and went through the routine, not only feeling the stretching of the exercises, but incorporating some of the energetic awareness Rick had taught me into the movement. The experience was quite different than usual, and I finished feeling tenacious and capable. I could resist any pull from the clinic. I didn't need to go there any more.

I repeated those two phrases like a mantra, over and over. My fingers touched the silver pendant, and I could almost feel a little pulse of energy from it. Knowing others in the community were working to protect potential victims made me feel better, too. If only we all felt brave enough to come out in the open.

But no one wanted to end up like Ben.

~*~

I woke shortly before dawn, feeling a definite call to rouse.

Lying still for a moment, I listened for a clue to what had woken me up. No phone chime, no doorbell. Nothing scratching at the windows. Puzzled, I slipped on a light robe and checked the living room for something out of place. The door was still locked and no one was even on the street outside. Nothing.

With a sigh, I went back to bed. A sudden stab of sciatic pain drove me upright again. I straightened, stretched, yoga style, and twisted in an effort to relieve the pain, but it wouldn't go away. After several minutes, I surrendered to the pain and headed for the kitchen for my medication. The earlier exercise session hadn't been very strenuous; what would have provoked this? I fumbled with the prescription bottles, took enough of each that the pain should subside.

As I started back down the hall, another stab of pain went down my lower back into my leg, sharp enough to make me stumble into the wall. "Damn it!" I bent over, stretched, lifted my leg, everything I could think of to try to relieve the burning agony. Then I saw it. Her.

A smoky apparition which resembled Francesca Ruprei, right down to her tucked chignon, floated about 10 feet in front of me. Sure I was hallucinating, I closed my eyes, opened them again. She was still there.

The apparition extended a hand toward me. "I can help you," she said in a hollow voice. "The Goldstone can make your pain disappear." The hand waved and the pain was instantly gone—for a few moments. The hand waved again, and it returned even stronger than before. "Come to the clinic now."

In a flash of understanding, I knew what had sent Lily Kimball out into the snow, what had killed those other women. That force lurking in the dark was worse than I'd ever believed. And this time it had come for me.

"No!" I said. Anguish forced her words out in measured voice. "I—will — not. Never—again."

"Come to the clinic now," the thing repeated. The compulsion entered my mind, and I found my feet actually taking steps toward the door. I grabbed hold of the amulet I'd made, still around my neck, and fought for control. *I will not. Will.*

Not.

I cast about in desperation, thinking of natural forces, things that were strong, unyielding. I thought of Niagara Falls, of the power of that water rushing over the precipice. I thought of the Santa Ana wind. I thought of the hardness of granite. All these things I added to my mental image of "barrier," trying to protect myself as I leaned against the wall.

The smoke shadow flickered, and the pain's intensity increased. "How much can you stand?" said the thing, its eerie voice taking on an amused tone. It actually smiled Dr. Ruprei's smile.

"I can take anything you can dish out!" Breathing through the pain, I hoped I was right. I'd taken enough medication to deaden the usual pain. Ten minutes. In ten minutes it would work. Could I hold on that long?

"Why do you fight us, Sara?" the shadow asked at last, in a more normal tone. It could have been the doctor speaking to her, a friend's voice, a caring voice. *She seemed so reasonable.* "Our destinies belong together. Don't you see that? When you come to us, we will join as one. You will know power as you've never known. You can serve a greater good. "

The smoke shadow moved closer to me eyes glowing red, hand out again. The voice was silky and seductive. It promised so much, gifts beyond my expectations, love, life and much more. All I had to do was go to them.

"You are one of us," the voice said, back to a more hollow, distant sound. "If you will not comply, measures will be taken. This is your last warning."

No. I squeezed the amulet harder, until it hurt my fingers, drew my attention away from this thing in front of me. "No!" I cried. "You're not real. You are not welcome here. You have no power." I concentrated, pulled together what psychic strength I could find and flung it at the Ruprei-thing, releasing my terror in a blood-curdling scream. "Get out of here. Leave me alone!"

The apparition vanished, leaving wispy strings of smoke that faded into the shadows. The pain disappeared with it.

I slid down the wall, drenched in sweat. I'd done it. I'd stood up against Ruprei and won. Granted, it was a projection, and likely weaker than the doctor in person. But I'd done it.

An anxious knocking started on my door. "Sara, honey? Are you all right?"

All the noise must have disturbed Thelma downstairs. I groaned and went to the door. There she stood, curlers askew and bathrobe misbuttoned in her haste to come upstairs. "Did I wake you? I'm so sorry." I bit my lip to keep nervous giggles trapped inside. "There was a …um… mouse."

"A mouse?" The old woman was horrified. "Where did you see a mouse?"

I pointed vaguely in the direction of the sink. "It ran under one of the cupboards. I'll get a trap after work today, all right?" I patted her arm, hoping she'd just go home. "I'm really sorry."

Thelma, however, was becoming more agitated, not less. "No, dear, it's my fault. I can't imagine —a mouse. I have never had vermin infest this house. I'll have an exterminator here first thing." She fussed over me. "Are you all right, dear? You look awfully pale."

"I'm fine. I'm just going to try to go back to sleep. I'll be fine. Good night." I closed the door over her protests and went back to bed, though I doubted I'd actually sleep any more.

I rubbed my new good luck charm with gratitude. Had it saved me from Lily's fate? As the beating of my heart slowed, I became aware of another sound. Soft music. With a frown I turned to the CD player on my dresser. I'd put a couple of CDs in before I went to bed, just because the silence was too frightening. But that music…

I opened the player and froze as I saw it was the disc Dr. Ruprei had given me. Was this it? Was this what had invited the woman into my home? Had I done this to myself? I grabbed the offending disc, prepared to break it in as many pieces as I could, but a more reasonable inner voice reminded me it would be evidence.

Hands trembling, I returned it to the case. I studied the insert and the print on the disk itself; it seemed to be professionally packaged, not a homemade creation. How many of these had they made? With the amount of money they'd spent on the office itself, one would expect they could afford plenty of these. They could have stockpiled them for shipping anywhere.

Then came the chilling thought that there could be other clinics like this around the world. Perhaps the Goldstone was the tip of the iceberg. How much energy did they need to create the power to perform their malevolent ritual? Could they need more energy than could be gathered from one site? Were others waiting to come join together, as the Ruprei-thing had commanded me?

With a shudder, I tucked the CD away in the back of my dresser with the copy of Ben's photos. I'd have to take action with these bits of evidence soon. Clearly Ruprei thought she could bring the battle to me. But I couldn't let that happen. I'd have to take the war to her, and end it. Once and for all.

CHAPTER TWENTY-SIX

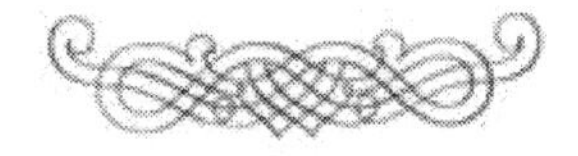

Jim O'Neal and his wife Kim threw a big Fourth of July party, complete with illegal fireworks sent by a friend from North Carolina. Gloria was otherwise occupied, but Dedra came to the barbecue, looking rosy and radiant. I was pleased. The difference since she'd left the hospital was astonishing.

"Didn't you used to work at the *Courier*?" I said, crossing the back yard to meet Dedra.

"Very funny." Dedra's skinny pink sundress and hairbow projected an image the exact opposite of that she had carried since her hospitalization. She once again looked like a college senior, ready to graduate and take on the prime challenge of life.

"New vitamins?" I asked.

"New doctor," Dedra confessed. "I've been to see your Dr. Paulsen. He gave me samples of this medication that's really working. Besides, he recommended this old German woman out on Oak Street that does massage. *Regular* massage. Between the two, I feel great."

They walked over to watch O'Neal fussing with the burgers and ribs, and muttering about man and fire. Chris Brown came over to join them, announcing his intention to down a record number of beers in the first hour of attending a company picnic. Dedra launched into him with a verbal barrage, and I relished its tone. It was the old Dedra.

Chris razzed her about stepping out on Ted with the handsome Dr. Paulsen, and she laughed. "Stay out of my private life."

"A private life? What's that?" Chris said. O'Neal handed him a plate and he began loading it up with food.

O'Neal got in on the fun, as I'd known he would. "Ladies and gentleman, as members of the Fourth Estate, we, of all people, should know there is no such thing as a private life in this day and age. The present government's policies on domestic spying should underscore that." He bowed deeply. "Now, let's get to the important stuff." He stabbed a chunk of ribs and dropped them on his plate, starting the remainder of the feeding frenzy that occurred whenever news people got near a buffet.

Since the company was educated and well informed about current events, the dinner conversation flowed easily from one subject to another. I was able to relax and steer conversation away from the stalled investigation and anything about the clinic. That was a welcome relief. I got to sit back and listen instead.

"So has Gloria offered you a position when you graduate?" Chris asked Dedra.

"Not yet. I've still got summer session at school to finish, though." Her eyes sparkled. "Why? Have you heard a good rumor?"

"I'm up for a good rumor," O'Neal grinned. "Anything with blood or guts is a plus."

Chris shook his head. "Gloria's been all wrapped up in something, but she hasn't given most of us a clue." He shot a look at me.

"What?" I reached for more potato salad.

"Just thought if something was going on in the newsroom that you might share."

"There's nothing going on."

Dedra smiled. "What's going on with Sara isn't in the newsroom. She's got an admirer."

"Oh?" Jim's wife, Kim, grinned. "Now these are the kind of rumors I like. Who?"

"You know," Chris said with a noticeable lack of enthusiasm. "Gorgeous blond doctor, most eligible bachelor of the year. Figures. Just figures." He sighed and consoled himself with another beer.

"Can we drop the subject, please?" I said. I turned to Kim. "Thanks for having all of us over, by the way."

"I like to meet the disreputable characters my husband spends so much time with."

Chris snorted and raised his hand. "Guilty as charged." He reached across the table and stabbed another burger. "Who's got the mustard?"

Dedra passed it. "How can you hope to attract a young lady of quality while you're such a barbarian?" she asked pointedly.

Chris stopped in mid bite. "Mmmph grrrtf dkrrrrrrph," he said.

"What?" Kim, Dedra and I spoke simultaneously.

After he finished chewing, he said, "It's my philosophy. If a woman doesn't love me for who I am right now, there's no point in changing for her."

"You're pretty cynical for someone who's still under thirty," Kim observed.

"Let me illustrate my point. Dedra here probably knows me as well as anyone in this town. Would you go out with me next Friday night, Dedra?"

"Sure," she said.

Chris fell off the picnic table bench.

"Chris!" Dedra cried, jumping up to see if he was all right. I could see from where I was sitting that he was fine, just laughing hysterically.

When Chris finally got himself upright again, he muttered, "The odds *never* break in my favor. How could that have happened?"

"That is not the explanation, my son," O'Neal said in an affected wise old man voice. "This is the moral of the traditional story: 'be careful what you wish for; you may get it.'"

That brought everyone to laughter, and I let the sun warm my skin, feeling stronger, thanks to my work, these friends, and Rick Paulsen.

~*~

The following Monday, Gloria called Dedra and me to her office, and once again Fresh Air blocked those listening from behind the closed door. Then she dropped a bomb.

"Dedra and I have been talking about the clinic," she said. "I've told her about your investigation."

That concerned me. As torn as Dedra had been about the clinic, not always truthful about being involved, I would have been reluctant to share the details of the investigation with her. I was suddenly glad I'd kept the information about the pictures to myself.

"She wants to help," Gloria said with a broad smile.

"That's great." I forced a smile I didn't feel.

"Gloria told me about her sister Marnie and the others who died. I almost died, too," Dedra said with grim conviction. "If it hadn't been for you—"

"Let's not start all that again," I said quickly. I didn't know how much Gloria knew about that. The fewer, the better. "Gloria, what do you have in mind?"

"With Dedra's cooperation, we should be able to get a first hand story someone will listen to. That, with your statistics and personal experiences, should convince the powers of the need for an unbiased criminal investigation." Her Blackberry went off and she looked at the message. "Lord! Publisher's meeting five minutes ago. Scat, you two!" She shooed us and hurried out.

"We should get our stories straight," I said. "Want to come to dinner tonight? I can throw something together by…six?"

"Free dinner? How can I say no?" She looked at her watch. "I have an assignment this afternoon out at some factory. A new fertilizer product they want to tell the world about."

"Sure, now they want to talk to you. If they had a toxic leak, they wouldn't want you anywhere near the place!"

Dedra laughed. "Yeah, right? If I've got time—no, maybe I'll call the doctor and cancel. Anyway, I should be done for sure before six. You're an angel. See you tonight."

~*~

I put the last touches on the pasta salad with tuna and checked again to make sure the glasses were clean and the white zinfandel chilled. Two long stemmed roses, one pink, one white, occupied a tall slim crystal vase on the white clothed table. All that was missing was Dedra.In the bedroom, I removed the apron I'd been wearing and changed into a sundress, red with printed sunflowers, something cool for a steamy July evening. The minutes ticked by. No Dedra. I uncorked the wine and poured a glass, returning the bottle to its ice bath. Sipping as I watched out the window, I half listened to the local news on the television in the background. As it came to the weather forecast, I decided to check in with her. She might have gotten a better offer, and as scatter-brained as she was, forgotten to call with regrets.

But Dedra's cell rang without answer; I left a message. She was probably on her way.

I flipped over to the network news, refreshed my wine, then called again, both her cell and her house. *Still no answer.*

Twenty minutes later, I was fit to be tied. Either she had rudely ignored our friendship for a quick date with someone else, or something bad could have happened. I hadn't forgotten the last time I'd found her at home. That image spurred me into my car on the way to Dedra's place.

But as I came to the steel blue house with the chipping paint, Dedra's car was noticeably absent. I got out and knocked on the door. No answer. It was locked. So much for that. She must have gotten a better offer.

I went home and covered the salad, then put it away. Munching on a handful of green grapes, I sat down with my laptop, reviewing some of the pieces on energetic transfer Rick had given to me. I continued to call Dedra's cell every half hour, but quit leaving messages after the first couple.

About nine-thirty my phone rang, and I pounced on it, prepared to give the girl a piece of my mind. But it wasn't Dedra, it was Rick. He sounded stricken.

"Honey, I think you'd better come down to the hospital right away," he said. "It's Dedra."

My stomach felt filled with ice. "What? What's happened?"

"Come now," he said. He hung up.

My mind buzzed as I rushed to the hospital. Rick hadn't given me details, so I considered the possibility that she'd had an accident on the road, or at the factory. What worried me most was his tone, and the fact he hadn't said she would be all right. My eyes clouded over with tears as I pulled into the lot, and screeched to a halt in the no parking zone outside the emergency room entrance.

I jumped out of the car and rushed inside. Brendon Zale, in uniform, was talking to the nurse at the desk. He stopped when I came in, and tried to get my attention, but I didn't want to deal with him. I demanded to speak to Rick, and the nurse paged him.

Brendon tried again. "Sara, I really should speak to you—"

"Leave me the hell alone." I hoped my voice was cold enough. From the way he almost jerked back, I guessed it was. I spied Rick coming through a door and ran over to meet him, leaving Brendon in my emotional dust.

"What's happened?" I asked. I studied his face for clues, but he just looked away. Not a good sign.

"Come on." He led me back into the treatment area, back along the hall to a room with a door that closed instead of a curtained area. As he opened the door, I saw Dedra lying on white sheets, her skin without color, eyes closed. The nurse in the room snapped off the silent equipment on the far side of the bed. Rick took my hand. “Sara, I’m so sorry,” he said.

Sorry? Why? Dead? She couldn't be!

My brain leapt from one intuitive realization to another. “No, I don't believe it.” I pushed past the nurse and grabbed Dedra's clammy hand. Despite the disgust that filled me, I held it tight and tried to repeat what I’d done before, concentrated as hard as I could on Dedra’s healthy being. “Come on, Dedra,” I pleaded, squeezing harder, fighting tears that choked me. “Come on, Dedra. Come on, damn it.” My voice tightened in panic as I felt no change in the hand I held, still cold and limp as a dead fish.

“She's gone,” Rick said quietly.

“No, you said I could do this.” I fought his arms that reached for me, tried to comfort me. “I won’t believe it.”

“It’s true, honey.” He finally disengaged me and pulled me close, rocking me from side to side until I calmed down. “We did everything we could.”

“Why didn't you call me earlier?” I demanded as the tears finally came. “Maybe I could have helped her then. What the hell happened?”

Rick shrugged. “We don't know. I just came on. Dr. Lucian was on the earlier shift. Said a paramedic brought her in about six o'clock. She was diaphoretic, blue fingernails, not getting oxygen for some reason. No obvious injury. They tried everything.” Rick gestured at the noiseless machinery. “But nothing helped.”

“But she was just fine when she left the newspaper office.”

“When was that?” Rick reached for the chart and made a note, then handed me some tissues.

“About three. She was coming to my place for dinner.” I wiped my face and pulled myself together. “What paramedic?”

“One of the Eastern paramedics. I think you met him before, when you brought Dedra here last time. Ted Frantz?”

“But—” Ted wouldn’t have let anything happen to Dedra, not as crazy about her as he was. He would have remembered what I’d done, too. He’d have called. What was going on?

“Come on, let's get out of here.” Rick guided me out the door. I took one last look at my friend, then the waiting nurses returned to the room to take care of the business of death.

He walked me back out to the lobby, his arm around my shoulders. “Was Dedra still treating at the clinic?” he asked. “These symptoms suggest—”

“Who knows?” A bitter taste hit my tongue. On that subject, Dedra didn’t tell the truth. “Last I heard she was seeing you.”

He nodded. “One of the few times that she took your advice. I thought she’d been doing much better. This is a real shock.”

As we approached the glass doors, I saw Ted and Brendon engaged in hot discussion at the far side of the waiting area. Ted looked up sharply as we approached. Experience likely told him what Rick would say before the words came out, and he turned away in despair.

"She's really gone?"

Rick stepped forward and laid a comforting hand on his shoulder. "I'm sorry. We did everything—"

He whirled back around and shoved Rick's hand away. "Don't you touch me." His eyes blazed with anger. Brendon took Ted's other arm, holding him back.

Rick, on the other hand, had retreated behind professional cool. He crossed his arms, showing Ted he was no threat. "Of course, I understand. I know you two were close."

"Get away from me." Ted looked ready to tackle him. I looked at Brendon, wondering where this hostility came from, and I saw he was just as tense as Ted.

"Perhaps you should give him some space, Doc," the officer said.

Rick nodded. "Very well. Sara, do you want to come to my office?" He gestured back in the other direction.

I debated whether to accept. I preferred finding out what might have happened. "I'll be along," I said.

A twitch ran along Rick's jaw, but he accepted what I said. "I'll be waiting for you." He turned and walked away, the nurse at the desk snagging his attention before he could go.

I watched Ted intently. "Am I on the shit list, too, or can I ask what happened?"

He eyed me a long minute, and didn't speak until Brendon elbowed him. "I ran into her downtown. She said she was on her way to your place, but she had a few minutes if I wanted to catch a beer."

His skin flushed a little, giving him a semblance of color. "We were at Flanagan's, having a couple of beers, just talking about—I don't know what. Nothing. Everything. She kept reaching for her chest like it was paining her. When I asked her what was wrong, she just put me off. I managed to get hold of her wrist at one point. Her pulse was racing, but she insisted she was fine."

Ted started to pace. "I wanted to get my bag and check her out, but she refused. She said she'd just come from the doctor's." A jerk of his head in the direction Rick had gone. "She got mad, so I dropped it."

"She didn't say she'd been at the clinic?"

Ted shook his head. "She just said the doctor had just checked her out, that's all. Not 'she' or 'he.' She was down by Paulsen's private office, so I thought that's what she meant."

"What happened next?" Brendon prompted.

"All of a sudden, she grabbed at her chest like she couldn't breathe. Then she went down, and I called the crew to bring her here. They wouldn't let me in the back because I wasn't family. No one would listen to me when I asked them to call you, either."

"I wish they had," I said sadly. "You know, I found out she was going to the clinic and not telling anyone. This was a month ago. She could have still been there. The fertilizer factory is out Declan Highway. She could have just stopped on her way back." I felt like hell and covered my face with my hands. "It's so unfair. She was full of life just the other day."

Brendon spoke up. "Sara, can I give you a ride home?"

"No. No, my car's outside." I glanced through the door. "I think it's parked illegally actually. Are you going to ticket me?"

He shook his head. "I'll take care of it. Just don't be long."

I nodded. "Ted, I'm really sorry." I went to hug him, and he pulled me close to whisper in my ear.

"What's the matter with you? Can't you see what he's doing?"

Startled, I tried not to yank away. "Who?"

"Your wonderful Dr. Paulsen."

"No, Ted, he's been trying to help Dedra."

"Has he?" Ted shoved me away, disturbed. "More likely, just finishing the clinic's work."

I knew Ted was distraught, as I was. Did he really mean what he was saying? Rick had always seemed like he wanted to protect these young women, not to harm them. "We'll talk about this later, all right, Ted?"

"That's a good idea, Ted," Brendon chimed in. "Let's talk about this again when we've had time to deal with the loss, all right? We can go to the station for you to file your report."

"Yeah, whatever." Ted continued to beseech with his eyes. "Sara, stay away from him."

"Take it easy, Ted. I'll give you a call." I backed away from him, not sure what else to say. Brendan watched me a moment, then led his friend outside. I was alone.

The room swiftly seemed too close, and I stepped outside the sliding doors, letting the night air fill my lungs. I couldn't believe she was dead. I couldn't believe she was dead *now*, just when she had agreed to share her story with the world, to bolster our suspicions about the women who had died.

I couldn't ignore the words of that ghostly apparition. A warning had been issued. Had this been the result? Could I have stopped this somehow, by sacrificing myself? Not likely. They would they have taken Dedra and the others anyway, to satisfy their needs.

That feeling of something lurking poured over me again. Was even Gloria's office no longer a safe place? After all Gloria had been through, I couldn't imagine that she would be in on the clinic conspiracy. Maybe it was wired, or bugged or…

You're not paranoid if they're out to get you.

I shivered in the humid night air. Someone must have known. Melissa Jones. Maybe she overheard us talking about dinner and called the clinic to warn them. Maybe Dr. Ruprei and the others had perfected a technique for delayed onset of symptoms, one that wouldn't leave a hard to explain body on their doorstep.

I breathed deeply, trying to clear my mind and slow my heart.

A security guard drove by slowly, eyeing my car. "I'll move that," I called, realizing I really had no desire to go back inside, Rick or not. I needed time. I drove away and pulled onto the berm of the highway after I'd gone less than a mile. Someone had to break the bad news to Gloria. Looked like that someone was me.

CHAPTER TWENTY-SEVEN

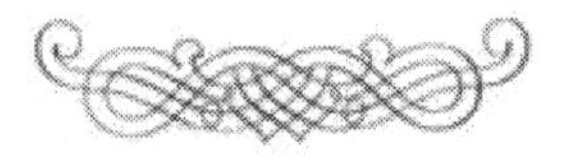

Despite my misgivings about Rick Paulsen, he had knowledge that would help me that I didn't seem to be able to find anywhere else. He'd been able to open places of strength inside me. He'd been able to teach me to use my own energy, to manipulate it. I needed to meet with him. But this time, on my own terms.

First, I had to choose a place where I'd be strong. I felt safest in my apartment, away from prying eyes, but the last time we'd been there…whoo. As much as I'd enjoyed that, I didn't want a repeat. Not yet. Maybe if we got through this. A rundown of alternative sites—definitely not Rick's place. Maybe his office at the hospital? That made me frown. Still not private enough. My place it was.

Rick agreed to come, even acquiesced to my conditions, including a promise that we would leave the bedroom door closed and work entirely in a professional manner. "The work is the most important, Sara. Wherever you choose." I was sure I heard regret in his voice.

"Seven p.m. tonight. There's no time to waste." I hung up, already psyching myself up to get into the work, as he said. With Dr. Ruprei willing to come to my home in the middle of the night, with Dedra dead, I had to be ready to withstand anything.

The rest of the day passed in a blur. I hardly even noticed Brendon Zale, who tried to flag me down at the convenience store when I stopped in for iced coffee. I murmured some excuse about being late for deadline and brushed him off. He could report back to the clinic that I was a busy, busy bee.

It had been hot outside that day, but inside, it was much cooler. I'd run the air conditioning when I'd gotten home that afternoon; I turned it off now so it wasn't a distraction. An overhead ceiling fan would circulate that air. At seven sharp, Rick came to my door and I was ready. After some awkward small talk and a hastily-gulped glass of iced tea, I took the same seat I'd had when he'd come the first time, my back leaning against the sofa for support. I wanted to be comfortable enough to last as long as I could. Too much time had passed already.

Rick smiled, his blue gaze warm, and reached into his jacket pocket. He took out a huge chunk of quartz crystal and set it on the coffee table beside us. He then slipped off his jacket before he came to sit in front of me, knees touching mine. "The time for games is done. Tonight we're going to dig deep."

I took a deep breath, feeling my heart skip around a bit. As much as I wanted this, some part of me that was still sane wanted to be as far away from it as possible. But this wasn't a matter that required thought. This path was fueled by feeling. I'd have to delve into new territory to empower myself sufficiently to challenge Dr. Ruprei.

Rick took a deep breath and released it, all the while looking into my eyes. "You're right. Your inner strength will be the key, and you can only reach that by letting your heart fill with your essence." At my surprised look, he smiled. "Sometimes you think so intensely, it's like you set the words into my mind."

"Oh, sorry," I said, embarrassed.

"Don't be." His boyish grin was designed, I was sure, to set me at ease. "Sara, I can sense that you know where we must go. You must access your core, open it to the outside. I'm ready to do some hard work with you. I think it will be hard, too." The smile faded. "First you must set aside your logical mind. It's not what you're used to doing. What you do every day involves using that not inconsequential mind, and putting your feelings aside. This work is the opposite."

He took my hands, held them, palms up, rubbing his thumbs into the center of my palms. The sensation ran up my arm into my shoulder. "You have to let yourself feel. Every single moment. Be fully present in each moment. Concentrate on what's happening around you. There will be no time for distraction when your battle comes."

I listened carefully, his words ringing true. "I don't intend to give her a chance to suck me dry again."

"I'm not sure your conscious intent has anything to do with it," he said.

A dark thread in his voice sent a shiver up my spine. "So I'll be hyperaware."

"That's a good start."

I shifted, trying to find a more comfortable spot. "There's something I haven't told you."

"Oh?" Rick watched me, his perfectly straight back seemingly effortless. I was envious.

"She came here. Dr. Ruprei." His expression was immediately fascinated, and I told him about my middle of the night visitor. As I got to the end of the story, I noticed my fingers twitching, and a quiver in my jaw had to be stilled by biting down hard on my lip. I hadn't yet conquered my fear.

"That would have scared the hell out of me," he said. "You handled it all by yourself. That's amazing." He squeezed my fingers, let them go with a soft caress.

"If I hadn't had the amulet…" I trailed off, not wanting to think about it. My hand went to the pendant, which I'd worn 24-7 since that night.

"Like I said, you're amazing." He stretched up to the ceiling, leaned deep over to the left, to the right. When he came back to center, he got down to business. "I know your enemy. I can help you become strong enough to fight what will come —what is inevitable." His eyes seemed to darken as he spoke. "Do you believe that?"

I nodded, unable to speak at the tautness of his voice. I realized Rick was frightened, too. What experience did he have with Francesca Ruprei that would bring him to such a level?

He got up a moment and took a vanilla-scented candle from the counter in the kitchen and turned off the fan. He set the candle behind the crystal and lit it. "Breathe," he said. "Relax and breathe."

As had happened before, after awhile, our rate of breathing gradually became synchronized, creating a harmony, a haven of well-being. We continued to build that safe space with our breath and our intent. After several minutes, Rick spoke softly, directing me again in exercises to detect and accept the expanse of my energy field. I became aware of aspects of myself I usually ignored, holding onto that heightened state, working at it.

"Let go, Sara."

"I'm letting go!" I felt the irritation pull me right back to the present, the moment. I stiffened, annoyed.

"When I said you had to work at it, I didn't mean you had to force it. Forcing this will not get you into that space. You have to let go." He reached across, tapped me on several hot points on my body. "Relax. Try again."

Frustrated, I blew air out from between my lips. When my lungs were empty, I inhaled slowly and tried again to breathe regularly until I could return to the proper state. Mindful of his reminder to release, release, release, I felt myself go a little deeper this time into relaxation.

In a voice soft as a feather's touch, Rick said, "Good. Now, let's expand ourselves into this space. The whole room. The crystal will help us do that. Open your eyes and focus on the crystal, on its energy."

We both looked at the crystal, the candlelight shooting translucent arrows of rainbow colors through it. I felt a warmth run over my skin. My sense of well-being rose as the seconds passed. I felt a little tingle even in the pendant hanging around my neck. This was genuine, not the rebound "high" I'd gotten from a treatment at the Goldstone clinic.

The thought of the clinic brought a sudden strong impulse to go there immediately. I struggled to keep my body from responding.

"What is it, Sara?" Rick studied my face, concerned.

"I want to go. To the clinic." My mouth twisted in a frown. I didn't want to go. But suddenly it was all I could think about.

"Do you?"

"No." I fingered the amulet. "No."

"You can resist, Sara. Feel the warm light. Feel the safety in this room. You can overcome that compulsion. They have learned they can use your energy to stimulate your will. They want to subjugate it to their needs. Resist." He nodded encouragement.

I balanced resistance against his previous command to relax and let go. He must have sensed my internal battle. He reached out to cup my chin in his right hand. "Dr. Ruprei knows you have the power to defeat them," he said resolutely. "You're not getting it from me. You've always had it. I sense you've worked hard over the years to hide it, because it frightened you. You didn't understand it."

What was he talking about? I'd always been independent, able to count on myself. I needed to be. Sometimes it was one of my faults. Jesse always said so, anyway

"Breathe with me again," Rick said. His gaze was intense as he drew his consciousness around him like a white cloak. "Let's see if we can find the source of this power."

Heartbeat quick as a hunted doe, I sat back and set myself on the same mission as Rick. If something within me caused Ruprei and the others to single me out, I should discover it. I should be able to use it for myself.

"Try to choose a metaphor to allow this knowledge to reveal itself," he suggested softly. "Something that comes to bloom, something that opens." He settled in, fingertips just touching my knees.

I let my mind wander a moment, until I pictured white metal gates in the front of my heart and mind. I imagined them solid and strong, tall and broad, keeping my secrets safe inside. Then, in my mind's eye, I saw myself walking up to the gates with a key in my hand. I slipped the key into the lock and turned it. I could feel every click as the key twisted in the metal. The last click freed the catch and the gates slowly opened. A cool breeze came from within and I walked inside.

The scene was familiar, an outdoor setting. As I studied the landscape, I recognized a tree, the lane. This was a day I remembered, the day I'd turned twelve. My father had finally decided I was old enough to care for a new puppy, a bouncy golden retriever. I'd named him Jake after a dog I'd read about in a book. We'd spent every waking hour together outside of school, exploring and playing. He'd made up for a childhood lonely without siblings.

That day we'd gone for a walk in the cornfield, both young things stretching our legs, farther than I usually went, chasing Jake and playing tag. I should have noticed how far we'd gone, but by the time I heard my mother's voice, it came from a great distance, her voice whipped on the wind, which had picked up considerably.

I noticed then the dark clouds sweeping in from the west over the Indiana cornfields. Lightning leapt from cloud to cloud, from cloud to ground. Thunder crackled along the edge of the sky, rolling echo after echo. All children raised in the country knew the danger of sudden summer storms. I knew I had to get home—right then.

"Come on, Jake," I'd called to the furry ball of energy still bounding around my feet. He followed me, at first, then he got spooked, stopping to bark at the sky, then he ran away, ran in the other direction. I saw with alarm that the clouds were coming on fast. One eye on the threatening sky, I chased after the dog, tears of frustration and fear rolling down my cheeks.

"Jake, come on. We have to go back. Jake?" But the dog ran toward the west, toward the storm. I had no intention of going back without him. I ran after him, helpless to control him, calling his name.

Jake suddenly came to a halt, tail up, ears perked. I seized him, holding tight to his collar, meaning to pick him up, but he wouldn't let me. He started barking, then froze. He was a handful even when he wasn't freaking out. I tried to pet him, soothe him into coming with me, but something had his attention. He sniffed the air, waiting.

I remember how the hair on the back of my neck prickled violently, causing me to jerk sideways. Trickle spread rapidly to the rest of the hair on my body. My nose burned with a sharp chemical odor. A loud crack and flash of light, a stab of pain, and then blackness.

When I woke up, I lay flat on my back, aching through every bone. Raindrops drenched my face. I was soaked. Momma was going to have a fit, I thought. I pushed myself upright, dizzy. What had happened? Why was I there?

My right hand hurt. A lot. Turning my neck with some effort, I realized through fuzzy thoughts that where it hurt was red and black. Rain pelted me, but I couldn't hear anything. The eerie silence created a slow-growing panic in my gut.

What had happened?

Finally I got control of my thoughts long enough to direct them at the motionless animal lying next to me. I thought I'd die, right there. "Jake!" I shook him, but he didn't respond. The grass around the dog was blackened, too.

Clues clicked into sequence, puzzle pieces locking together, each one a little faster than the last. "Jakers. Oh, no." The crack, the flash. We must have been hit by lightning. My throat clogged with tears, overflowed onto skin wet from the rain. I picked up the limp, soaked body and held him close. "You can't be dead. You can't be!"

I sat there, too stricken to move, holding my dog, sobbing. I half wished the lightning had taken me, too, not wanting to go on without him. I don't know how long we were there in the cold downpour, because time seemed to extend out, expand. A small warmth started inside me and spread outward, keeping me safe as the storm raged overhead, filling me, filling Jake.

As I was about to give up, I felt a small twitch in one of the dog's legs, then another. Slowly the warmth spread in the dog, and he gave a sudden, genuine squirm. With a small yelp, the dog tore himself loose from my arms. He lurched away, stumbling as he took his first steps, but he was walking on his own.

He *lived.*

At first I was delighted I hadn't lost the pet I'd wanted for years, and crawled after him, squishing in the mud, calling his name. He danced away from me, barking, though I couldn't hear him, or my own voice, even. I let him go. If I'd just been given my life again, I wouldn't want to stop moving, either, I knew that.

I was also old enough to know that normal people couldn't make something dead live again. Something had happened to me, too, when the lightning struck. Something abnormal.

Jake ran back to me, past me. I felt heavy footsteps run up behind me. My father lifted me up, big as I was, and turned me to face him, both of us dripping. I saw his mouth move, and understood some of what he was saying. He and my mother had been worried. He'd been looking for me. I could tell he was frustrated that I didn't respond, but my mind was still trying to wrap itself around what had happened. I held out my hand to him, now really starting to hurt.

He looked at it, at the dog's similar injury, and the ground, where a spot was blackened.

"My Lord Jesus," he said, falling to his knees next to me. I could tell by his eyes something was very wrong. He snapped his fingers for the dog. Jake ambled awkwardly to him. He examined Jake's coat, then took my hand again and studied it.

He gathered me into his arms. I felt vibrations in his chest as he spoke. When I didn't respond, he held me away from him, staring into my face. He was a man who didn't show fear, especially not to children, wanting to appear strong. But he was afraid.

"Are you all right, Sara? Talk to me."

I tried to read his lips, thought I'd managed it, but couldn't seem to provoke a response from inside my exhausted body.

"Did the lightning hit you? Can you hear me?"

I couldn't answer. I watched the dog move around more steadily in the grass.

Finally my father hugged me and carried me back to the house. The dog followed, limping a little, as he would the rest of his life, which extended into my college years.

At the emergency room, the kindly old doctor asked if I'd noticed anything unusual after the accident. I thought about my father's awed face and told the doctor about the hearing loss. Nothing else. I never told another soul about the dog, and set myself to forgetting the incident. It wasn't normal. *It would never happen again.*

Abruptly my focus returned to the present, to my aching back, to Rick sitting close. As I'd relived that experience, now it fit into my memories, where it belonged. How could I have forgotten something that must have profoundly changed my life? Deeply shaken, I felt the horror once again on my father's face, and wondered if he'd always been waiting for me to manifest some other horrible power. I'd never let myself.

Not until Dedra.

The coincidence hit me like a second bolt of lightning. The power to keep Dedra alive hadn't come from the clinic. It had come from within me, trapped inside like a genie from the Arabian Nights, waiting for the magic words of release. The treatment at the clinic must have unlocked or enhanced the energy I carried.

But it was mine.

As I opened my eyes, I found Rick observing me. "Take your time," he said. "These visions sometimes need to be sorted thoroughly."

"Okay." My voice, a near-whisper. Inside, though, I roared. My power. I sensed it now. It moved within me. I shook hands with it, embraced it. Perhaps I wouldn't have control of it right away, but I would practice. I would learn.

I reached for Rick's hands, held them with gratitude. His face showed initial confusion, but warmed as I explained what I'd seen.

"We did it. We opened the dark places." He beamed, and pulled me close for an impulsive hug. "You've got control over your whole self. It's done. It's done." He let me go and stood up, one long smooth movement like a spring being released. "You've done well, Sara, very well."

He reached a hand to help me up, and I felt a tingle as our skin touched. "Thank you for helping me." I stood up, stretched and went to the window. No one was watching from across the street. Progress on all fronts. I felt like I'd just won the Indy 500.

"You're the one who did the work. I'm so proud of you. Now, nothing will stand in our way," he said, jubilant.

It wasn't till much later, after we drank celebratory glasses of zinfandel and he'd gone home, that I wondered just who he was referring to.

CHAPTER TWENTY-EIGHT

The next week, I found out that Dr. Ruprei was the featured speaker at an awards luncheon for the local Business and Professional Women's organization. Gloria, a long time member and officer of the group, had invited me to join on several occasions, but I'd declined. There wasn't a woman on the roster under forty, and their meals were just barely a step up from that rubber chicken Gloria had referenced. This time I wanted in.

Gloria wrangled tickets for us both, saving her disapproval for an intense stare and a staccato "You'd better know what you're doing!"

"Don't I always?" I flashed her a cocky smile.

Since I'd discovered the missing part of my history, I'd followed up with more reading and exercises, on my own. Rick had offered to come by again, but though I genuinely felt appreciative of his effort to help me, I wanted to keep our lives separate until after I finished the investigation. He'd said he understood.

"I'm sure this will be behind you very soon, Sara, and you're worth the wait. I'm really looking forward to being able to get to know you better." He even offered to help get information or even give me a ride to the clinic, if I wanted one, but I put him off. Not yet. He still appealed to me, and I would never forget the mind-blowing encounter after the clinic. So I wouldn't close that door altogether.

The day of the luncheon dawned, sunny and hot. Nearly August, and it showed. Women gathered at the county's low-key country club for the luncheon, most in cotton dresses or light linen jackets, if they were brave enough to fight the wrinkles. I'd never seen so much coral lipstick.

I was a little surprised to see Brendon and his cohort Tom the crabby cop on site. "What's up with that?" I asked Gloria. "None of these old ladies seem to be particularly dangerous."

"The doctor was concerned because of recent buzz about the clinic," Gloria said with a tiny smirk. "I can't imagine why."

Gloria had taken Dedra's death hard, but had pulled it together much faster than I'd expected, even more determined to see the clinic shut down. I had to ask if she was the one who intended to attack Ruprei when she was finished with her speech.

She eyed me. "Really, Sara."

"I can't believe you all would honor her with some woman of the year award anyway, knowing what we know. She's a killer."

Some ladies passing by me turned sharply to stare as I spoke. I bit my lip a moment and smile. "Killer shoes. Aren't they?" I pointed to Gloria's chunky black pumps. Not looking convinced, they moved on. "Sorry," I muttered.

"Sometimes things happen for a reason." Gloria scowled. "Can you stay out of trouble while I sit with the board?"

"Yes, I can stay out of trouble." Already bored before the yammering started, I wandered inside to the main room, where dozens of round tables had been set with white dishes and red and blue floral arrangements. Young men and women in servers' outfits of white shirt and black vest and pants moved around the room with large trays, placing small salads on each of the plates. The hubbub of women's voices tangled, danced and rose through the room.

I found a seat out on the far edge of the assemblage where I could sit by myself, but had a good view of the head table. Surveying the crowd, I picked out FiFi LeMew and several of her library cronies; Thelma McCracken, who had her bridge pals close by her, her table full as she smiled with a rueful expression and apology for not saving me a seat; several other women I'd met around town who looked familiar. But there was only one woman I'd come to see. When she walked in, I felt my spine straighten.

Ruprei marched to the podium like she was a queen, Brendon and Tom trailing in her wake, watching the other BPW members cackle and preen as they passed. Brendon took up a position right behind the doctor up front, and Tom circulated through the room, a sharp eye on everything and everyone.

The awards ceremony proceeded apace. The salads, each with one cherry tomato and one black olive, were replaced by croissant sandwiches as the eager wait staff did their jobs. Several women gave uninspired talks. Dr. Ruprei spoke about women as business owners, how women had to work many years to be able to create a successful business, as there were often men waiting to steal the glory out from under them. I smirked a bit, thinking of Talman, but I couldn't imagine he was much of a threat. He was just an administrator, despite his charisma. This woman was the dangerous element I'd prepared to take on. I watched her, purpose burning within me.

She knew, too. Every once in awhile, her gaze would fall on me, as if drawn there, and she would look quickly away. I hoped she was afraid. I really did.

When the event had finished, I got up when she did, meaning to go outside and confront her in the parking lot. Nothing final, just to let her know I suspected her hand in Dedra's death, and to warn her against coming back to see me again. I didn't know how the final battle would come together; a mere skirmish was all I had in mind.

I made my way toward the door, coming up almost right behind her, Brendon between us as she left the building, women stopping on both sides to shake her hand. *Don't touch her!* I wanted to scream. But she just worked the crowd, touching woman after woman, I'm sure sucking just a little bit of energy from each.

The women would go back to their offices, thinking about a nap and decrying heavy luncheons at mid-day. And the doctor? What would she do with all that delicious power for herself?

The thought made me sick, and I was glad I hadn't eaten much of my lunch.

Finally we cleared the group. I quickened my step to catch up as she hurried for her large black SUV, Brendon on her heels. He took a fast look over his shoulder, and a satisfied expression crossed his face. Damn him! He was going to stop me, I knew it.

As the doctor came to the little cement curb where her vehicle was parked, Brendon reached out to help her over it, his right hand in hers. She tripped, and he stumbled too, their hands going upward as they fell. He fumbled at the hem of her sleeve. She hit the ground fairly hard, although he avoided stepping on her. I stopped about six feet away. She didn't get up.

Brendon stared down at her for several long seconds, just watching, then he looked up at me, eyes wide, breathing hard.

I looked down at the doctor again. I'd expected she'd skin a knee or something, the way she tripped, but she still hadn't moved. I looked curiously at Brendon. He didn't move, either. I saw no mark on him; on her, a scrape on one of her hands that oozed blood and looked like small bits of rock had dug their way in, and a small wound on her left temple eerily reminiscent of the one on Lily Kimball's head all those months ago.

As I heard an outcry from the club behind us, I knelt down and felt along the doctor's neck for a pulse. There wasn't any. "She's dead, Jim," I whispered. I looked up at Brendon. "She's dead."

Just like that. No fanfare, no pyrotechnics. Just—gone.

A rush of footsteps came up behind me, a flutter of women in flowery dresses, and someone called an ambulance. No one offered to do CPR; but as she hadn't had a heart attack (had she?), it wouldn't have been appropriate. Brendon went into crowd control mode, as Tom joined him. Tom seemed a whole lot more worried. If I'd had to nail it down, I would have described Brendon's expression as relieved.

People milled around, commenting, pointing, everywhere. The ambulance arrived with lights blazing, but shut them off once the medics had examined her. As the volunteer force (not Ted Frantz, fortunately) carted the wicked witch away, I watched, the anti-climactic end of the doctor a puzzle. The blow to the head must have caused some sort of concussion. I could almost visualize the graphic a television crime show would have used, bone fragments shattering, splitting apart, driving into the brain, causing cerebral hemorrhage. *All that energy didn't save her, did it...*

Tom and Brendon canvassed the crowd, taking statements from anyone who'd seen the incident. I moved slowly among them, taking a few notes myself, but very low-key, not wanting to draw attention, and not wanting to give anyone a statement of my own. I noticed Tom watching me, and he finally came toward me with purpose in his step. As I avoided him, Brendon grabbed my arm.

"I'll take her statement," he said firmly.

"All right. Then get that other newspaper woman." He gestured at the front of the building, where Gloria waited with some of the elderly club members.

"Yes, sir." Brendon drew me aside, but into an open space in the middle of one of the parking lanes in the lot. He surveyed the area around us. I checked myself to see if I'd lost any energy from his touch, but I couldn't tell, as keyed up as I was.

"I really don't have anything to tell you," I said to him.

His gray eyes were the warmest I'd ever seen them. "I'm not going to ask you anything. But I'd appreciate it if you would keep talking while I scribble on this pad." He took out a notebook not unlike mine.

Now he'd lost me. He'd told Tom he was taking my statement, but he wasn't asking questions. "Are you all right?" I asked finally. "Did you lose a marble or two when you fell down?"

He struggled not to smile. "You make it hard to look professional, Sara." He continued to scribble words down.

"What is it you're saying I said?" I snapped. Suspicion made my muscles start to tighten up. I didn't like when that happened.

"That you came out and saw the doctor trip over the cement block. That I went to help her up, but she wasn't breathing. That you're the one who determined she was dead." He stepped closer, and I could see that was exactly what he'd written.

Nearly right, but strange. "I would have figured as her lap dog, you'd have at least done mouth-to-mouth."

"Lap dog?" He seemed genuinely shocked. Realizing he was showing emotion rather than doing as he'd been told, he slapped the steel curtain down again and kept writing.

Something didn't add up. Playing along until I could catch up with the program, I gestured over toward the spot where the doctor had fallen, then up to the building, as though I was giving a whole rundown.

He nodded, kept writing. "All right. Thanks, Sara." He looked around for Gloria, but hesitated before he went to speak with her. "You should go home. There's nothing more you can do here." He walked away.

As Brendon spoke with Gloria, some thirty yards away, she turned to look at me, then turned back toask him a series of agitated questions, accompanied by jerky gestures. He glanced over at me and shook his head, then started writing on his pad.

A frown creeping onto my lips, I grunted and went to my car. When I pulled out of the parking lot, I looked back at the building. Gloria and Brendon were the only two left, still in avid conversation.

~*~

That night, restless in my apartment, I decided it was time to take the camera back to the funeral home. Safer now that Dr. Ruprei was gone. I stole a look out the window and saw no one watching under the streetlight. Maybe it really was all over.

I sorted through my drawers for black slacks and a long-sleeved black shirt. After I was dressed, I looked at myself in the mirror, and almost snickered. Spy work didn't really become me. All I had to do was get into the funeral home and return the camera to the cabinet. In a small town, I'd be surprised if the place was locked up, but there had to at least be a window left unlatched, a fire escape, something. Just get in and out. That was all.

Piece of cake, right?

I tucked my amulet under my shirt before I left.

Just before eleven p.m., I parked several blocks away from the funeral home, in the opposite direction from where I'd parked before. Making my way through the yards, I got as close to the building as I could before coming out into the open. I sprinted for the back of the building.

As I came around the corner, I started checking the windows. All locked. I looked for some kind of fire escape, but I didn't see any. My pulse pounded in my ears. Damn. How was I going to get in?

I inched along the wall, past the back entrance, before I realized that there was a stick in the door. It was already open.

Stunned at my good fortune, I peeked in the crack. Who would have left the thing open? Only the security lights were on, the kind that lit up the inside so police could check for intruders. I didn't see any one, but there was a strong odor of embalming chemicals. Someone must be airing the place out. If I was quick, maybe I could be finished before anyone noticed. Checking the camera in my pocket, butterflies thick in my stomach, I slipped inside.

Listening for activity, I moved quickly down the corridor toward the embalming room. I took a quick look around the corner to see the light was off. Whoever was working wasn't in there. I set clear in my mind where I'd seen Ben remove the camera. I just had to go in, open the drawer, put it back. I took a deep breath, cleared my mind and went.

Halfway across the room to the left, four or five feet right. My fingers trembled as I reached for the drawer's handle. My other hand slid into my pocket, feeling for the camera.

A bright light flashed in my face. "What the hell are you doing here?"

I covered my face with my hands, backing away from the flashlight beam that pierced my eyes. "Brendon? Is that you?" I ran into the table behind me, felt cold flesh under my fingers and screamed.

"Shh! Hush. For God's sake, Sara, get hold of yourself." Brendon grabbed me by the shoulder and covered my mouth with his other hand. I fought him, trying to get some advantage, finding my grip on my new energy a ragged edge. Moaning when I couldn't speak, I swung my fist, closed around the camera for extra weight, in his direction.

He cried out when my fist connected with his head and let go, backing away. "Please stop. Look at what I have. Look." He swung the flashlight to the right, to reveal the body on the table, sheet pulled down away from its withered and wrinkled face, right arm exposed. The skin on the arm was purpled, mottled as only one other I'd seen had been. Despite the discoloration, I recognized her—Francesca Ruprei.

"What are you doing here?" I hissed. "Did they send you? From the clinic?"

"No." He held out his hand. On his palm was a metal disk several inches across, perhaps a quarter inch thick, with unusual letters and markings on it. "I came to get this back."

I blinked. I checked the doctor's arm and saw an imprint of that disk in a distinct bruise. Just like Ulrike's.

"What's it doing here?" I was careful to stay out of reach.

Brendon cleared his throat. "I didn't have an opportunity to retrieve it. Too many people around at the club."

"Retrieve it?" I looked into his face, studied what I could find amidst the shadows. "That means you left it there."

He nodded slowly.

"Is that what killed her?"

He nodded again.

"And Ulrike?"

"Yes."

I nearly choked on relief. "You're not with the clinic?"

"Not at all. I'm a hunter."

CHAPTER TWENTY-NINE

He shone his light at my hand. "What are you doing here?"

"Oh. This was Ben's camera." I pointed at the cabinet.

"You had the camera? Why would you....pictures of...?" His words ferreted out some possible connection. "Fine, whatever. Get it back and let's get out of here."

As he illuminated the corner of the room with the cabinet, I put the camera away and then stole a glance back at the doctor's corpse. "What does that disk do, exactly?" I asked.

"Come on!" he said, annoyed, and dragged me out.

We crept to the corner and then hurried out the back door, closing it tight behind us. As I wound up to ask more questions, he seized my wrist and hurried me away down Sullivan Street before I could get them out. I wasn't convinced I could trust him, but he'd gone a long way to proving himself knowledgeable about the vampires. Rick had identified a "hunter" as the one who'd killed the Grand Master—surely the term, along with two dead vampire bodies, wasn't a coincidence!

We got to his truck. "Get in," he said.

"Not so fast, pal. How do I know you're not—"

He climbed in the driver's side. "I'm leaving here now. If you want to keep talking, you'd best get in too." His keys slid into the ignition and the headlights came on as the car did.

Torn, I swallowed my pride and took the leap. If it was a mistake, I'd end up on a slab pretty quickly. I jumped into his passenger seat and he drove away from the funeral home into the night. Half an hour later, we were drinking coffee at a Denny's in Findlay. The midnight crowd was loud, the waitresses busy. We wouldn't be noticed—or remembered.

In that elapsed time, we'd sorted out who was who, I'd changed from my black turtleneck into a police-issue T-shirt Brendon happened to have in his truck, and I'd heard a story that, if I'd heard it before I came to Ralston, I would have thought was inspired by some very pricey hallucinogens. But knowing what I knew? Made perfect sense.

Brendon Zale had been born Bela Zagravescu, of immigrant parents in Boston. The 'occupation' of Hunter, if that's what one would call it, had been passed to him from his grandfather Dmitri. During his youth, when his parents thought Brendon and Dmitri had been camping weekends at a fishing hole, the boy had been learning a range of ancient skills to rid the world of psychic vampires.

Not just any vampires, he made clear. This group in particular. Brendon's grandfather had been the Hunter who had killed the grand master Sheila and Dr. Ruprei had discussed, that one dangerous day.

"You mean they've been around that long?" I said.

"Some of them the same, others new converts." He stirred cream into his cup, his finger sliding along the steel spoon. "I mean, look how old Ulrike was. She had to be 100. The doctor was even older. If my grandfather was right, she was over 250 years old."

"But how did he know? How did *you* know?"

"His grandfather had taught him, as he taught me. In the eighteenth and nineteenth centuries, these evil men practiced their wiles on the local peasants, becoming strong, becoming rich, and then traveled to the New World. Here they refined their techniques, learned about the human body. Doctors and other practitioners were seduced into the mix. Each addition made them more deadly." I hesitated to ask my next question. The answer might be more frightening than I was prepared for. "How close are they to their goal? Bringing back the man your grandfather killed?"

"A month ago, I would have said it would be any day. They'd drained several women in the weeks before that. The Kimball woman among them."

I eyed him. "That's why you became a member of the force. To be able to gather information without provoking attention."

He shrugged. "It was as good as any. Your job would have been just as appropriate. I wasn't sure when you first arrived if…well, if you might not be a Hunter also."

"What? There's no Hunter clan secret handshake or something?" I was only half kidding.

"I never learned one," he replied.

Stymied by his literal interpretation, I went back to the previous question. "Has the situation changed?"

"I have to believe it's so. The three of them, the women, they'd come together from across the country. But with two of them gone, their power has to be severely weakened."

I frowned. "Won't they just come back to life, too? Isn't that why the clinic reclaimed Ulrike's body?" My fingers pulled the paper napkin in front of me to bits at the same speed my mind was leaping from point to point, seeking some certainty to cling to.

"No. This is the difference between the era of my grandfather and this one. Just as their malevolence has become more specialized and adapted, so has mine. These deaths are final." He reached in his pocket and took out the metal disk, held it out to me. Just before he dropped it in my hand, he looked me in the eye, unsmiling. "If you're one of them—" He released it.

I hadn't thought about magic to be used against the vampires being able to hurt average people off the street. Was I considered average, after my sessions with Rick? I could give energy, I could take energy. Would this kill me, too? I went to jerk my hand back, but the disk dropped in my palm before I could.

And nothing happened.

His slow smile told me he'd read the panic in my eyes. "I know about you," he said.

"Know what about me?" I was still wrestling with the thought I could have died.

"Ted Frantz," he said as if that explained it all. As I stared at him, with what I'm sure was a blank look, he leaned closer. "He and I talk. He's been concerned about the women in this town for many months. He told me about you and Dedra."

With gradual understanding, I nodded. "I didn't do that on purpose."

"Ted said you'd seemed stunned. But he thought it was very important. He suggested I take an interest in you, and stay close, to make sure nothing happened to you."

"What?" I thought back over the weeks that had passed and Brendon's near-constant effort to ask me out. I didn't know if I should be grateful, flattered or insulted. "You mean that's why you wanted to date?"

He actually blushed. "Well, maybe at first. But by the end, I thought you were something special. I just wanted to. Even the more you said no, it made me crazy."

Faced with the options, at that point I chose flattered. What the hell. Examining the disk, I saw letters of a foreign language as well as symbols that looked mystic. The disk seemed light for metal, though it had a dull gray finish. "What's it made out of?"

"Silver. Like your amulet."

That raised an eyebrow. "How do you—"

"Judy told me you'd come in. If you hadn't gone to her when you did, I would likely have found a way to make sure you had a protective talisman you could carry with you."

So the jeweler had been watching for me. How big was this conspiracy, anyway? While I pondered, I turned the disk over, saw the markings were on both sides. "What does this do, exactly?"

"The markings spell out a very old Romanian litany, a prohibition against vampiric energies." He smiled. "Those, I got from Grandfather."

"So you have the disk, and…?" I waved it at him. "What then?"

He reached across the table quickly and took the metal from my hand, tucked it safely away again. "Better not to flaunt our tools." He drank from his coffee cup. "The vampires have biological cell markers that react with the silver. It releases the energy trapped in the cells, the energy that keeps them young and strong."

I thought back over the markings on the bodies. "You have to touch them with this?"

"Once it contacts their skin, the reaction begins. As you've seen, the process takes some time. Several hours."

I'd certainly seen that with Ulrike's body, as she had appeared normal until she'd been removed from the IGA. Not until the next morning had Ben noticed the change. I had pictures. "Damn it."

"What?"

"I didn't take any photos of Ruprei's deterioration." I smacked my forehead. "You scared the hell out of me and I forgot all about it."

"Why would you need photos?"

"To cause an investigation, to close down the.... Oh." I bit my lip. In all likelihood, the clinic would shut down now anyway, with the loss of two of its practitioners.

Ulrike. I thought about the IGA again. How I'd seen Brendon kneeling by the fallen woman, checking for a pulse. No. That hadn't been what he was doing at all. He was getting the disk back before it had been discovered. He just hadn't had an opportunity to do the same in front of the gathered group at the country club.

"I had not meant for the hunt to take so long," he said, a rueful tone lining his words. "The vampires have become more clever. They very seldom go about in public. The woman at the grocery store, I had been following her for weeks, waiting for that opportunity. After she died, the others became even more cautious. That's why Gloria Wilson set up her nomination for that award."

"Gloria did?" That was a real kick in the pants. Ben, Judy, Gloria...exactly how many people were on board here?

"Many people are working behind the scenes to overcome the chokehold the clinic has on this community, Sara. You're just the one in the line of fire. Your bravery has kept the lights off others of us so we could make this happen." He shared a faint smile.

"And Rick Paulsen," I said. "He's been spying on the clinic also."

"I know you've been seeing him. He continues to affiliate with the Goldstone. Both he and Chal Talman were of this community before Ruprei and the others came."

"Really?" Rick and I hadn't talked about Talman much. I had no idea.

"Yes." He paused as the waitress came by to refill our cups. I took the moment to survey the restaurant for familiar faces. I saw none. "I followed Ruprei and Ulrike from Boston. Sheila Morgan joined them here after two years. Paulsen arrived about the time I did. He studied with Talman before joining the staff at hospital."

"Studied what?"

"The same thing he's teaching you. Energy manipulation."

I shifted under his steady gaze, a little uncomfortable with what he knew about me. Not that I would have denied anything he had said, but I just wondered if he knew that much already, what else did he know? Had he crossed over from casual observation to something more intent? Unnerved, I asked him. "So, what? Do you have my place wired?"

"Not yet."

I nearly dropped the cup in my hand, but fortunately he caught it.

"You wouldn't!"

"I trust now you will not make it necessary." He released my hand and the cup, setting both on the table. The sincerity on his face showed me he meant exactly what he said. When I didn't answer, he added, "The needs of the community outweigh the needs of one person."

"Spare me the Spock crap, okay?" Displeased with the proposed invasion of my privacy, I leaned back and crossed my arms, a bad taste in my mouth.

He grinned, showing he knew the reference. I should have known. "Like I said, we have struck a blow that should slow them down considerably, if not stop them outright."

"Good onya, then, bro." I nodded my approval. "So. What next?"

"I don't know. I haven't gotten that far. Perhaps it is up to the vampires to make the next move." He sat uncomfortably on the vinyl bench, neither confidently forward or slumping in defeat.

"I'd say you should keep after them while you've got them on the run." Consternation dug a trench in my brow. "What about the dead girls? What about Lily? What about Dedra? You can't just walk away from what's happened to them!"

"What do you suggest I do, Sara? The police chief and at least one officer are clinic devotees. I cannot pursue justice for those women through my office, any more than you can force it by your writing!" He looked stricken. "This was the first chance I'd had at Ruprei. I did what I could do."

Thinking, I nodded and finished off the coffee in my cup. "It's a good start, Brendon. It is." I looked up at him. "Or would you rather I called you Bela?" I chuckled. "That sure doesn't fit you. It makes me picture Dracula, not van Helsing."

"Bren is fine." His smile echoed my amusement. "I should take you home."

"Can I have one of those disks? Might come in handy."

He shook his head. "Only those who have been trained know how to use them correctly. In the wrong hands, they could be dangerous."

"Too bad." I sighed. The amulet was certainly something, and it made me feel safer. But anything else I could have would add to the protection, I was sure. He'd finished his coffee and so had I. "Yep, our missions are done for the night. Let's go."

Brendon drove me to my car, and I went on from there to my apartment without encountering anyone in the least wicked. The thought crossed my mind to call Rick, see what his thoughts were about what had happened, but the adrenaline was wearing off and I was about beat. I took a hot shower, letting the water wash away the day, and my bad memories, knowing that Francesca would not bother me again. I had the best nights' sleep I'd had in years.

CHAPTER THIRTY

When I arrived at the office the next morning, Melissa Jones looked like hell. Her hair was stringy, hanging loose, and she wouldn't look anyone in the eye. I bit my lip to keep from smiling. The beginning of the end. Without Dr. Ruprei to provide cohesion for that energy pool, it was all beginning to disintegrate.

Jim O'Neal smelled a crime story that never formally materialized, as both deaths were categorized as natural by the coroner's office. As far as I knew, no one ever got pictures of the doctor's body. I held onto what photos I had of the other, even though I wasn't sure what I was going to do with them. Maybe, as I'd told Brendon, when I was all wound up, we should stay on the clinic people, push them while they were weak. If Melissa was any example, the rest would soon fall by the wayside, too.

Gloria called me into her office after deadline, her cigarette-heavy conversation a fishing expedition for information. "So, I saw you talking to Officer Zale after the incident at the country club," she said.

"I saw you, too." I sat back in my chair and eyed her, with a little smirk. "Nice set-up."

A speculative look crossed her face. "What do you mean?"

"I mean you seem to have a lot of irons in this particular fire." Watching her face go from puzzled to worried, I finally smiled. "Don't worry. Brendon and I talked last night. About everything."

"Everything?"

"About the reason he's interested in the clinic."

"Ah." She nodded, seeming to approve. "He finally brought it up."

I couldn't help but laugh. "Um, we kind of ambushed each other, actually." I explained our encounter at the funeral home. I didn't confirm to her that he'd confessed his part in the deaths of Ulrike and Ruprei; I didn't need to. We debated the value of a story in the paper, even if it was just to soothe the families of the dead women. If they could know for once and all what had killed their loved ones, would it put their doubts and pain to rest, or just open up old wounds?

"Frankly, Sara, I think you'd be better off to give that place a wide berth. If it's going down the toilet, so be it. We don't need to flush it along." She tossed her cigarette butt out the window before too much of the August heat seeped in.

"Maybe you're right. Let them crumble away to dust."

When I came out of the editor's office, O'Neal said Rick Paulsen was waiting to see me. I hurried along to the courtyard outside where he'd been sent.

His face lit up as he saw me. "Hey, you look great!" He swept me up in his arms and gave me a kiss.

I was a little surprised, but ready for some celebration after all. "I meant to call you yesterday, but I just got sidetracked. You heard then?"

"I heard." He hugged me again, face shining with relief. "She's no longer a threat. Whatever you did—"

"Me?" I pulled away from him.

"You were at the club yesterday, right? FiFi said she'd seen you follow Dr. Ruprei outside." He stopped and studied me, unsure.

About to tell him what had really happened, something held me back at the last second. I remembered Brendon congratulating me for being the face of the resistance, if you could call it that, someone to divert attention from everything else that was going on. Bren and I had talked about Rick with no clear delineation of whose side he might be on. That suggested caution. I grinned. "Okay, you're right. I should know I can't hide anything from you."

"I knew our work would pay off." His blue eyes sparkled with delight. "An ace in the hole, that's what you are, Sara Woods." He hugged me again.

He certainly was enthusiastic about this, I thought, still a little surprised. "I'm glad you're pleased," I said.

"Pleased enough to buy you a cup of coffee. Maybe some lemon meringue pie, too." He winked.

"Pie? Wouldn't miss it. Come on." I led him back through the building to the front door, where I stopped at the reception area to mark myself out with a push pin, then we took his car to the diner. Rick never stopped smiling.

When we walked into the diner, a bell hanging on the door announced our arrival. Half a dozen other patrons, small-town observers, glanced up as we came in, identified us, surely clicked through whatever gossip was attached to our reputations, and then returned to their food and conversations. Rick chose a booth away from the windows and called out to Sandy Stone, the owner, who often served as waitress, cashier and even short order cook once in awhile. "Sandy, coffee and pie for two."

The black-haired woman peeked out from the back through the small pass-through and nodded. "Coming up, Doc."

I took the side of the booth that faced away from the door, wanting to concentrate on Rick. Since we'd agreed to hold off on a relationship until after the clinic issue was settled, what had happened was significant on a personal level as well. We might want a little privacy.

He stopped to say hello to a pair of older patrons, inquiring about the health of one of them. They seemed smitten with the handsome young doctor and flattered by his attention.

Rick came to sit across from me, still radiating good feeling. I was caught up in his warmth and gave him my hand across the table when he beckoned for it.

"I'm proud of you, Sara."

I blushed. "Thanks. I mean it. Thank you for taking the time to teach me."

"Thoroughly my pleasure, and a little self-serving, if you must know." He let go of my hand as Sandy brought our coffee and pie. It looked delicious.

"Thanks," I told her. "You're amazing. This pie…wow."

"She's something else," Rick said with a grin. He dug into the tart pie with a real appetite.

I did the same. I wasn't a real baked-good freak, but pie never failed to appeal. When I was a kid, my grandma had been a baker, and each holiday was filled with pastries of all flavors. Sandy's lemon meringue came real close to hers. Rick and I both ate every crumb, then relaxed to sip coffee, letting us wash it down in style.

"Where were we?" I said, with a little guilty laugh. "I lost track." I thought back to the conversation. "We were talking about what you'd taught me."

"Yes. We've opened up your energy core so it can be tapped. You got Francesca once before, caught her off guard. Now you've done it again." He smiled. "I expect you must have drawn quite a bit of her energy into you this time."

He still believed I'd killed her. I just smiled back and shrugged, as if modestly, using the coffee as an excuse, drinking most of that cup before setting it down. I remembered the end of our former exchange. "You said teaching me had been something self-serving for you. Did you mean something special by that?"

"Did I?" He glanced at the door as the bell rang again. "Oh, right. It means so much more to have a partner who's *simpatico*, you know? Interested in the same things, who have studied the same course. People who understand what you're all about inside, you know?"

"It's hard to find someone like that," I said, thinking ruefully of Jesse, feeling my thoughts start to wander.

"Sometimes, even if you do, if you try too hard, you can destroy what you're trying to save."

I nodded. "I know what you mean. It's possible for everything to unravel so easily." As I spoke, dizziness mushroomed up inside me, a wave of fatigue nibbling ever-faster at my focus. I blinked and rubbed my eyes. *Talk about unraveling…what was going on?*

"Exactly. I knew you'd understand."

I thought about the chance for us to be together, wondered whether I dared ask him point-blank at this point. I could scare him off. At the same time, I wasn't sure a long-term relationship with him was what I really wanted. Now that I knew Brendon Zale wasn't just an obsessed stalker, we'd seemed to hit it off the night before.

Of course, that could have been just the warm afterglow of a vampire killing. Who knew?

"Sara?"

"Sorry. Woolgathering." I forced a smile, the wooziness a little stronger. The floor felt like it shifted, tilted a little bit.

"Sara?" A little more intense. His voice seemed to come from far away.

I grabbed for the edge of the table, looking for support, and knocked my cup off. It fell in slow motion, and broke into several pieces as I watched, frozen in place, nausea nipping at my stomach. *What was happening?*

"She'll be fine," came a voice from behind me. "She'll be just fine." Chal Talman slid into the booth next to Rick. "You did well, love," he said, and kissed Rick on the lips.

Horrified, unable to move, I prayed one of the other patrons would catch wind that something odd was happening, considering the sound of broken glass, and hell, the fact that two men had declared themselves openly gay in a small-town, white-bread, church-fearing community.

With relief, I saw people come into my line of sight. One was that good-looking city councilman Dedra had always raved about. The coroner, Jim Reed, too, and FiFi from the library. *Do something!* I silently commanded them. *Help me.* I couldn't make my mouth move, or even generate sound. My body was fading from my control as the seconds ticked by.

But, to my horror, they did nothing. They stood and stared, joined by Sandy, Thelma's friend from the IGA, and lastly the police chief and Officer Tom, who wore an expression I'd never seen on his face before: triumph.

Chal, his eyes chocolate brown once again, smiled with indulgence, with tolerance. The smile of a parent who needed to correct a wayward child. "Little Sara. Who would have believed you of all people could have caused us such trouble?" He waited for an answer he had to know I couldn't give. "That's all right, dear. We'll set the matter to rights. We'll get our energy back. And much more besides. Much more."

His eyes filled with malice as I felt the last bits of consciousness pull away and everything went black.

CHAPTER THIRTY ONE

I came awake lying on a plastic examination table in a large medically equipped room. From the paintings on the walls, trademark red and blacks of Francesca Ruprei, I knew I was at the clinic. That meant I was in serious trouble.

I quickly assessed myself. Sandy must have put something in the pie, in the coffee, somewhere. It remained in my body, because I still had no control over my muscles. I flashed back to the last time I'd been here, when I'd been so drained I couldn't get up. To the time Ulrike had put me in some kind of trance. Both of those times, though, I'd felt weak. I didn't now. My heart felt strong. My vital force was spread throughout my body. If I could just move…

I was wearing some sort of white gown, something out of those awful virginal sacrifice movies. *And my amulet was gone.*

Scoping out my surroundings, I noted several large rectangular windows along the ceiling of the room. It was dark. I must have been here for hours. The blackness outside was shattered every few minutes by bright white lightning. I heard the crash of thunder following each flash.

Flash.

Crash.

Flash.

Crash.

In a long-practiced habit, I counted the time between them. All my life I'd prayed that each time I counted, the number of seconds would expand, meaning the storm was moving away from wherever I was. Tonight they weren't. The storm was growing closer. The paralysis in my limbs apparently extended to my fears as well. My normal dread of lightning storms was pleasantly muted. The rush of adrenaline in my body was firmly devoted to my clinic-oriented predicament.

When the light flashed, I tried to find anything familiar in the room, but found none. I must not have been here before.

It was dark. After hours. What time was it? Was Gloria looking for me? Was anyone?

A slow realization came to me, a murmur of voices, not close enough to recognize. I strained to hear them. I didn't want to encounter anyone, not here, because anyone could be a traitor, an evil force… Rick's face appeared in my mind, unbidden, and I felt sick. He'd seemed to mean so well, kindly caring for me—damn it! He'd washed dishes! I should have known he was too good to be true!

The rush of anger seemed to jolt something back into working order, because my hands twitched suddenly and I could feel my fingers, move them, curl them slowly. Same with my toes. The drug was wearing off. If I could hold off whatever Chal and Rick had planned, maybe I could save myself.

Yes. *Save myself.* Calling for help seemed to be out of the question at this juncture. And with the police in on things, I could bet they'd sent Brendon far away. No wonder I hadn't seen him that day.

The voices moved closer, synchronizing into a slow chant. My heart beat picked up, and fear pricked my muscles, urging them to move.

What was I doing here? Could this be it? The ritual Francesca Ruprei had promised? The one intended to raise the master? Or was it Ruprei they intended to bring back to life?

Don't panic.

I might as well have urged myself to quit breathing. Panic seeped into every crevice between my nerves. Ruprei had asked me to join their little group, and I'd refused her cold. Rick had said something about her, what had it been? Yes. He believed I had sucked Ruprei's energy from her. They must think I still had it. Since I had not joined them, there was only one logical next step: the clinic must intend to use me as life force fuel for their little Frankenstein endeavour.

I forced my system to slow, relaxed as best I could with deep breathing as the droning voices drew closer. As I loosened up, feeling crawled up my arms, tingling like they'd been asleep. Perhaps whatever they had given me was wearing off, or the less I fought it, the more I could do. Either way, if I kept my wits, maybe I had a chance of escaping the fate they intended for me.

Someone turned off the light in the hall as the chanters approached. Lightning flashed outside, the thunder almost overhead. At first I planned to act unconscious, to play possum as long as possible, but at the last second couldn't keep my eyes closed. I had to know what was happening.

More than a dozen people crowded into the room around me, wearing red and black hooded robes. Each carried a tall black candle that gave off a putrid fragrance. As the last person entered the room, the overhead light was turned off. The figures closed in to form a perfect circle around the table with me in the center, hoods pulled forward to disguise the wearers. Candlelight caused eerie shadows to waver across the darkened figures and the walls. *Crash.*

The person standing next to my head on the right side reached up to remove the hood, revealing himself as Chal Talman. I'd never seen him look darker, more malevolent. At some silent signal, those around the circle removed their hoods as well, one after the other, exposing the people I'd seen at the diner, and several others, including the nurse from the emergency room and the city mayor, as well as Melissa Jones, who looked a little stronger by candlelight. The last one to remove his hood was Rick Paulsen, on my immediate left. He smiled down on me with love.

"Bastard," I whispered, surprised my voice was once again mine.

He smiled, looked across the table at Chal.

Talman looked around the circle with that powerful gaze, meeting the eyes of each follower. "We have come together for one purpose, and one purpose only. To gather the forces of the universe to our own control. To bring back our master to lead us. Francesca Ruprei had begun to stray from the Master's path. She had begun to believe she could claim all the power for herself! She has been punished! Now she is fallen!"

Flash.

I continued to lie perfectly still, but I could feel strength returning to my body. I wondered if they needed me to be fully charged, awake and powered up in order to suck all the energy out of me. If so they'd wait. If so, I'd have a chance to escape.

"I have been chosen as the one to lead you, to lead us into the future." Chal's face didn't show it, but there was victory in his tone. He took another survey of the group, visually checking in with each member of the group, then back down at me. The others stood with their candles, staring hungrily at me.

Flash. Crash.

Those were almost instantaneous. I realized the storm was right overhead.

"We shall bring the Master back to us, and he shall lead us into the world," Chal intoned. The others chanted, "We shall bring the Master back to us, and he shall lead us into the world."

"We shall choose the strong and devour the weak."

They repeated his words. As he continued to lay out a chanted plan, it sounded to me like the vampires intended to spread out from here, eventually placing themselves in power, as they had with the model in this little town, reducing most of the country's population to a source of food.

That couldn't happen.

Flash. Crash.

The gathered ones were aware of the storm as well. With each echo of thunder, they grew more restless, stretched a shoulder, raised up on toes, drawing in audible breaths. Their agitation added to mine. The situation threatened to overwhelm me. There was no cavalry this time. I had to do something. But what?

My mind raced as my body started to return to me, faster and faster. Adrenaline must have retired the effects of the drug, because the struggle for control grew easier. I couldn't let them succeed.

I could only hold them off for so long. Rick had showed me how to shield against casual intrusions by energy seekers. But there were a dozen of them here, all trained, all pros at it. No way I could withstand them all.

Crash.

As the numbness wore off, my dread of the storm grew. Much too close for my comfort, it was clearly immense. The wind was audible outside, and I could see branches blowing violently.

The devotees continued to preen and curl, stretching lazily like cats, gathering their energy. They would kill me in the next few minutes unless I could stop them.

Come on. Think!

I tried to remember what would kill vampires. Didn't have any wooden stakes or silver bullets. No precious stones. No flame-throwers.

Crash.

The lightning was simultaneous with the thunder, so close it made me jump.

At the same time, the nearest window was breached by a large branch from outside. A gust of wind shot through the room, extinguishing most of the candles. In the dark once again, I tested my muscles, found myself ready to move. *Get ready!*

"What the—" a man said. "Who's got the cursed matches?" There was a whisper of activity as the candles re-lighted, one by one. Chal appeared unruffled as his flock came back to focus once more.

The wind continued to blow, whistling now through the broken window. I studied my fear of the storm, realizing what remained was not the mindless terror I'd dealt with since I was twelve years old. I'd found the source of that fear. I'd incorporated it into myself, into my energy.

Flash.

As the lightning illuminated the room for several seconds, I felt a little tingle, as if it was speaking to me. What was lightning? It burned. My dog had been evidence of that. The sudden remembered odor of wet dog and burnt flesh filled my nose. It burned.

Fire.

Chal laid his left hand on my forehead, and right hand on my hip. Rick moved to the same points on my left. Light flickered on their faces, creating eerie shadows. Here it came. If I was going to do anything, it had to be now.

I closed my eyes and mentally reached up and out, picturing the storm, the lightning, calling it, drawing it to me. I felt more than a little tingle. I pulled on that power with all my might, summoning it. A large crack sounded from outside the window. A brief thought flitted through that what I intended would likely mean my own death as well.

But if I was going to die, it should be in saving the rest of humanity.

I twitched and forced one hand up onto Chal's chest, over his heart, then did the same to Rick.

"Yes, Sara." Rick grinned. "Help us. Build the bond, release your energy for the Master."

"Go to Hell," I said. "Take your friends with you!"

I yanked that mental control for all I was worth, using every bit of energy I had within me, right down to my core, as well as all I could pull from both men, dragging the power from the sky above down to me. Chal seemed to choke on the words he'd opened his mouth to utter. A huge boom overhead brought the ceiling falling in around us, a broken tree exposing the room to the rain and wind. The candles went out again.

"Now!" I yelled.

As if in obedience, lightning blinded me and I felt a punch in the center of my chest, a hot, liquid punch that flowed through my body, my arms, my hands and into the two men. They screamed, a horrible sound that faded from my observation, as I was pinned onto the table, jerking along with them. I caught glimpses of the others coming close to help, several others, and in the reflected light, bright as a photo flash, I saw them touch the men and then, helplessly, begin to jerk and writhe as well. Fire shot from their outstretched hands to some of the others, to the curtains, to other points of the room, and the room began to burn.

The lightning bolt crackled, then faded, the smell of ozone and burnt flesh overwhelming. Rick fell away, to my left, his face a rictus of pain. Chal let go, reaching for the blackened spot on his chest, struggling for comfort and finding none before he fell. Deafened by the lightning, I could hear nothing, but saw the few remaining others, Mark the city councilman, Rona, trying feebly to get out the door. It was blocked shut by part of the ceiling structure. They were trapped.

I felt myself fading, too, as the fires burned, consuming the room. At least I'd taken the vampires with me. So tired, unable to move, I closed my eyes, ready to rest.

CHAPTER THIRTY-TWO

Light stabbed my eyes. I moaned and tried to block it. I couldn't.

"Hold still!"

As my perception gradually solidified, I felt motion under my back. Heard a screaming siren. Felt a warm grip on my hand. I couldn't focus.

"Sara? Sara, wake up!"

"She's coming around, Bren. Calm down." I knew that voice. Ted Frantz. Ambulance medic.

Our motion stopped and activity buzzed around me. A door opened, someone got out, I moved smoothly, on wheels. A moment later, there was heat, and rain, then bright light again, as we sped along a hallway.

"Sara? Let me go in."

"We'll take care of her, officer. Please wait out here."

Ted's voice, throwing off a litany of numbers and words, among other voices, as we moved. Was he talking about me?

Was I alive?

A blur of medical activity followed, transferred to another bed, people poking me, hooking up monitors, stab of a needle into the back of my hand. "Miss Woods, we're going to sedate you," someone said, and I tried to protest.

Don't send me into the darkness again!

But it happened before I got a word out.

I woke up sometime later, weak, in a white room, like the one Dedra had used at the hospital. Several vases of bright flowers sat on a table next to the bed. I could move, some, and I experimented a little, finding wires and tubes kept me prisoner.

"Sara?"

Brendon came into my field of vision. I'd never been so happy to see someone without blue eyes in my life. "Hey," I whispered.

"Hey." He gingerly took my bandaged hand, looking relieved. "Gloria was here earlier, but she had to go back to work. You're doing well, the doctor says, considering."

Pieces of memory started to flicker to life. "Considering what happened?"

"You were in pretty bad shape when you came in."

"How…?" As bigger pieces of memory came into focus, I remembered the realization that I was going to die. Something had intervened.

"How did you get here?" When I nodded, he took a seat on the very edge of the bed, not letting go. "Do you remember what happened at the Goldstone?"

"Some." My mental picture was fuzzy. Something about a storm, and fire. "Are they dead?"

That made him smile. "As far as we can tell. The visiting coroner's identifying the bodies found in the fire." He ticked off the names of those identified, including Melissa and Rick; the rest matched those I'd seen.

"Yes. That's them."

He paused, looking out the window. "I almost didn't make it back in time." At my prompting look, he took a deep breath. "Tom and Dick had sent me over to Seneca County to pick up a prisoner, but something didn't ring true. I just had a bad feeling about it, so I turned around and came back. Drove into that damned storm. I checked with Gloria and Thelma, but no one had seen you. Someone at the paper remembered you said something about pie, so I went down to Sandy's to see if you'd been there. Place was locked up and dark. At dinnertime on a weeknight."

He shook his head. "Definitely not right. So I headed out, looking for where trouble might be happening. Lucky I found it."

"She drugged me," I said.

That raised an eyebrow. "Sandy? No way. Damn. I'd never have picked her."

I stretched, feeling medicated. A heavy weight rested on my chest. A thick bandage. "What happened?"

"You had some seriously bad burns," he said, his smile fading. He held up my hand. "Contact points, I'd guess. Lightning must have channeled right through you, and it burned where it went in, and where it went out. You didn't have a heartbeat at all when I got there. The shock must have stopped it."

He must have arrived just as the incident happened; or else I'd be brain-dead.

"I had to climb down through the hole in the ceiling to get you. The firefighters nearly took my head off." He chuckled. "Guess I'm a little stubborn, too."

I decided to allow myself to be grateful. "Always the hero," I said with a faint smile.

"You're the hero this time, Sara Woods," he said. "Brave as hell, if a little bit crazy. I can't imagine taking that risk myself, but you came through in spades. You know, we make a pretty good team."

"But the vampires are gone. No reason to work together any more."

His face fell a little. "You still owe me a date."

That brought a soft laugh, quickly followed by a growl. "Do I? Don't make me do that. Ow."

"Sorry. But I mean to hold you to your word. As soon as you get well." His brow furrowed, and his attention faded.

"What is it?"

"I was going to wait until you were up and around to ask."

"Had enough games. Spit it."

He nodded. "I found the trail of another Bostonite. She's begun another psychic cell, in Colorado." He paused. "If you're interested in collaborating."

With a groan, I closed my eyes. "Do they have a paper there?"

"I'm sure we'll find you something to do, love. Now, get some rest."

The thought of him leaving disturbed me, and I tried to hold onto his hand, difficult through the bandages. "Don't go," I said.

"Don't worry, Sara. I'll be here when you wake up, and for as long as you need me."

As I drifted back to sleep, his hand warm in mine, I hoped that would be for a very long time.

ACKNOWLEDGEMENTS

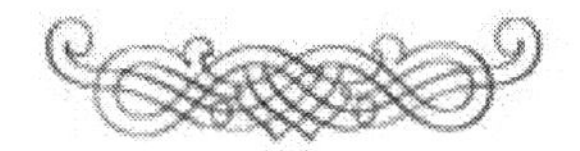

This book couldn't have been written without the years I spent at the *South Dade News Leader*, in Homestead, Florida, which, at the time I worked there was a daily paper. The camaraderie and great reporters and editors I worked with really laid the foundation for this tale. Several of the reporters in this story are drawn from those in real life; I was careful to withhold the names of the not-so-innocent. :)

I also want to thank the teachers and students at the Full Spectrum Healing Circles I attended for the lessons I absorbed in self-awareness and self-healing, as well as information on some of the techniques I used in the story.

One of the main pieces of music I listed to while writing this book was Andrew Lloyd Webber's wonderful *Phantom of the Opera,* and I suppose obvious parallels can't be helped. The music is inspiring, and it will always be part of my life because of this.

Thanks, too, to those who help heal me on a daily basis, including my long-suffering chiropractor Dr. Brad Jackson, who always welcomes me and takes good care of me, even when I aggravate my condition in a less-than-intelligent fashion, and my husband, who also helps maintain my spirits, creativity and determination with his loving support.

I so appreciate my editor Matt Silvestri, my publisher Frank Hall, my cover artist Karri Klawiter, and all the family at Hydra Publications for making this such a smooth process and a group effort. I'm looking forward to a long association with all these folks!

Finally, thank you, thank you, thank you!!! to the Area One Pennwriters critique groups, who regularly review my work, provide thoughtful commentary and support one another as we all work along the path to our chosen avocation of writing. I couldn't do this without you.

ABOUT THE AUTHOR

Lyndi Alexander dreamed for many years of being a spaceship captain, but settled instead for inspired excursions into fictional places with fascinating companions from her imagination that she likes to share with others. She has been a published writer for over thirty years, including seven years as a reporter and editor at a newspaper in Homestead, Florida. Her list of publications is eclectic, from science fiction to romance to horror, from tech reporting to television reviews. Lyndi is married to an absent-minded computer geek. Together, they have a dozen computers, seven children and a full house in northwestern Pennsylvania.

Lyndi is also the author of:

The Elf Queen, 2010; *The Elf Child*, 2011; and *The Elf Mage*, 2012; all from Dragonfly Publishing

http://clanelvesofthebitterroot.com

The Elf Guardian, coming from Dragonfly Publishing in 2013

Triad, Dragonfly Publishing, 2012

The Horizon trilogy—*Horizon Shift*, 2013, *Horizon Strife*, 2014 and *Horizon Dynasty*, 2015, from Dragonfly Publishing.

Her website is http://lyndialexander.wordpress.com, and you're invited to stop by and check out the news, contests and other events there. If you'd like to contact Lyndi, you can reach her here: lyndialexander at gmail dot com. Please feel free to ask questions about the characters, upcoming booksignings and anything else that fascinates you about her books.

Made in the USA
Charleston, SC
10 September 2012